BEST LESBIAN
ROMANCE

BEST LESBIAN ROMANCE

EDITED BY
ANGELA BROWN

CLEIS
PRESS

Cleis Press Inc., P.O. Box 14697, San Francisco, California 94114.

Printed in the United States.
Cover design: Scott Idleman
Cover photograph: Samantha Wolov
Text design: Frank Wiedemann
Cleis Press logo art: Juana Alicia
First Edition.
10 9 8 7 6 5 4 3 2 1

Lori L. Lake's "Paige" originally appeared online at Khimairal Ink, www.bedazzledink.com/khimairal-ink (volume 1, July 2005).

Contents

1   *Shooting Snow* • LYNNE JAMNECK
19   *Stepping Out* • CHEYENNE BLUE
30   *Paige* • LORI L. LAKE
43   *Not the End of Liner Notes* • JEWELLE GOMEZ
53   *Nobody's Heart Is Broken Now* • SARAH COATS
65   *Wish Granted* • SANDRA BARRET
78   *The Attic* • K. I. THOMPSON
84   *Dreamtime* • FIONA ZEDDE
92   *Bright, Blowsy Poppies* • MAGGIE KINSELLA
102   *Chances Are, or Murphy Was an Optimist* • SAGGIO AMANTE
112   *Under the Skin* • LISA FIGUEROA
120   *Sivonya* • TERESA LAMAI
127   *All You Can Think About* • RACHEL ROSENBERG
139   *The Petrified Girl* • KATHERINE SPARROW
156   *The Love Boat* • AUNT FANNY
176   *Mo'o and the Woman* • ELSPETH POTTER
182   *In the Heart of Egypt* • ANNE LAUGHLIN
202   *WLSB* • SANDRA BARRET
212   *Pretty* • LESLIE ANNE LEASURE

228   *About the Authors*
233   *About the Editor*

SHOOTING SNOW

Lynne Jamneck

A pril 26

"Cigarettes. I need cigarettes."

I stuck my hand resolutely beneath the messy pile of papers, envelopes, and photo prints. The craving took hold of me nearly every day, but reality reminded me that I'd finally—at the behest of my health—quit smoking three months ago. They say after thirty there's no turning back the damage the stuff inflicts. I pulled my hand back. I'd be damned if I'd admit that turning thirty had not only turned me prematurely gray but had also killed my self-control.

Instead I withdrew a tin of mints from beneath the mess. Looked at it. Snarled at it. Sucking on a piece of candy didn't come close to sucking on nicotine. I sighed. Please, God, send me a distraction.

Of course, nothing happened.

I played with the miniature green tin, turning it to inspect the ingredients. *Sugar-free*. Good. *Artificial flavor*. Bad. That was the extent of the nutritional information.

The phone rang. I tossed the mints into an open drawer and answered.

"I got you a gig," the voice on the other end said. His tone was annoying as ever, but the severity of it had been dulled by familiarity.

"Who the hell are you? Brian Epstein?"

"That's funny. Seriously, this is a good one. I think you'll like it."

"You didn't book me on a road trip through Texas again to shoot photos of seedy bars and local yokels, did you?"

"C'mon, that wasn't so bad, was it? Besides, you got to see the president play golf. Even took a damn fine picture of the guy."

"Yeah, and it made a damn fine dartboard in the end."

My manager sighed. "Whatever," he said. "Listen, you're going to Greenland."

"I am? When did you plan on telling me that?"

"Han, I just did."

I hate when he calls me that. For the better part of ten years, Fodor Grimsby has been my manager, and he still doesn't call me by my proper name. But I've stopped reminding him. Every time I do I gnash my teeth, my blood pressure soars, and I prepare myself for a panic attack two weeks down the line.

I leaned back in my chair and plunked my dirty CATs on a solitary clean corner of my hurricane-torn desk. My scuffed jeans needed a wash. Big deal—I needed a vacation. I decided to humor him. "What's in Greenland?"

"Ever heard of the Greenland Ice Core Project?"

"That would be a no, Grimsby."

"Thought as much. If it'll make you feel better, neither had I. Until this morning."

"Uh-huh…" I swiveled my chair so I could look out the bay

window behind me. Two robins were fighting over a fat, wriggling earthworm in the grass. They were making such a racket they didn't seem to notice the worm was getting away.

"GRIP was a multinational European research project, organized through some European science foundation, roughly between 1989 and 1992. Ice-core drilling. You like taking pictures of animals, don't you, Han?"

"What do animals have to do with an ice-core project?"

"There's a scientific team going to Greenland to investigate the effect GRIP and others of its kind have had on deep-sea mammals and fish in the area, animals..." I heard him shuffle some papers. "Yeah...mammals and fish. Anyway, they're looking for a photographer. They phone me, I phone you. That's why you have an agent, see?"

"I thought an agent was supposed to call other people and tell them about the genius talent of his clients."

Grimsby ignored the jibe. We have that kind of relationship. "It's not like you've got anything else going. Just last week you told me you were getting bored."

"It's not true. You know me, Grimsby. I'm a fickle bitch."

He laughed. "Yeah, but you're constantly moaning about needing a vacation, which you always scorn when one comes along. So how about it?"

I swiveled back to face the heap of junk on the desk and dropped my feet to the floor. "Isn't Iceland pretty cold? You know how I get in extreme weather."

"Greenland, not Iceland."

"Is there a difference?"

"Who knows. But hey, it's a once-in-a-lifetime opportunity, don't you think? And Han..." His voice turned serious, the way it always does when he talks about money. "The pay is really good."

I rummaged until I found a tooth-marked pen. "Give me the number. I want to speak to them first before I agree. Damn it. Hang on. Pen won't write." I knew Grimsby wouldn't trust me on remembering, because my short-term memory was shot to shit.

Once I'd taken down the contact information, I said good-bye and dialed the number. An answering machine picked up. So much for speaking to G. Skerret. Damn Grimsby. Just like him to give me an initial instead of a name.

I picked up the phone again. Grimsby answered on the fourth ring. "What did you say they wanted me for?"

"They want you to take photos. Of animals."

"Then I guess I'll take photos. And Grimsby, if you're convincing me to do this just because of a fat commission, I'll kill you."

"Yeah, yeah. Famous last words."

A week later I found myself with three small suitcases on a tiny airplane, debating my sanity. As luck had it, I had the seat right next to the propeller, which—apart from making an awful racket —looked as if it would tear off at any second.

Admittedly, the view was spectacular. My pocket-size tourist manual confirmed that Greenland was currently almost halfway through summer. The closest city to where I'd be staying was the capital, Nuuk, a west-coast city south of the Arctic Circle that experienced midsummer temperatures as high as fifty degrees Fahrenheit.

With me was a man named Terry Carlisle. He was thickly bearded and rough skinned and had eyes the color of cobalt. Probably early to midforties. He'd met me at San Francisco International where he introduced himself as my escort to Greenland and the campsite. Carlisle was a scientist, some kind of expert on isotopes—whatever you call that—and talked nonstop about things like climate change and other environmental gobbledygook. When I asked him if this was a government-sponsored trip he laughed and said no. "Private funding."

I asked him who G. Skerret was, and he told me George was the lead scientist on the project and was waiting for me at the base. George was writing a book apparently.

Great. Cooped up in the freezing cold with a bunch of scientists who knew more about the world than I did and had degrees to prove it. Hang on—didn't I always maintain that life experience is the most valuable degree you can hold? Sure, that's the sort of horseshit I tell myself all the time when I'm surrounded by people who live and breathe textbook intelligence. I won't deny it: sometimes it irks me. Then again, no one ever told me not to go to college.

Once the airplane landed, Terry and I were whisked into a canopied truck that looked suspiciously like a Russian GAZ-66. I prayed silently this wasn't a sign of things to come. The quasi-military vehicle could only take us so far. The rest of the way we had to plow through on foot. It didn't take long for my legs to turn freezing cold, then completely numb. Grimsby's voice kept looping perversely through my mind: *Make sure you take enough warm clothes. Fleece. Take lots of fleece.* Of course, I hadn't.

Terry Carlisle led the front of the pack. Two others had joined us. Carlisle had introduced them to me in the truck, but I'd already forgotten their names. All I knew was that one, a young male who seemed to be biologically melded to his iPod, was a student from UCLA. The other, a woman with cornrows and the ingratiating ability to smile throughout the entire trip, was a biochemistry student from the University of Cape Town in South Africa.

A flurry of snow whipped at us from the front as I struggled with my camera equipment and battled to see two feet ahead.

Where the hell were the sled dogs?

May 7

"Don't worry about it too much."

The words were clear, but I struggled to see. "Worry about what?" I heard myself say woozily. Slowly things began to come into focus. "What the hell...is that noise? Is that coffee?" I sat up and realized I was in a hospital bed. My neck was stiff, but I was warm. I rubbed my eyes. Reality started to bloom.

I was in a small room with another person whose back was turned to me. I tried to figure out who it was, but the heavy parka and winter cap threw me off. Did I imagine it, or was it a woman's voice I'd heard just now? The student from South Africa?

"How do you take your coffee?" the voice asked as I swung my legs off the bed.

"Black. No sugar."

"Of course."

What was that supposed to mean? "I usually do sugar and cream. But something tells me I'm going to need the extra kick today." I took in the small room. Three beds, all the same cramped size. One in the opposite corner, two against the wall. I was sitting on one of the latter.

"What am I not supposed to worry about?"

She turned around, a mug of coffee in each hand.

Holy shit.

Two long strides and she was next to me. She held out one of the cups. "Careful. These tin mugs are hazardous, and we make the coffee hot around here." She sat gingerly on the bed next to me. Adolescent nervousness mocked me. "Georgia Skerret." I shook her hand. It was surprisingly warm. She looked at me from across the top of her blue mug. "You passed out. That's what I meant. You shouldn't worry about it."

I eyed her skeptically. "*Passed out?* How embarrassing."

She smiled as if she knew something. Her eyes were the same hue of mint green as her heavily padded parka. "I thought you might feel that way about it."

"Oh?" I stretched my legs. "Why is that?"

She got up from the bed. "Toast?"

"Um...thanks. I'm starving." I really was.

She talked while she worked. "I know all about you. You hate being uncomfortable. I've read the interviews. I'm completely surprised you actually came."

I was intrigued. "So why'd you offer me the job in the first place?"

"You're the best. Nothing else will do." She plucked hot toast from a dangerous-looking toaster and slathered it with butter. It smelled heavenly. I heard a rattle to my right, and Terry Carlisle stuck his head through the doorway.

"Hey, George, looks like the weather's clearing. Maybe we could go out sooner than anticipated."

"Told you so."

"I'll get the gear ready. Hannah, nice to see you up and about." Then he was gone.

I waited. "George?" I asked, smirking.

"Han?" she countered back, not looking at me. *Damn Grimsby.* "You'd better get your gear ready. When the weather's good we have to move fast. And make sure you bring enough film. I fired the previous photographer because he thought there wasn't anything interesting about snow."

Previous? I felt slighted at the thought. "I'm ready whenever you are."

"Good. Grab that parka on the wall behind you. A former

researcher left it here. It smells faintly of fish, but I'm sure you'll agree it's better than hypothermia."

"Right." I was sure she could hear the sarcasm in my voice.

"By the way, I'd like you to take photos of the crew too."

"I thought as much."

"Don't worry about film. We trek out regularly to Nuuk for supplies." She stopped short and looked at me like I was something interesting.

I waited then asked, "Anything else before you leave so I can change into something fresh?"

She grinned. "You're not at all the way I imagined you'd be."

I smiled tightly and pulled off my cold socks. "Let's hope that doesn't put you off."

"Let's hope not."

What the hell was that supposed to mean?

June 27

Conveniently, no one told me that the sun never sets from May 25 to July 25 here. There's light around the clock. At nighttime—which you can tell only by looking at the clock—long shadows and warm, soft light from the low-hanging sun make everything look dreamlike. Ghostlike. Beautiful.

George tells me there are probably northern lights shining here all the time, but we can't see them because of the constant brightness.

There's snow as far as the eye can see. Somehow you don't realize the extent of it until you're seeing it for the first time. Until you're in it.

Icebergs rise up to one hundred meters above the arctic waterline. George says that up to ninety percent of an iceberg is hidden below the water. She wants to take me to Illulisat to see the world's most active glacier, which moves twenty-five to thirty meters a day.

August 4

George and I have warmed to each other after a not-so-unexpected shouting match. We broke the ice, so to speak.

It had started slowly one Tuesday night, around one of Terry's perfect bonfires. I suspect everyone else saw it coming long before George and I did. They were courteous enough to slink away before we eventually started yelling at each other at the top of our lungs. Me on one side of the lapping, dancing fire; George defiantly on the other. She accused me of being an ignorant Brit. I called her a smug Canadian with a superiority complex.

We both wanted to be in control. I had no business wanting to be in control in the first place, since really I was her employee. But I was used to working alone, being my own boss. I had difficulty accepting the circumstances. And I felt she was patronizing. I told her so.

In the end, we found mutual respect through our equal capacity for blindly refusing to back down. In the end, we shook on it. Those nightly campfires had ended up provoking me in more ways than one.

October 19

I have rolls of film that need to be developed. After several months I can now remember the names of the two students. Glen and Melinda. Usually once every three weeks Terry and one of them hike out to Nuuk for supplies. Coffee and fresh bread, mostly. Sometimes a little fruit. Peanuts if we're lucky. Terry likes to spoil us. He's much more emotional than I first took him to be.

Sometimes George, Glen, and I go off to find the animals

while Melinda and Terry stay at the base. Melinda's interest in climate change makes her follow Terry around like a hungry puppy. Glen's iPod headphones are pretty much glued to his ears. I've learned to tap him on the shoulder if I want to ask him something. It's very clear, though, that his main interest is the wildlife. I've become aware of his presence more when I'm shooting film. He doesn't talk much, but he's a keen observer.

I'm *extremely* attracted to George.

Somewhere between getting used to the slush in my boots and listening to George relate Greenland myths around the fire it just happened. I'm careful how I look at her. I don't want to cause any friction.

Ignorant as I sometimes am, I've learned exactly how many different types of whales there are here. The waters of Greenland include the two largest of the species—the blue whale and the fin whale. Since I've been here, we've spotted not only those two kinds, but also humpbacks, minkes, narwhales, belugas, and sperm and pilot whales. Ironically, we haven't seen any Greenland whales.

The beasts seem curiously attracted to George. The times we've been out in the water they appear out of the blue, and always on George's side of the boat. I got the shit scared out of me the first few times. They swim up so close to the boat. Once, a humpback breached so near to the hull it sent the whole thing up a couple of feet on the roll of a gentle wave. On another occasion a pod of orca spy-hopped in a circle around the boat. They came out of the water vertically, exposing almost the entire top half of their bodies and momentarily staying that way in a manner similar to humans treading water. George had come to stand close to me then. She said they did it to observe boats. It definitely had felt as if they were inspecting *us*—but not in a menacing way. I'd been so enthralled by the behavior of the seven giants that I only became aware of George's fingers lacing into mine when she leaned over and said, "Did you know that the orca is actually the largest member of the oceanic dolphin family?" I breathed slowly, my heart racing. Then she explained to me how, when it comes to the clicks and whistles they use for communication, resident orca pods have their own regional dialects.

What a strange, curious, and beautiful world. Sometimes it seems completely foreign, as if Greenland and San Francisco couldn't possibly exist on the same planet. The roughly two million seals that populate the Greenlandic waters. Walruses. Reindeer and polar bears. I haven't seen a wolf yet, but we hear them all the time, especially at night. And three days ago we saw a small herd of musk oxen near a river valley where they'd been living during the summer months. Soon, in anticipation of winter, they'll move to a higher elevation to avoid the deep snow.

On their last trip, Terry and Melinda surprised us all by coming back to camp on a sled pulled by twelve baying dogs. It makes fishing a lot easier. George is fond of making holes in the snow and waiting for the fish to appear. I've got a few excellent shots of her yanking a halibut (at least I think it was) out from the cold water while it flopped madly at the end of her fishing spear. She and I have made deliberate eye contact like that a few times. Me watching her through the viewfinder of my six-year-old Nikon and her looking back at me through the lens.

December 7

The winter darkness is equally as fascinating as the perpetual daylight is in summer. For weeks the sun doesn't rise above the horizon, and a dusky, murky twilight prevails. The landscape is a sea of white snow and frozen sea. From time to time the stars and moon illuminate patches of white. Pristine and never-ending whiteness that goes on seemingly forever.

We were into winter barely a month when a dire ice storm hit.

It began unremarkably. This time, Terry, Melinda, and Glen all decided to go to Nuuk together. I suspected the younger two of the crew were both starting to feel the itch of cabin fever. To my surprise, I've grown accustomed to the living circumstances out here in the cold.

It had taken the three longer than usual to get to Nuuk because we'd been moving steadily north toward Illulisat over the last three months. Terry had suggested they fly straight to Illulisat instead of going to the capital once again but was overthrown by a two against one vote from Melinda and Glen who wanted to take one last visit to Santa's house in Nuuk. Melinda figured that if she asked him really nicely Santa would send her some African sun in a bottle. Glen wanted a new iPod. His old one was about to give up the digital ghost any day now.

George and I were tracking a polar bear when we first noticed the snow was coming down harder. It was only the third bear we'd seen since I'd arrived, and we were both keen to get as close as possible. George wanted to take blood samples, which I at first thought was crazy. She told me she could handle it, I didn't need to worry. When she slung the heavy tranquilizer gun over her shoulder and winked at me my trust was cemented.

The bear was a couple of ice mounds ahead of us, sniffing the air and ground as he went along. I'd grown so used to swiping snow away from my eyes that it wasn't until I was completely covered by a film of white dust that I noticed anything out of the ordinary. The wind had picked up, too, and the temperature had dropped. Soon we were standing almost two feet deep in fresh snow. We were probably about a kilometer from camp.

"We have to turn around!" George shouted above the wind, which had pitched itself up to a violent, screeching whistle.

"That's probably a good idea!" I was shivering hard already.

The bear had just been there moments ago, but when we looked again it was nowhere in sight. Gone, or camouflaged inside the white.

"Follow me!" She pointed in a direction—I wasn't sure whether it was north, south, or what. Everything looked the same. My heart skipped, and a hot flash of anxiety gripped my chest.

"Just follow me, okay?" I felt her hands squarely on my shoulders. Her eyes looked into mine. "Trust me?"

I nodded.

"Okay," she smiled.

She pulled, I pushed. The wind howled and heaved at us. If we hadn't been trolling through three feet of snow, the force of it would probably have pulled us off our feet. The cold clawed its way tenaciously through my gloves, my boots, my clothes. *What the hell? Keep your chin up, Hannah.*

She led me to the old research station where our team recently had set up camp. It was just two small square little houses, but it was better than the tents we'd had to use on so many occasions. I fell through the door and onto a bed, shivering as if I'd just been dipped in the Greenland Sea.

"You have to sit up." George pulled me until I managed to keep myself in an upright position. I felt her tug a fur blanket around my shoulders, and then she jammed a hot tin cup into my hand, steadying it so I could take a sip. I almost spilled it on the floor. Coffee. Hot. And something else.

"Shot of Famous Grouse." I was aware of George's hands on mine, rubbing softly. "Jesus Christ, Hannah. Now will you start dressing warmer? You'll catch your death out here trying to prove to me how tough you are."

I took another sip of the spiked coffee. "Shitty whiskey. Next time tell Terry to bring us something decent." I didn't have to look at George to know she'd have that curve of a smile around her lips. "Besides, I stopped trying to impress girls in high school."

"Is that right?"

Is that right? I mouthed behind her back like a snotty sixteen year old. *It's your own stupidity for not doing as you're told.* It's a hard habit to break, but somewhere along the line I would have to accept that—about some things, at least—others knew better.

"Drink your coffee," George said. Her back was toward me, and she was fiddling with the gas stove. She seemed to be struggling with it. The wind hammered at the windows and pummeled snow. "Fuck!" She rose to her feet, kicked the stove, and threw a wrench, narrowly missing the bottle of Grouse on the floor.

I laughed, or tried to. "We got all the way back here and now there's no gas?"

George grabbed the bottle of whiskey and said, "Get under the blankets. In the bed." This time I did what she said. We piled all the blankets from the three beds onto one. There was no way either of us would venture outside and into the second building for more. By now the wind-chill factor must have been well below freezing.

George got into bed with me, and we huddled close. Her body heat sought mine. She made me take another mouthful of whiskey then helped herself.

"I wouldn't have taken you for the kind of woman who needed to booze a girl up before bedding her," I said.

My attempt at humor to relieve my own anxiety only made George circle her arms around me tighter. "Shut up, wiseass. Terry and the others will be back in the morning. The storm should pass quickly. Usually when it comes up so suddenly it works itself out pretty quick."

"I'm cold."

Her arms wrapped tighter around me. I couldn't help thinking, *I could die like this.*

The teasing was merciless, of course.

The morning after the storm, Terry, Glen, and Melinda found the two of us still snuggled tightly beneath the blankets. George had been right. By the time Terry shook us both by the shoulder there was no sign of the storm that had caught us so unaware the night before. Terry was pissed we'd drunk so much of the whiskey. I had a hangover.

Thank god Terry fixed the gas. Melinda made me some coffee while Glen and Terry unpacked the supplies. George made herself scarce.

I watched as Melinda spooned two, three, then four generous helpings of sugar into my mug. "You want to give me diabetes?" I asked her.

Melinda snorted. "Just drink it."

"Fine." I'd never gotten used to her South African accent. I didn't want to. It was original.

"So tell me, Hannah," she said, "how long are the two of you going to dance around each other?"

"Excuse me? Dance?"

"You heard me. That woman's in love with you."

I almost choked on my coffee.

"And don't deny your own feelings." She gave me a sympathetic look. "Really, it's quite transparent."

"Oh, pfff!"

Melinda slapped me on the back and grinned widely. "I couldn't have said it better."

January 5

"No, no. I like this one." George held the black-and-white print up against the light. It was a shot of Terry and Melinda examining some sort of core specimen beneath a microscope. George placed the print in one of the piles we were sorting. "Have you booked your flight back to San Francisco yet?"

I hesitated. "Not yet."

She continued looking at the photos. "Take the chance to do so while we're in Illulisat. Otherwise you could be stuck here for another nine months. We're heading out again pretty soon." She held up another print and smiled. "You actually manage to make me look photogenic."

"You are. Photogenic, I mean. What I mean is, you're easy to photograph."

The room was small but cozy. George and I had found a room in a bed-and-breakfast run by one of the locals. Terry, Glen, and Melinda had preferred the lodgings of Camp Brede-bugt ten kilometers north of town. I looked forward to sleeping on a decent mattress again.

I cleared my throat. "Fodor suggested, maybe, that I stay on."

George looked at me curiously. By now I'd memorized every line of her face. "Who's Fodor?"

"Fodor Grimsby, my agent. I know, it's a ridiculous name, but he's very proud of it."

George laughed, a look of realization flooding her face. "I thought his name was Frodo."

We both laughed, trying to dump some of the tension that pulled at us. I finally felt a little loose around the edges, as if I might find the balls to do something. George sifted through the photos again, and I took off my jacket. I'd come to realize over the last few months that wearing little clothing was a privilege.

"There are so many wonderful shots here, Hannah. It's going

to be difficult to pick the ones I'd like to use for the book."

I crossed my arms, content with the compliment, and looked at the prints on the table. We stood so close I smelled the lingering scent of soap on her skin. "I can't help it," I said. "I rarely take a bad picture."

George raised an eyebrow without looking at me. "You're full of it, you know that?"

I leaned in and kissed her because I didn't know how to contradict what she'd said. Or maybe I wanted to prove to her how right she was.

At last. After catching myself thinking about her at night before falling asleep, while building a fire, while making coffee or scraping the scales off a fresh halibut with cold, red, swollen hands.

When I pulled back, uncertain, George released a tight breath. I took it in, absorbed it. "Don't you dare wait another eight months before doing that again," she said.

I laughed, my forehead still against hers, overjoyed. George kissed me again, her warm hand on my neck, breathing lust into my open mouth. I said something pedestrian like "More," and she took me to the bed. We didn't waste a lot of time with clothes. We pulled them off quickly, in a rush, hands shaky. After all this time, we were so hungry for each other that we forgot about lunch only being available between one and two, and that dinner wasn't served until seven thirty. We skipped that too.

April 20

I can now almost track a polar bear by myself. To prove this, George sometimes lets me walk out in front. She claims it gives the added bonus of her shoulder or the side of her face not winding up in one or more of the shots. Secretly, I think it's a pity. I like those.

I haven't been back to San Francisco in twelve months. Grimsby says I've gone native.

He's using my apartment. Says the rent's cheaper than his old place, but I think it's because of the skinny blonde two doors down. She's an aspiring actress.

Curiously enough, I miss Glen, even though he didn't talk most of the time he was here. Melinda's coming back in three months along with another scientist from Baltimore. Seems she too fell in love with the ice.

George's publisher wired a telegram to let her know she's getting rave reviews for the book. They want her to do another one. Oh, and they like the pictures, too.

The distraction I asked for turned out longer than expected. From the looks of things it could go on forever. What with listening to George telling me stories about indigenous spirits by the roaring fire at night and the two of us making love afterward in a small, creaky bed. What's not to like? I know. I hide my true feelings behind my phony butch boldness.

I've heard it said many times that the snowfields are a bleak, harsh, and cruel place. Mostly it's people who've never lived here who say so. Once I was one of those. Then again, once I thought I knew everything.

STEPPING OUT

Cheyenne Blue

"It's the air here." The teacher's enthusiasm is contagious. Her skinny body seems to burst with the desire to share her passion. "We have less pollution. Our soil may be poor, but with care, we can grow some of the most flavorsome food in the world."

Irene dumps herbs into the mortar and starts grinding. It was a good idea, this women's cooking course, here in the Victorian high country. Six women, all enthusiastic amateurs like herself—moneyed, like herself, she adds with wry honesty—here to learn, to improve their skills and cooking creativity, with the added bonus of a holiday in the Australian bush. Miriam Stockard, a retired restaurateur, runs the course at her property on the edge of the Great Dividing Range.

Irene has come alone. This is just one of her "filler times," as she likes to call them, a chance to occupy herself in a most convivial way. It's too easy to be alone in Los Angeles. And she's a "women only" course junkie; maybe, just maybe, she'll meet someone special.

There's nobody promising at Wannaroo, though. Nobody except Miriam herself.

Irene watches surreptitiously out of lowered eyes as Miriam circles the room. The morning light touches her wild hair, burnishing the silver streaks, mingling them with the gold to create some fantastic new alloy. Miriam wears a faded T-shirt, baggy shorts, and Swedish massage sandals—unconventional garb for a chef. The light catches the sun-bleached hairs that cover her tanned forearms like the pelt of a large cat. Her hair spills out of the fuzzy ponytail that barely contains it as she leans over Lucy's bowl to take a taste of her seasonings with a finger. Miriam must be over forty, Irene muses, but her wiry frame, tanned nut-brown by the Aussie sun; quick way of speaking; and unconventional approach make her appear younger.

Sometimes, she imagines Miriam is watching her too, with swift glances out of the corner of her eye, but she puts it down to wishful thinking. Miriam is probably making sure she isn't using too much salt.

The class works quietly for an hour. Outside, the liquid notes of a magpie overlay the buzz of cicadas, providing a musical backdrop for Miriam's muted voice as she encourages and draws out each woman in turn. The course fosters a creative approach. No slavish following of recipes, no automated adding of a pinch of nutmeg and a sprig of parsley; here they invent, mix, blend, experiment, embellish. Melding flavors that challenge the imagination, often supplementing them with the bush tucker they gather outside. Lilly pilly and tamarillo custard. Yabby ravioli with lime and shitake mushrooms. There are no limits, Miriam explains, no preconceptions. They are here to expand their horizons, challenge their creativity, become artists.

Irene watches Miriam, and challenges her own creativity by imagining what she would do to her if they were naked under the lazy ceiling fan in the high-ceilinged bedroom with the verandah that opens to the world.

The women break for morning coffee each day around eleven. Miriam's daughter, Janey, carries in freshly baked scones and dishes of Miriam's homemade jams. There's a running competition to guess the ingredients. Irene takes it seriously, savoring the flavor, trying not to be fooled by the color.

Quandong? she wonders idly, spreading some on a wholemeal scone. Maybe loquat—the hard yellow fruit from the old spreading tree in the backyard. She smiles at Janey, who steadies the plate with a twelve year old's concentration. "A dollar if you'll give me a clue," she whispers in mock seriousness.

Janey's hazel eyes open wide. "I can't do that," she says. "Mum would kill me."

The evening is molten, and saturated by an abrupt thunderstorm that starts as if someone has opened sluice gates. Irene sits quietly in the covered verandah, and listens to the rain lash the corrugated iron roof. The air is so liquid that she cleaves through it and her sweat shines on her skin.

She's alone. The other women departed earlier for a folk-music night in Beechworth—an evening of red wine and song. Normally, Irene would go too—the unforced spontaneity of instant companions is partly why she came—but she's behind on her diary. It lies untouched on her knees, its brocade cover damp from the night air.

The creak of the flyscreen alerts her to someone's presence. It's Miriam, a steaming mug in one hand. She opens the flyscreens so the air can move more freely, and props her bare feet on the rail. In profile, her face is serene as she stares out into the night.

Irene doesn't want to interfere; she senses Miriam is looking for solitude. After all, she's a vital presence to the smooth running of the course, encouraging the diverse group of women to mix, throw away their inhibitions, and enjoy themselves. She probably welcomes a rare evening alone. But Irene's pen rolls off the diary and drops to the floor with a clatter.

Miriam jerks, then calls out, "I didn't know anyone was here. You must think I'm rude, ignoring you like that."

Her face is smiling and open, so Irene picks up her diary and her glass of local Tokay and joins her. "I wanted to catch up with my writing." She raises the diary, and lets it fall back on her bare legs. "But it's pleasanter to simply watch the rain."

Miriam nods, and her face relaxes. "I love storms like these. When you can smell the earth, and the bush. It's when I love my home the best."

"Do you ever not love it?"

"Sometimes. Last summer there was a bushfire burning out of control in the foothills. It came down the ridge, and Janey and I had to evacuate. They got it under control, eventually, but when we came back we didn't know what we'd find. We were lucky, the house was untouched." She sips the steaming tea. "Then I hated this place. And in winter, when the air is so chill and crisp, and your breath freezes in your lungs, I'm not too keen about it. But I wouldn't leave it for anything."

"Have you been here long?"

"Nearly twenty years. Janey was born in your bedroom."

Irene thinks of the echoes of pain that must still linger in a corner of the room. She wonders who was there at the birth with Miriam. "Where does Janey go to school?" she asks instead.

"Beechworth. She gets the school bus from the end of the road. But now, it's the holidays and she's trying to earn enough to buy herself a pony. She bakes the morning scones, cleans up in the kitchen, and also works on a neighbor's property, helping with the livestock."

"She's a good kid."

"The best." There's a silence, broken only by the battering rain and a persistent mosquito. "What's it like where you live?"

A thread of genuine interest colors Miriam's voice, so Irene tells her about Santa Monica, and the insanity of L.A. life.

"You live alone?"

"Yes. For the last four years since my partner and I split. It was amicable," she hastens to add. "Julie moved to the East Coast to take a promotion."

Miriam nods, a sharp gesture, as if she expected nothing less. "Why are you here?"

Irene swirls the Tokay in her glass. "I'd never been to Australia." She sips, waiting to see if Miriam will notice the unspoken addendum.

"There must be cooking classes in L.A.?"

"Too many."

"Big city got too small?"

"Guess you could say that. I wanted different. To meet new people."

"Yes. Ours is a small world at times."

Irene notices her phrasing, but the evasive dance continues.

"Where are you going next?" Miriam scuttles over one of the clean glasses on the table and pours herself some of Irene's Tokay.

"Sydney for a week. Guess everyone should see the Opera House and the Harbour Bridge, right?"

Miriam's hesitation creeps into the room. A pause, too long to be careless, too studied not to be meant. And then she says, "Or you could stay here."

At first, Irene thinks it's a question. The Aussie accent tilts up at the end of the word, like a ski jump. She opens her mouth to say she's already seen the sights in this parched land of drooping gums and cackling birdlife, but then, in the other woman's face, she sees that no, it isn't a question. It's a statement of something offered, something known. She waits, studying Miriam's face. It's all there, a quiet knowledge, maybe a touch of wistfulness.

"How long?" she asks instead. "You've probably got my room booked for your next course."

"There's a week in between," says Miriam.

It's one of those times, Irene thinks, when you instantly know all there is to know about what's important. You can sift seamlessly through the layers of politeness, and the mouthing of words to the meaning behind them. Miriam isn't simply offering her bed and breakfast as an alternative to a Sydney hotel.

"What about Janey?"

"Janey's cool. She knows. There's no hiding around here."

"No." There isn't with Miriam. No facades, no games, no pretence. "That's what I like about you Aussies. Your directness."

Miriam laughs, relaxes. Offer down on the table and accepted. "It's our curse too. No polite place to hide when it goes wrong."

Their eyes meet, cling across the table. Emboldened, Irene reaches out a hand, covers Miriam's where it lies on the scarred wooden surface. She grips hard, and Miriam turns hers around, so they are clenched palm to palm. Irene studies the contrast: soft white city hand to narrow, sun-browned paw.

A clatter outside announces the return of the rest of the group. Reflexively, Irene jerks, her hand twitching before withdrawal. It's not that she minds, but she thinks Miriam might. After all, she's the leader, the tutor. But Miriam's hand bites down hard and so she lets it lie.

The rest of the women sweep in with a cacophony of good-natured comments. They throw themselves down on the battered overstuffed couches around the verandah and demand some of the Tokay. If anyone notices Irene and Miriam's clasped hands, it goes unremarked.

The group disbands in an exchange of email addresses, and a flurry of future plans. Elsie's going to Melbourne to visit her sister, Lucy to Sydney and her inner suburbs terrace; Alynna is also going to Melbourne to catch the plane to New Zealand, the others scatter like grass seeds in the wind.

Lucy asks if Irene wants to ride with her to Sydney.

"No," says Irene, simply. "I'm staying here awhile."

"No worries then." Lucy leans in, pecks her on the cheek, tosses the car keys from hand to hand. "Look me up when you do make it to Sydney."

"I will."

Cars chug off in clouds of dust. Irene watches the dust settle again, her hands gripping the verandah rail. She turns to find Miriam watching her. Irene's tongue-tied. The moment of knowledge when she decided to stay seems hazy. Had the Tokay dulled her senses, made a simple offer into something else? Maybe Miriam only wanted an extra week's board and lodging. But then Miriam crosses the worn boards to her side, rests a hand on her hip in an intimate gesture.

"I'm glad you stayed," she says. "I'm looking forward to getting to know you better."

Out of the corner of her eye, Irene sees the fuzzy down on Miriam's cheek. A wisp of hair curls around her ear, silver in the low sunlight, and there, on her own hip, is a small hand radiating heat and possession. Irene covers it with her own, and leans just enough so she can feel the warmth of Miriam's body against her side. It's like orbiting the sun. She's taller than Miriam, who leans her head down on her shoulder. They rest in this pose for long minutes.

It's a peaceful evening, now that the other women have gone.

Miriam reheats leftovers, and they eat them with a simple salad in the wide, modern kitchen. Janey chatters about a horse she's caring for—the owner wants her to ride it in a showing class. If she notices Miriam and Irene's closeness, she holds her silence. After dinner, the three of them take a walk outside, where the ground is hard and unyielding and the gum trees droop. The night sounds of the bush surround them.

Irene takes Miriam's hand again, threading her fingers through, and they walk through the tinder-dry grass, clasped hands swinging.

The next day they kiss. An almost-accidental kiss, one Irene carefully planned. She turns from the kitchen bench, rests a hand on Miriam's shoulder, leans in to hear what she's saying, and her lips find Miriam's in a nuzzling, questing way. As kisses go, it's short, but the spark arcs between them, strung fine and glowing in the humid air. The sweetness of it steals Irene's breath away, and she rests her forehead against Miriam's so that their breath mingles between them.

The day after, Irene knows she's falling. Fast, hard, and helpless for a woman she barely knows. Immediately the problems tumble in her mind: the distance—an Australian and an American—the culture, immigration requirements, Janey. If it comes to it, she should be the one to relocate. Miriam has a house, a daughter, a business, and Irene has so very little that is fixed and immutable. But it's too soon to think like that.

By the middle of their week, Irene knows she wants to stay. More than a week, more than a month. She wants to wake beside Miriam, turn to her, and kiss her sleep-slack lips. She wants to drop Janey off at the school bus and feel a parent's pride as she wins a ribbon with her horse. The thought of merging into Miriam's life is compelling. She wants to be a part of this place, this family, this community, even this laconic country.

The day before Irene leaves, they make love. It is a silent glide to Miriam's bedroom. There are no words spoken, no offer, no acceptance. They simply rise together from the battered couch on the verandah, hold hands, and walk upstairs. Miriam doesn't pause in front of Irene's door, as she had for the last few nights for their kiss; instead, she leads her past to her own room. It's a cool sanctuary of sea green, and the bed is wide and firm. Theirs is an unhurried loving, punctuated by the rhythmic whop of the ceiling fan, stirring air over their bodies.

When it's over, they lie side by side on their backs, fingertips touching. When Irene dares to look at her lover, she finds Miriam already staring at her with a curling half smile.

Miriam touches Irene's face, brushing her fingertips over her lips. "I love you," she says.

Irene's breath hitches, and for a moment she can't reply.

"Too soon?" The curling smile is still in place, but there's a fixed quality to it that wasn't there a moment before. "Blame my Aussie directness again. I—"

But Irene smiles, rolls, stopping her words with a kiss. "Not too soon," she says.

The day Irene leaves, they start making plans. Irene will return to L.A., sublet her apartment, organize her finances, direct her mail, contact the Australian embassy about a visa, cancel subscriptions, notify her friends, sell her car…. The list overflows her head, building a wall between them, brick by brick. What seemed so easy, so obvious is already a trial. The hurried conversation, held in the front of Miriam's battered old Holden as she drives Irene to Tullamarine airport, seems strained. But if they don't say it now, then Irene knows it will go unaddressed. So she pushes her worries aside and concentrates only on Miriam and how much she loves her.

Irene waits at the boarding gate at LAX. Any minute now, they will start boarding her flight to Melbourne, Australia, and she will wait until they call her row number. Then she will stand, fold her copy of the *Los Angeles Times*, leave it on the seat for someone to find, open her passport to the page with her photograph, and join the line to board the plane.

And then there will be no going back.

Her boarding card is damp from the sweat of her hand. She checks her waist belt for the umpteenth time: passport; some of the bright, brash Australian currency; a few gray American dollars, rolled and secured with a rubber band; the key to her apartment in Santa Monica; and the last email Miriam sent her. She resists the temptation to unfold it and read it once more, even though the words are already imprinted in her brain.

"Come," says the final sentence. "Just catch a plane. Janey and I are longing to see you again."

The desk attendant taps the tannoy and announces boarding for passengers needing assistance, those with small children, and those passengers traveling first and business class.

Irene stands, takes out her passport, and moves closer to the desk for the general boarding call.

Even as she shuffles along the aisle, she's thinking how much she'll miss L.A. The palm trees, the boardwalk, the vibrant street life, the myriad restaurants, the long hazy marine days. But her long scribbled lists of pros and cons are weighed and balanced and set aside.

Does everyone feel this way? she wonders, as she fastens her seatbelt and stows her magazine in the pocket in front of her. Does everyone feel they're stepping out into the stars without a space suit? She can always change her mind, and return; this she knows. She clings to the thought to help make the leaving easier.

But fifteen hours later, as the plane bumps onto the runway at Tullamarine; as she clears customs and immigration and wheels her trolley out into the arrivals hall; as she sees Miriam's dear face, and Janey's smiling one, her heart is singing.

PAIGE

Lori L. Lake

Paige Brandt came home on a Friday evening in the spring of 1988 after nine years in the joint upstate. I'd been up to the Skywater High School gym to work out and had stopped to gas up my VW. Parking at the pump closest to the highway at Stevens' Shell Station gave me a good view as the Greyhound rolled into town, stopped at the corner, and she got out. Her hair was shoulder length and blew in the wind. She wore jeans and a sweatshirt, and even from a distance, I saw her shiver in the cool Pacific Ocean air. She held a bag in her hand—that was all. A thick, brown grocery-type bag with the top rolled over and the whole thing creased as though she'd held it in her lap for hours, which she probably had. It's nearly two hundred miles from Central Oregon Correctional Facility to this little town of Skywater along the Oregon coast, population 932.

Paige had robbed the liquor store nine years earlier with Charley Yecke. They were caught before they even made it over the Washington border, which was probably lucky in some ways. No federal charges. I heard that both of them were high and drunk and completely out of it, sitting on the side of Highway 101 near Seaside. They didn't put up a fight when they were arrested, and Paige didn't have a chance when it came to trial before Judge Tremont. Though she was only sixteen at the time, they tried her as an adult over the protests of her mother and the legal-aid attorney. In a twenty-minute open-and-shut case, her fate was sealed.

The world kept turning while she did her time. I graduated from our shit-hole high school, a place that never gave wild girls a chance. And Paige was definitely a wild one. By fourteen she'd been drinking and smoking and running with boys four or five years older. Her mama worked at the candy store, pulling taffy, making divinity, cooking up chocolate for fudge and truffles. Nobody knew who Paige's daddy was, and her mama had never married.

Sometimes I thought of her, wild-haired Paige Brandt who stole $760.48 from Pitney's Liquor & Spirits and spent less than $100 of it before she and Charley were captured. Didn't seem like it was worth it.

News rippled through town that Paige was back. All day Saturday I heard plenty of conversations over the counter at Sweet Lands Candy, where I work.

Paige couldn't go "home" anymore. Her mama had died the year before. Ovarian cancer. Paige's granddad let her have a room. Mrs. LaBounty was scandalized to have to live across the street from them. Mr. Steele said he'd bought a new box of shotgun shells, just in case.

I've worked at the candy store ever since senior year in high school. Paige's mother taught me well. I still miss her.

Monday morning, bright and early, I stood at the window of Sweet Lands Candy assembling the ingredients for five colors of frosting. Three trays of cupcakes had come out of the oven an hour before, and I was fixing to frost and decorate them with little crosses and Jesus faces. Dixie Shenk was due to pick them up sometime after nine a.m. for the kids in her daughter's class at Holy Redeemer.

If you work long enough at a candy store, eventually sweets no longer hold your interest. I've long since stopped caring about jelly beans and peanut clusters, all-day suckers and saltwater taffy. Tourists come and tourists go, and they can take the damn candy with 'em. I'm pretty well sick of it.

Paige tapped on the window at 8:55, five minutes before we open, and a thrill of worry sped up my spine. Even though I had wanted to be—had intended to be—less judgmental than the rest of the townspeople, I couldn't help it. She caught me by surprise, before I had the chance to properly compose myself. I met her eyes, and I know she saw the momentary fear. Her face closed off and took on a hardened scowl.

She was dressed exactly the same as the day before, but not holding anything at all, not a gun, not the paper bag, just herself. She crossed her arms over her chest and started to turn away, but I shook my head and mouthed, "Wait."

I had sticky crap all over my hands, so I gave them a quick rinse in the metal sink, then wiped them on my pink apron as I went around the counter. Mr. Tilden didn't need to know I opened up early. He was off to Portland to buy another truckload of sugar and oil and whatnot. I flipped the OPEN sign and unlocked the door, and she shuffled in, bringing the smell of salt air with her. The fifty years of pain in her eyes looked bad on her twenty-five-year-old face, and her dark eyes didn't burn with the intensity they had in high school. Instead, she reeked of fatigue. Her light-brown shoulder-length hair looked like it had been hacked with pinking shears. I was surprised at how pale she was, her high cheekbones not even carrying a hint of color. "You been down to the beach?" I asked.

She shook her head. "Too cold."

I imagined it would be, since she wasn't wearing a jacket. The sweatshirt was dark blue and not particularly thick. She must have been wearing it for a long time for it to appear so worn.

Paige stood in the store, her eyes taking in the shelves of candies, little-kid toys, gum, and racks of fancy candy behind glass. I couldn't remember when Mr. Tilden had cleared out the tables in the alcove and replaced them with two rows of red shelves, but I knew Paige couldn't have ever seen the change. She turned her back to me, moved over into that alcove, and ran a hand over a display of glittery Barbie candy packs. I suddenly realized she wasn't here to buy anything, but to take in the place, as though she were breathing it in.

I didn't know what to say, so I went back around the counter, to the worktable by the window, and resumed frosting the cupcakes. Every once in a while I glanced over, but Paige seemed lost in thought.

Outside, foot traffic increased in front of my friend Robin's bakery across the street, and I wished for a nice, steamy cappuccino. A big RV hauling a fishing boat pulled up in front and blocked my view. Three teenaged kids spilled out of the back along with three adults from the front. They dodged across the highway to the bakery. I didn't notice Dixie, and she startled me when she came in.

"Good morning, Dixie. And good timing, too. I'm just ready to wrap these up for you." I sealed up one box of cupcakes.

Dixie glanced over at Paige, then frowned and moved up close to the counter. In a voice not low enough for Paige to fail to hear, she said, "What's *she* doing in here?"

I shrugged and turned away, my hands fumbling with the flaps for the second box. I got it together and quickly filled it with the remaining cupcakes, then stacked and carried them over to the counter. "Anything else you need?"

Dixie pressed her lips together and shook her head. I took her money and rang up the order. She slid the boxes off the counter and headed for the door in a hurry. "Keep the change, Jillian."

I stood holding the two quarters as Paige turned and sauntered toward the door. She saw Dixie and said, "Here, I'll get that for you," and reached for the door handle.

"No," Dixie said sharply. "I can get it myself."

But by then Paige was pulling the door open and stepping back. Dixie shot her a look of pure malice as she raced out, nearly running into one of the kids munching on a doughnut near the RV.

So that's how it's going to be, I thought. I didn't know what to say, and when Paige met my eyes, I looked away.

"You went to Skywater High, didn't you?"

I nodded. "Graduated in 1980."

"You were a year behind me." Paige gazed over my head at the Coca-Cola clock. "Have you worked here long?"

"Since my senior year."

Her gaze dropped abruptly, and the eyes that met mine were filled with such longing that I very nearly felt my soul sucked right out. "You knew her." It wasn't a question, but a statement of wonder. "Oh! You must be Jill. She wrote about you sometimes."

I felt my face grow hot. Paige's mother sent letters to the prison with my name in them? How strange. I didn't know what to say.

"You're not hiring here, are you?"

I shook my head. "Sorry. We're full up at the moment. But lots of places will be needing summer help soon."

She turned away. "All right then, thanks."

"You're welcome, Paige."

For a moment she looked startled that I called her by her name. She trudged toward the door, and I watched her go. I didn't think she'd have an easy time finding work.

Days passed, and talk didn't let up about "that vicious felon" and "Aggie Brandt's sleazy daughter." In the Coffee Café, I got an earful from four older guys who sat behind me. Almost made me too sick to eat my omelet. The checkers at Fenton Foods carried on a continual conversation with one another about Paige as they rang up my groceries. In the Laundromat, a woman with three preschool-aged kids running around raising hell complained that she didn't feel her children were safe in Skywater anymore. Obviously Paige's arrival was the biggest thing to happen in town since the Weed & Feed got held up last fall.

One day I drove up to Florence, thirty miles up the coast, and Paige Brandt was a topic of discussion at the Dairy Queen where I stopped for a cone.

Only my mother seemed to have any perspective. "People change in nine years, Jillian. That girl went into jail a scared but cocky sixteen year old, and now, after all this time, she's probably a different person. People shouldn't judge her until they get to know who she is *now*."

I agreed with my mother, but the two times I had seen Paige in town, she'd stalked by me, her face angry and hard—like she wanted to kill somebody. Really, the townspeople here are merciless. I don't know how she stayed. I'm not even sure why I had.

A couple weeks went by, and talk around town died down, then turned to the Turnbull girl's pregnancy and whether senior baseball shortstop Jack Clark was the father or not. I heard so many heated discussions on the topic that soon I was sick to death of it, but here was Mr. Kaiser, standing at my counter asking for truffles while yammering on about malicious girls who deep-six the sports careers of well-meaning athletes. Give me a break. As much as we needed the business at Sweet Lands, I just wished the townsfolk would buy their candy and go somewhere else to gossip. Thank god it was closing time.

As Mr. Kaiser was leaving, Paige came through the door. She wore a navy-blue windbreaker and jeans. I looked at the clock and saw that it was two minutes to eight, then turned to finish wiping down the fudge table.

I got that funny feeling you get when someone is staring— sort of a shiver of apprehension. When I looked up, I saw Paige looking at me from the alcove by the miniature *Finding Nemo* lunch boxes. She turned away, but not before I saw her look of embarrassment.

I asked, "Can I help you with anything in particular?"

She glanced up, blushing, and shook her head. Her face was hard to read, but she looked reflective, like she had something to say but couldn't quite come out with it.

Just then, Mr. Tilden came up from the back room. "Jillian, I've got one last receipt. Have you cashed out the—hey!" He glared toward Paige. "What are you doing in here?"

Paige's face went slack, her eyes hard and narrowed. Before she had a chance to answer, Mr. Tilden was at the door, pulling it open. "You can just take your thievin' self right out the door, and don't come back."

I raised a hand and said, "Mr. T…"

"Hush now." He nodded toward the clock. "It's after hours.

Who knows what she has in mind. C'mon, Brandt, get out."

Paige took a deep breath and moved slowly toward the door. Her hands were balled into fists, and she shook with fury. She stopped at the doorway. "I didn't want your crass shit anyway."

He grabbed her arm and forcefully pushed her out. "I catch you back here, your ass is grass." He slammed the door shut, turned the lock, and pulled down the CLOSED shade.

Out the main window, I caught sight of Paige standing on the sidewalk to light a cigarette. She looked toward me as though she wanted to tell me something, but I was hard pressed to know what it could be. Her head went up, and she squared her shoulders before she walked away fast.

Exasperated, Mr. Tilden put his hands on his hips and faced me. "I don't understand how Aggie could have been such a wonderful person, and her daughter is the exact opposite. How is that so?"

I didn't know how to answer, but I don't think Mr. T would have cared what I said.

"If that tramp shows up here again, Jillian, you are to call 911. You hear me?" I nodded, and he said, "Okay, finish up here, and I'll see you in the morning."

My boss retreated to the rear of the store and left me with the last of the day's pans to wash. As I stood over the sink, I saw a flash of red outside. Paige stood at the window looking down at the trays of goodies I had so artfully displayed there. When her eyes rose to meet mine, they were full of such sadness and longing that I had to look away.

Working all day in the candy store is hard on me. I'm shy, and the steady flow of customers and their demands makes me feel like they're sucking all the sweetness right out of me. Whenever I get the early shift, I like to jog or walk along the beach in the late afternoon. It's great stress relief, even when the weather is bad, and I get some time to myself. I take a change of clothes to work for those early mornings, and most days, when I get done at 2:30, I try to get at least half an hour of exercise, then go home and wash away the salt from the ocean and the sugar from the shop. Once the high school lets out for the summer, the gym is open to the public three days a week. I often go up there to shoot a few baskets, lift weights, and don gloves to smack the punching bag. On a day like today when it's raining, I usually stay indoors.

I drove my VW up to the school. Built in the '50s, it's a rabbit warren full of dark hallways and shabby rooms. I don't think they've painted since I graduated. It smells of dampness, dust, and floor cleaner. Mel and Jorge, the custodians, had cordoned off the gym to reseal the wood floor, so I took the stairs to the upper loft where the Universal Gym sat surrounded by benches and free weights. The windowless room had never had proper ventilation, and it was much warmer than the sixty degrees outside. All was quiet and no one else was working out.

Feeling energized by the prospect of solitude, I stepped across mats to the far wall, set down my little workout bag, then sank to the floor to stretch. I had changed back at the store into shorts, a T-shirt, and a black Mickey Mouse sweatshirt. I shifted into a hurdler's stretch, then a variety of other contortions to loosen up. My legs were fatigued from standing most of the day, but my arms felt strong. I decided to focus most on upper body lifting.

I started to rise and heard a distant rhythmic pounding. *Bump-bump-bump*...pause. *Bump-bump-bump*. Through the door and down the hall was a room, hardly more than a twelve-by-twelve-foot box, where two huge boxing bags hung in the corners. I opened the door and ducked in the dim room before I realized it was Paige Brandt pounding the hell out of the big black bag. She wore red shorts and a baggy gray T-shirt, and when she turned, brown gloves on her hands, her face glowed so red that she looked like she'd been crying. I hesitated. She whirled away and slammed a fist into the bag. Huffing with exertion, she struck at it again.

I watched, fascinated, until she paused and turned. "What are you looking at, candy girl?"

I glanced away, heart in my throat. Paige resumed her assault on the bag, so I went to the corner and rooted around in the box full of gloves until I found a pair that fit. The gloves were bulky and a little unwieldy, but the rules, posted prominently on the wall, required that no one work the bags without gloves. The insides were stiff and rough against my palms, and I flexed my hands to try to loosen them.

I went to the left bag and gave it a halfhearted poke. Paige peppered her bag with jab after jab, then leaned in, steadied the swinging bag with her left fist, and bashed away with her right glove. I let fly a volley of punches, but I couldn't stop watching her out of the corner of my eye. I wondered if they let women box in prison. I wondered if she'd had to defend herself there. Suddenly, I wondered if I was safe in the same room with her.

As if to answer my question, she squared off and faced me, fists curled up against her chest. "What is wrong with you—with *all* you people?"

Now that I looked closer, I saw that she had indeed been crying. Her chest heaved, perhaps less from the exertion with the punching bag and more from emotions I easily read in her face. "I can't speak for the rest of the town."

She stepped nearer. "I shouldn't have come here."

"What?" I didn't understand. Did she mean she shouldn't have come to the gym? Or to Skywater? I let my hands drop to my sides as I studied her. She brought one glove up to her forehead as though to brush bangs out of her face, but the glove was too bulky.

"Paige." I moved forward, mouth open, but not knowing what to say.

"You think you're better than me." A glove reached out, tapped me on the shoulder, bumping me back. When the next jab came toward me, I blocked it with my right arm. "Not one person gives a shit what I've been through."

I blocked another jab and met her eyes. "You wanna beat someone up, Paige?" She didn't respond. "Go on—hit me. Just stay away from my face."

She lashed out, a roundhouse that whacked me high in the left shoulder. Holding my gloves high, I braced myself for another hit. Instead, I saw misery well up and leak out her eyes. She turned her face away, defeated.

An unexpected rush of heat started at my throat and traveled straight to my groin. I reached out and touched her chest with the top of my glove. I moved closer, pushed her with the glove again. She stepped aside, alarm showing on her tear-stained face, and I followed as she backed toward the closed door. "You want to hurt someone, Paige?"

She shook her head. "I gotta go."

Once again I met her eyes, and before she looked away, I felt a fire rise up in my belly. For a moment I couldn't breathe. I tightened my fist in the glove and socked her in the shoulder. "Come on, Paige. You're being a chicken."

Now her eyes blazed, and she brought up her fists. I shoved her back against the door. "Jillian, I could hurt you badly. Don't provoke me."

I grinned and cuffed her again, a light blow to her other shoulder. She struck out and caught me by surprise. I didn't have time to react as the brown glove sank into my midsection and ejected all the air from my body. I let out a gasp and would have fallen to the ground had she not grabbed me. "I'm sorry...sorry...so sorry. God, I'm sorry! How many times do I have to say it?"

We stumbled, clutched together like two prize-fighters in a clinch, but there was no referee to part us. When I got my breath back, it exploded from me in a fire of panting. My whole body was electrified, every nerve ending quivering. I wrapped my arms around her middle and squeezed, pressed my face into her neck, sucked on salty skin. She stiffened, as though surprised.

"Paige," I whispered as I pressed her against the door, moved my knee between her legs, and heard her moan.

Her arms tightened around me, the gloves against my shoulders. She was leaning so hard against my gloves that they were pinned against the door behind her. I was able to slide my hands out. I reached up under her T-shirt, caressed her ribs, kneaded firm moist breasts, and pressed my ear against her neck. The pulse point there raced as fast as my breathing.

She moved against my leg and made a whimpering sound, like a wounded animal. I froze and leaned back slowly, afraid of what I would see in her eyes.

Her irises were huge, a well of deep brown pain. "You smell like she used to, Jill. Just like cotton candy." The brown gloves came up on either side of my head and pulled my face toward her. Soft lips covered mine, drank me in, devoured me. Somehow she got her boxing gloves off, and her hands went up my shirt and unhooked my bra. Hot palms glided around to cover my breasts, and I gripped her waist, my thumbs digging into her hip bones.

She shifted her hips forward, moved her knee, and suddenly I was impaled upon her leg, the center of me rubbing against her with abandon. She cupped my behind, moved me up higher, and I pulled up my shirt. Her mouth found my right breast and sent shock waves to the hot bundle of nerves between my legs.

It was all I could do to hold on then. I was a throbbing, pulsing being; feeling a high I had never before experienced; eagerly tasting her tongue, her mouth, her neck. My hand found its way into her shorts, down into the patch of soft hair, to the moist wetness within. She gasped and gripped me tight. "Oh, Jillian," she said. "Like that, Jill, like that…"

We moved together, breathing as one, fighting gravity. I came first—with lights and explosions and a humming sound in the distance that I realized was my own voice. I didn't want it to stop—the punch and pound of her knee against my center. As the throbbing dissipated, she, too, called out, saying my name over and over, and she could no longer hold us both up.

We slid down the door, me still straddling her thigh, my face pressed into her neck. My knees touched the floor, and she twisted, slid a boxing glove out of the way. She gripped me tightly, her hands caressing my back, under my arms, alongside my breasts. I felt the fire all over again. "You're good." I gulped. "Very good."

In a voice filled with wonder, she asked, "How did you do that to me, Jillian?"

"What?"

"That! This." Her eyes met mine, and she looked completely flabbergasted. "How?"

"I guess you stopped fighting."

Mr. Johnson gave Paige a job at the Shell station the next week. She worked there six long years until he sold it to her when he retired. Ten more years have gone by, and Paige still owns it.

And me.

NOT THE END OF LINER NOTES

Jewelle Gomez

It would only have been more stereotypical if she'd answered "James Dean."

But first I noticed the wink of her T-shirt just at the neck. Thin lavender stripes marched across the field of pale-green polished cotton leading me right to that sliver of white. My breath caught somewhere in my diaphragm. The shirt topped a pair of well-worn jeans that were really being worn well. Not that kid kind of tight jeans that makes anyone larger than a size ten feel like a blimp. But the kind of worn denim that lovingly drapes the body of a woman prepared to change a tire, cook a meal or dance.

"Should we," she said, not a question at all. Her arms opened in front of her in front of me. She waited.

You rarely ever get to watch a person wait. In fact, people hardly wait anymore. At least not as still as she did.

People don't do a lot of things anymore. That's why I'm

taking the dance class—Swing and Salsa 101. For colored girls who've considered suicide when the rainbow is enuf, this is nothing. For a colored girl raised in Wisconsin by members of the War Resisters League, a colored girl who's just seen her first gray hairs—this is a leap. But not growing is dying, they say.

I'd been curled up on my couch alone, if you don't count my cat, at my favorite time of the day—twilight—and it came to me as I was reading liner notes. I may be the only person in my set who possesses a turntable. (I am the only person who still uses the word *set* in that way.) Ella Fitzgerald was singing and I was reading what a music critic had to say about her, about the songs (by Gershwin), about the climate in which the recording was made. An entire world rolled out of my little speakers in front of me and I needed to engage. I wanted to dance! I leapt up from the couch but realized I didn't know the steps.

So, having no girlfriend and knowing no local bar that has a swing night, I found a class. Queers don't have marriage, but we got classes in everything. At first I just walked by the storefront building a couple of times, not stopping. I could hear music coming through the venetian blinds, from behind the painted window that read, AKIDO CLASSES FROM 3-7 PM and DANCE FROM 7:30 TO 10.

I harrumphed at myself for the ridiculousness of the idea—me taking dance classes! I hadn't been in anything remotely resembling a dance position in more than a decade. There was that time I tripped on the curb, went flying into the middle of Valencia Street, and was almost hit by a low rider. It was kind of like that aerial dancing I saw at a concert at Yerba Buena Gardens once. But except for the loud radio in the urgent care center when they were putting the cast on my ankle, it wasn't much of a musical experience.

Even when I was with what's-her-name, in those four years I

don't think we danced more than twice. She thought Our People danced, laughed, talked, and wore red too much. All except for her, of course, who did none of those things with any frequency. It was like *she* was raised in Wisconsin, not me.

I was in love with her brain, so it didn't much matter at the time—and she could do the horizontal boogie. However, once she was gone I started laughing and talking, loud too. I pulled out all of my record albums and spent the next few years reacquainting myself with them.

Nina Simone, Novella Nelson, Jimmy Rushing, and some of those I bought later but never played around the house when what's-her-name was on the scene: Joan Armatrading, Ferron, Sarah Jane Morris. It was like a reunion. But they sure did make me want to dance.

So I walked by the storefront a couple of times, then I went in early when the sweat of the martial arts class was not yet blown out the door by the giant fan they kept at one end of the floor. I grabbed a brochure and split before the instructor, draped in her white gi, could ask me anything. She smiled broadly at me from across the room, as if the sheer force of her cheer would drag me back. I guess it did, because I came the next week, signed up, and now here I was.

I couldn't tell if the nighttime dance teacher was related to the afternoon martial arts instructor, but they had a similar way about them—crisp, direct, with dazzling smiles. For the first half hour of the class I stood by the wall, in the exact spot, metaphorically speaking, that had terrified me all through high school. I could no longer imagine what I'd been reading on that record jacket that had propelled me off of my comfortable couch and into the glare of potential humiliation.

I watched the instructor, a friendly looking full-bodied woman with unnaturally black hair to match her deeply black clothes, as she worked with half the class on leading then the other half on following. Being bi-sensitive she was careful to allow people to work both sides of the fence.

There were ten of us: four lesbians in addition to me. Not "L Word" lesbians but solid representations of our city's most vibrant neighborhoods: the Mission District, the Haight, Bernal Heights, and maybe the Avenues. I couldn't look in their direction to confirm for fear I'd flame up like a barbecue; I didn't want to feel like I was on the make. Then there were three American ethnic (maybe straight) guys who seemed to have wandered in from another movie; perhaps they'd gotten gift certificates for Father's Day.

There was the one sprightly queen who was thrilled by all of us and appeared to have taken the class before. And the other student who looked as terrified as me: a deeply quiet person who was in transition, but I wasn't certain in which direction.

We each took turns being twirled around by the cheerful dark cloud and it was surreal, but I thought I shouldn't smile, much less laugh. So I just tried to pay attention to their feet, not their faces, and not trip when it was my turn.

Then the instructor recued the music and waved her arms as if she were starting the Arthur Murray ballroom competition. We were meant to swing into each other's arms like Ginger and Fred stepping out onto a soundstage that was dressed up to look like the Riviera. This was the moment that most of us of a certain age remember with an agony of adolescent discomfort that tastes like something gone sour in the refrigerator.

My feet felt as if they were imbedded in fast-drying cement— a vendetta finally settled. I didn't look around me, only at my shoes, which had been carefully chosen to provide just enough slide but no slalom. I think everyone else was hesitating too, but your vision tends to go at times like this.

Then I noticed that the transperson and I were glued to the wall while everyone else was milling about. S/he was wearing dark linen pants on very long legs and impossibly high heels. In a lovely contralto that could have belonged to anyone s/he said: "I...uh...I'd say let's dance, but I'm trying to break the old habits...learn to do it the other way 'round...not lead...you know."

I looked up into her tentative gray eyes and realized she didn't want me to think she wasn't asking me to dance because I was the only colored person in the room. Funny how you can hear a whole paragraph in the space of a single musical note.

"You go, girl!" I answered as she sucked in her courage, gave her high heels a shake like a newborn pup, and sauntered over to the bulky Italian guy. That left me with the wall all to myself.

Then I heard a voice say, "Should we," and it wasn't a question. That's when I saw her T-shirt.

I stepped into her arms, since there really was nowhere else to go, except back up against the dreaded wall, and I comforted myself with the fact that she couldn't be such a great dancer if she was here too. I expected her to count off the steps under her breath like the kids did in the Our Gang comedies when they were stuck in this kind of situation. But she started having a conversation. With me!

"We've met, you know."

Again it wasn't a question, which was good because I was unable to answer anyway; my throat was unaccountably dry as if a flash fire had just rushed through me. She drew me close, and I felt the firmness of her breasts against mine. I wanted to see what color her eyes were. But I couldn't because her hand on my back was hot and cool at the same time. And her breasts were pressed into me in that gently insistent way that women's breasts do.

"Not too officially. You were staffing the registration table at the Breast Cancer Action town hall meeting last year. I helped hang the banner when it fell. It was kind of a madhouse."

I did remember an incredibly efficient woman coming to our rescue, but it was only an impression—hands, arms, aura. Me and what's-her-name were just breaking up, so most of that day was a blur. But I still couldn't speak, so it didn't matter. Our feet were moving as they should, or at least the woman in black had not pointed out our failures yet.

I smiled.

"So what brought you here?" she said, pulling back a little.

I was extremely disappointed—such a direct question required a verbal response. I took a deep breath, so deep it made me cough.

"Sorry," I said.

"You all right?"

Her eyes were level with mine, English toffee I thought, wondering if that was really a color. Her skin was alabaster.

Holy Mary, mother of god, I was in the arms of a white woman whose skin I thought was like alabaster! Okay, maybe it wasn't like alabaster. I don't really know what alabaster looks like. Maybe it was more like ivory—the ivory on my adopted father's great old piano. Warm and soft like it's been touched so many times it wants more.

She was *looking* her question now.

"Yes, just something in my throat."

I tried the breath thing again and a voice came out. I explained about the liner notes and was so excited that she actually knew what liner notes were that I couldn't hear what she said next.

The music stopped. The instructor in black did a couple of steps with a brave soul who volunteered to learn something complicated in front of nine strangers. We stood side by side and watched. Except I wasn't really watching them; I was thinking, *This can't be happening and what is the "this" that can't be happening?* I vaguely remembered this type of feeling from somewhere in the past.

"Here we go," she said with a laugh in her voice as the instructor in black started the music again.

And I thought, *Well, this is definitely happening.*

Usually I don't think about "this" much. A date here and there has been fine with me since what's-her-name. I haven't been much into the couple thing since then. My time is way too precious to me. And when it's date time I'm usually the one who does the picking. Seeing how poorly I'd picked last time, I wasn't rushing. But I can't stand hanging on the wall even if it is only at a dance class.

"I really miss liner notes." This time I was able to locate my voice without a search warrant.

"Yeah, they're great history."

"Great photographs too! They take you so deep into the music."

"That's what got me here," she said. "I wanted to be more *in* the music, not just listening to it."

"Umm. I like that idea, being in the music."

I felt self-conscious about my hand sweating on the shoulder of her starched shirt. But I'm not one to carry a hanky, so that was that. I tried to look at her without her seeing—no small feat when you're dancing together. Her dark brown hair was slicked back dramatically as if it were 1956. And her eyes were closed. So I shut mine. She pulled me just a little closer then, as if she could feel my eyes closing.

We made it through the music again, and I began to wonder if she was a shill or a ringer or whatever they're called. She danced way too well for this to be her first lesson. Maybe she picked up girls at dance classes and then left them slaughtered in Golden Gate Park.

I hate when my imagination runs away with me. That's why I avoid horror movies at all costs. If I didn't, I'd see men in hockey masks in every shadow. When the instructor stopped the tape to announce she was moving from the cheek-to-cheek tempo to some real swing I wasn't sure if I was relieved or disappointed.

"I started taking this class last year but had to drop out when I got a new job. I was too wiped out. You're bringing it all back for me."

The severity of her haircut was totally broken by the sparkle of her smile. English toffee twinkled at me.

The next series of steps looked more complicated, maybe just because they were supposed to happen fast. The instructor made people change partners. The queen was loving being able to switch-hit. First he led a curly-haired Irish guy, then he let a beanpole-tall dyke lead him. My wall-sister moved out of the arms of a guy who was as big and solid as a firefighter. Her partner looked as reluctant to break up the duo as she did. But we regrouped and practiced throwing each other out and back and ducking under each other's arms without being decapitated. Swinging to music that had been twirling on turntables for more than fifty years made my heart feel good. I'd have to ask the instructor for the names of the bands she was playing. My new partner was good: brusque and efficient. She kept fiddling with her long hair, though, as if she hoped to be spotted by a talent scout for "Dancing with the Stars." We were hardly a showstopping duo, but I was getting the hang of it.

"Okay, we'll go back to a slow tempo just to finish up and see if you can remember the steps. No fear!" she said, glowing with good cheer.

The room took a collective breath trying to recalibrate from *hi-dee-hi-dee-hi-dee-ho* to "Moonlight in Vermont." Across the room I saw the young woman excuse herself politely from her partner as everyone decided how he or she wanted to end the session. She made her way back toward me comfortably, and I was in her arms just as the music started.

"This makes me want to pull all those records out of storage."

"You've still got records?" I stumbled.

"Sure. I figure CDs will never beat out vinyl for natural sound. And who the hell can read that tiny print?"

I realized then that she wasn't really much younger than me. It was the clothes and the haircut that gave her that boyish aura. But listening to her voice and really looking I could tell she and I were contemporaries. Damn, I hoped we wouldn't both break out in a hot flash at the same time; the fire sprinklers would blow.

She held me close like she had before and I wasn't sure if it was her heart beating or mine. The softness of her cheek, the heat of her against me, her breath at my ear, the firmness of her hand on my back were all a kind of communication. Our bodies were talking, which was just as well because I was pretty sure my voice was gone again.

The music ended and people were moving around us, gathering coats and bags. The instructor was gathering her black swirl of clothes around her as she announced what we'd be working on next week.

Well, that was that, I thought, *I'm out of here.* No time for fiddling with slick dyke dancers on the prowl. Still, we stood together, like teenagers used to linger with each other in the vestibule before they had to go upstairs to their parents.

"I actually know your name."

"Really," I said, immediately suspicious.

"Emma. I asked that day at the BCA event."

"After Emma Goldman."

"Well, she said she wouldn't come to the revolution if there was no dancing. So I guess you'll make it."

"What's yours?" I said, thinking, *Not only does she know what liner notes are, she quotes Emma Goldman. She* must *be a serial killer.*

"Jo. Jo March, actually."

The hint of a grin on her mouth was uncertain. How could she know I'd been in love with Jo March for the first ten years of my reading life? Well, I guess most girls who read *Little Women* are in love with Jo March.

"You're not joking, are you?"

"No. Corny, stereotypical, but truly my name."

"I always wanted to know more about Jo March." I couldn't believe it when the sentence popped out of my mouth. But I couldn't suck it back in. I looked away from those caramel eyes and watched the rest of the class chattering with each other as they ambled toward the door and the instructor popped on the big fan. I waved at my wall-sister as she disappeared through the door smiling.

"I'd be more than happy to tell you," Jo said with a big grin.

Better than James Dean. A name I could roll around on my tongue. With any luck.

NOBODY'S HEART IS BROKEN NOW

Sarah Coats

Do it for me, Rachel. Please."

"It doesn't work like that," I said. "Magic can't give you everything you want."

She just looked at me, hunger and hope in her eyes.

"It's a love spell. It won't cure your dad's kind of heartbreak. It won't strengthen his valves and arteries. It won't let him live. No matter what, he's dying," I said, hoping for once I could convince her not to do something. It was never a good idea to mess with magic if you didn't have to, not even with the little spells. That was one thing the world had learned since magic had come back.

"It unbreaks hearts," Kirin said stubbornly. "I don't need him to live, I just need to talk to him one last time. Maybe it *will* work. Come on. Please, Rachel." She leaned toward me and put her lips over mine, slid her tongue into my mouth and flicked it around impatiently. A facsimile of a kiss. She pulled back and ground her teeth.

"Your mother won't like it. She'll find out." Something in my belly told me this was a bad idea. Real bad.

"She won't, not unless you tell her. No one will know."

Kirin's dark-circled eyes darted restlessly around her ridiculous childhood room. Rivulets of shimmer-string hung from the ceiling. Heart-shaped pillows lined the head of the bed. A chandelier set with full-spectrum bulbs encased in crystal sent rainbows spilling across the room. The fact that Kirin had grown up in this room should have been funny to me; instead it was just creepy. So much work—so much artifice—to hide the truth of what had gone on in this house. As soon as we had arrived here the day before, Kirin started looking worse and worse. Usually she reminded me of a crow, but today she looked like a rat trying to claw her way up from the sewers.

I sighed. "Your father will die, no matter what."

"I know, but they said he won't regain consciousness. The spell will wake him up. It has to."

It was flawed logic, but she was desperate. "Okay. You'll have to get the ingredients."

From under her bed she pulled out a cardboard box filled with the necessary icons. The wealthy always get what they want, one way or another.

There were a hundred good reasons not to do the spell and only one bad reason to do it. Her father, Samhael Dor, was the richest man in all of Seattle, a legend. Now he was dying of heart failure, and all the surgeons, chemists, and mystics in the whole world couldn't save him from death, though he had enough money to buy all of them, twice over.

In the box were three dragon's teeth, seven hen seeds, a jar full of lost words, an ounce of cocaine, and other oddities. I looked them over and tried to find something missing.

Kirin tapped her foot impatiently and stared at me with her

violet eyes, a present from her father on her sixteenth birthday. "At least one part of you will be perfect," he'd told her.

Eyes that I love.

A loud rap came from the door, and Kirin jumped up and pushed the box back beneath her bed then pulled down the duvet to hide it. She flopped down beside me and painted a phony innocent look on her face before saying, "Enter, Mother."

Stern as a seraph, Cloudia walked into the room and studied her daughter, then me. Though thirty years our senior, she presented a twin image of Kirin I found riveting to watch; silence and rage wrapped up in a pretty box of civility. Like mother, like daughter.

"A mystic was just here to tend to your father, and he sensed magical icons. What mischief have you brought into my house? I don't need this, not now." Her eyes flicked around the room then fell on me—the weakness in Kirin's armor.

"What has my daughter dragged you into, Rachel?"

Wrinkles of pain and suffering quilted her face, and I thought about her dying husband, two decades older than her. Samhael Dor, the man who had made billions in genesticides. Who had taken no responsibility when they had gotten away from him. What was it like to be his wife?

I stared back at Cloudia and blinked slowly, words outside the grasp of my tongue as I grew lost in her gaze and my own thoughts. She shook her head and looked away from me, dismissing me as unworthy of attention. Her intense gaze fell on her daughter.

"Oh, Mother, don't be silly," Kirin said. "I'm sure it's nothing. You're just trying to distract yourself from all your grief. You don't need to hide your pain from us." Kirin looked at me, her rodent eyes begging for my complicity.

A flash of anger, then a lake of ice covered Cloudia's

countenance as she looked around, frowning at the space's sugar-and-spice surfaces. The room was a mother's plea for a daughter who had never existed, not like she was supposed to. Or if she had, it was so long ago that none of that little girl existed at all anymore.

Kirin had snarled jet-black hair, tatty jeans, and a pale unsmiling face. Her pushed-up sleeves showed the black-inked words written into her body. She had tattooed herself in adolescence, gouged words into her thighs and arms with needles, thread, and ink. Words that were painful to read: DEVIL'S DAUGHTER. POISONED. ETERNAL RAGE.

Cloudia walked to the golden boxes that lay mounted in slots along one wall of the room. They were marked in swirling calligraphy with words like, SWEATERS, JOURNALS, and PHOTOS. She pulled out one of the boxes and threw off the lid. Kirin grinned sickly at me from behind her mother's back and rolled her eyes. Cloudia opened another one, then another, savagely.

"You're hysterical, Mother. Distraught with grief." Cloudia glared at her. "Like you always used to tell me, being emotional does not help," Kirin said wickedly.

"I will find out what you're hiding! You will bring no more chaos into this house! You will not steal your father's last dignity!"

"Such a fine and upstanding father. How could I upset him?" Cloudia pulled open more boxes.

"Leave!" Kirin ordered, just as her mother's eyes slid toward the duvet that hid the box. Cloudia walked toward the bed.

"Leave!" Kirin cried out with the voice of a fourteen-year-old, broken and powerless. She stood and blocked her mother from coming closer.

"You won't get away with anything."

They stood face-to-face, six inches apart. I studied my hands and pretended I wasn't there.

Cloudia turned and stormed out of the room. As the door slammed behind her, Kirin laughed falsely. I exhaled and fell back onto her bed. If wishes were horses, I would ride away and never come back here.

"Stuff with your mom is messed up."

"Yep. Let's do the spell now."

I looked at her and saw the woman I'd been dating for a year, but I saw a stranger, too. She was so different in her parents' house. Who was she? I should have known that by now, should have known all her family stories, but there was a lot of silence between us. Always had been. The night before, I had held Kirin's hand and stared at Samhael Dor with her. It was hard to see the monster that lay beneath. I could only conjure up a vague pity for him, because bad men live the lives they create and how could he have ever had a day of pleasure? Beside me, I had felt Kirin shrinking into herself as she looked at him. What did she remember?

Dor Genesticides had crossbred their poisons with local flora and killed all the green things in Seattle, making all of them dependent on Dor inoculations to grow. The entire city turned brown when I was five years old. There just wasn't enough money to pay for the parks or trees along the streets with all the funds it took to contain the contamination in the city limits of Seattle. The Dor name was a bad word on the playground of my youth: *You're such a Dor. Nothing but a Dor. Damned Dor.*

When I met Kirin, I couldn't believer she was his daughter; that I could kiss someone with that name. I had assumed *those* people inhabited a different world, washed white, barricaded from the rest of us. But there she was, at one of our clubs, sitting at the bar alone, separated from everyone else by an invisible wall. On the crowded dance floor I spun around in a trance, surrounded by friends all hopped up on Bliss cut with something strange that made us buzz and twirl and laugh, again and again. She watched me, her hooded eyes keeping time with my steps until I noticed her and was drawn, closer and closer. Until our lips touched, and I laughed into her mouth. Beyond butch, she was stone cold, or maybe I was feverish.

She took me tucked under her coat to her tasteful apartment with clean furniture, steel appliances, and not a roach in sight. She threw me down on her bed, and I spun around and around her, shocked by every taste and touch. I awoke with my head full of clouds and the sun shining in on us, two bodies wrapped together like paper and string. It was a rare, perfectly sunny Seattle day. I rose and made us pancakes, delighted to find real maple syrup, butter, and blueberries, as though she had bought them to welcome me home.

She walked naked from her bedroom and faced me, with her hands on her hips. The nightmare of her tattoos screamed out warnings: *You leave. Now.*

My weakness has always been for women outside my reach; women who, even if I stretch as far as I can, I will never touch. Who will never truly touch me either. "I made you pancakes. Get dressed. I'm Rachel," I told her.

"I will only make you miserable," she said. Her violet eyes drew me in and spat me out. She shook her snarled mane at me, but I stayed.

That day led to this one in a twisting curl of time that made her dear to me. She was right: I was never happy with her, but it was a sweet misery—a staring-in-the-window-at-the-lollipops-with-a-mouthful-of-drool kind of ecstasy. Kirin always kept me wanting more, kept me hungry for her. For no reason, she would go silent for days, grind her teeth all night long, then lash out at me out of nowhere. There was a bitter laugh for every time I cried. She would then be as nice as she knew how, but trouble was never far beneath the depths of her exotic eyes. She'd buy me things I had no use for, or make mixes of love songs with lyrics so far away from what we had that it would make us both laugh. She would scream at me, over and over, that I was nothing to her. Had I grown big as the tallest augmented basketball player, I still couldn't have reached her.

"Let's do the spell now," she repeated, needy of me in a way I hadn't thought possible. This wasn't the Kirin I adored. Even so, how could I deny her anything?

She rose and locked the door with a crooked clasp that was obviously something she had nailed up in her youth to keep the demons out. "Come, fair witch. It is time to do your work."

I looked in the box for some sort of excuse. There were trinkets that held no power in themselves, but reached into the world just beyond sight. I ran my hands uneasily over the dragon teeth and felt life pulsing inside. "It's a love spell, you know. Love's tricky. I'm not even very good with magic."

"You have better luck than most. Do this." Kirin drew the spell scroll from her vest pocket and handed it to me.

"What time is it?"

"The moon has risen," she replied.

I thought about the moon cycle and realized it was a new moon tonight. Powerful. "We'll have to go up to the roof."

Kirin scouted the halls in front of us as I carried the box and scroll. I held my breath at every corner and seemed to hear the clicking of Cloudia's heels following us, but she didn't, unfortunately, come to thwart us. The roof was flat and covered with a garden of real green grass. Every plant was well groomed, every tree perfectly pruned. After the green was gone, I used to dream about gardens like this. Children should have been playing up here, and old people should have been feeding pigeons. When was the last time anyone had enjoyed this place?

A stone path embedded with small lights led us into the heart of the garden. Illuminated statues watched silently as we passed them. A wind blew from the north with a contaminated metal smell, cold enough to make me shiver. *Go away, no good will come of this*, the world seemed to whisper.

Kirin spread out a blanket on a patch of grass. Already my fingers felt stiff and cold.

"Hurry, Rachel," she ordered.

As I laid out the items in the right order and read over the scroll Kirin held in her hands, I felt bone-deep that this would go all wrong. In magic, if nothing else, instinct is everything. Kirin's steely eyes glared at me. For her I would walk across a scorched earth of broken glass, so I would do this, no matter how futile or wrong. Chances were, nothing would happen. That's what magic is, most of the time.

I began. The song I sang and the objects I pushed apart and together spoke of heartache, of lost love. Nothing of a weakened aortic organ so thin and papery no replacement surgery could be attempted. Wind chapped my lips and stung my eyes as I sang of lovely boys and daring girls, of all that the heart had lost being restored, regained, made whole. I whispered his name, the intended, *Samhael Dor*, over and over. The spell was hard to follow; many of the words were difficult to pronounce or unknown to me. I stumbled through, then sang it again, a strength taking root in the icons before me. Almost too strong for me to hold. The spell went far beyond the normal poppy-seed panacea for heartache.

This was my last thought as the spell took me over and tossed me to and fro, whipped across my spine and bade me cry out the words for all to hear. There was nothing I could do but obey.

Magic ran through me and sunk into the grass I sat on, bleeding out in all directions. I sang and my voice grew hoarse. My eyes could barely stay open. The north wind grew and stole my warmth as I sang on pitifully, compelled to do so.

"Enough," Kirin finally whispered, and folded up the scroll she held before me with her shivering arms. When she finished, I was released and fell forward onto the grass, unable to catch myself. Kirin gathered me in her strong arms, and we walked slowly back to her room.

"Did it work?" she asked through chattering teeth.

Did it? Something powerful had happened. I nestled into her and tucked my head against her arm. Dreams flew at me so suddenly it seemed I must still be awake. Bright colors and bold noises rose up and then, in front of me, stood a miracle. My first love stood within my reach, so different than any other, so painful. Above us, colors and light exploded and showered down pinpricks of fire that burned our shoulders. A pinwheel spun wildly above her, making a gold halo around her head. She turned and ran. I followed her through green fields and alpine flowers. She moved just ahead of me and out of my reach. Not minding that I would never reach her, I ran and ran without growing tired. Then she was staring at me motionless, and I saw the truth of what we had been: awful for each other; destructive when we should have been tender, when we were both so young and vulnerable. She smiled, I smiled, and we held hands, a circle formed between us.

I awoke just as suddenly as I had fallen asleep. My hand was over my heart and I felt the calm lub-dub, lub-dub under my breast. Peace flooded through me at the memory of her. It had not gone well. It had made me doubt I could be loved, but all that doubt was gone now. A hurt I'd been holding within me for a long time was gone.

"Lights," I called out, then saw where I was, remembered what I had done. An instant later I realized the meaning of my dream. Spellbleed. Contamination. If my heart had been mended, so had everyone else's.

Where was Kirin?

I jumped up from the bed and ran from the room, though my body felt hollow and begged only to curl back in on itself and dream some more. Where was she? What had I done to her?

I ran as fast as my legs would carry me to the room where Samhael Dor lay dying, then paused, my hand on the door handle. I didn't want to see what was inside, didn't want to find out what I had done, that I was too late. I wanted to run and not look back, leave Kirin behind. But love, for once, was greater than fear, and I opened the door. Samhael's gaze met mine as I peered inside, eyes I had hoped to never see open. They were bright and honest as a child's. Had they always been so, or had I done that? I shuddered away from his gaze, unwilling to share any intimacy with the man. What right did he have of innocence?

Cloudia and Kirin sat on both sides of him. Each of them held one of his hands and held each other's to form a circle.

"Come, sit," Cloudia spoke with a steady voice. Kirin nodded. There was a chair at the end of the bed, far from them, where I perched myself.

Their attention returned to each other and Kirin spoke. My woman of impenetrable armor, yet her voice came out without any defenses at all.

"You stole my childhood," Kirin said. "I was terrified, always, of you, Father. I could never be perfect enough. Too fat, too ugly, too stupid. Everything I did, I knew you would always disapprove. I was so scared all the time of what you would say to me, what you would make me do. Remember when you made me memorize the Titan's Manifesto, then mocked me because I left out the word 'and'? And you, Mother, did nothing to protect me from him, like you weren't even there. There was no safe place for me in this house, ever."

Samhael looked at her. He saw her, what she had wanted so badly. But like this?

"Kirin," his voice held no more force than a breeze. "You are my only child, I expected so much from you. What did you become? Nothing useful. I tried to teach you, but you never learned."

"I chose to do nothing for my own gain. I chose to agree with your father, in everything," Cloudia said. "I'd like to think I would choose differently now, but I don't know if that's true. I'm truly sorry, Kirin. We never should have had you."

Samhael moved his hand a little, a gesture that seemed to indicate that all of this was unimportant.

Kirin was silent for a time then spoke again, "I'll never forgive either of you. You left no place for love to grow inside me."

Her father smiled and nodded absently while Cloudia sucked in breath and ran a hand across her chest. Pain, or its sudden absence? I wondered what all of them were feeling, after my spell. What had I stolen from Kirin? If only she hadn't made me do it.

Kirin nodded thoughtfully and her eyes met mine. I saw something stunned and strange in her look, and she gave me a small, half smile before she spoke again. "If there is a hell, both of you will rot there. If there isn't, you've wasted your one life."

Kirin stood and walked out of the room. I followed behind her. She didn't hesitate as she left the house and walked out into the middle of the night. Neither of us was dressed for it; the thin soles of my slippers became soggy and my body shook with cold. I couldn't speak to her as I walked behind her, didn't know if she knew I was there, or if she cared.

Could she ever forgive me? So much of her was built upon

her pain, and if it was suddenly taken away? What would be left? I didn't know a Kirin without hurt, and the thought of her unguarded and honest scared me. I felt the throb of my loss as I kept time with her footsteps, wondering, wondering what would come of this.

We walked unharassed through checkpoints I would have been turned away from if I weren't beside her embedded ID. We came to our apartment—her apartment? She fumbled with the key then opened the door. I stood numbly behind her, unsure if I was wanted, or even if I wanted her. Kirin turned and faced me, wrapped in so many shadows I couldn't see her clearly.

"What will we do now? Who will we be when the pain is gone and we can be free, if we want to? What do you want to do, Rachel?" she asked softly, in a way she had never spoken. She held out her hands to me and smiled without any guile, letting me see in. "First off, I love you."

Fear roared through me and I stood frozen. I had said those words to her, easily, often, without any thought she would ever reciprocate. And now that she did? This was not safe. This was not the woman I had chosen to be with, but someone else who wore her face and body. I stepped back. She watched me calmly. Her lips didn't turn down cruelly, nor did she look at me with disdain. Her arms opened wider, ready to embrace all of me. This wasn't how it was supposed to go. It felt hard to breathe, like something was lodged in my throat. But then I took a tiny step forward, then another until her arms touched me, held me, embraced me tenderly. I felt her heart beating through our T-shirts and felt the echo of my own heart, strong and certain, unbroken and brave.

WISH GRANTED

Sandra Barret

Teri pulled out of the steaming kiss to stare into Karen's chocolate-brown eyes. The unbridled passion reflected in her boss's dark face drew Teri closer. "We shouldn't do this," she whispered between nibbles on Karen's earlobe. Karen moaned, breaking down Teri's noble defenses.

"Please," Karen begged. "Don't stop. Teri. Oh, Teri... Teri..."

"Teri?"

Teri MacNamara snapped out of her delicious reverie to look up at the scowl that marred the beautiful features of her boss, Karen Lintal, CPA and partner at Winters and Rosheim Accounting.

"Um, sorry, what were you saying?" Teri felt a blush creep up from the tips of her rainbow-painted toenails to the roots of her dirty-blonde hair. Bad enough to be fantasizing about her boss, but to be caught at it? She needed a hole to crawl into and hide.

"Grab your pad and whatever you have left for a brain and bring it into my office. I want the notes on the Fiestan account as well."

Karen made a sharp turn, and Teri couldn't help but watch the sway of her black business skirt as it disappeared beyond the double-wide oak doorway. Teri sighed, giving up any hope that she could break the spell that Karen had placed on her libido. Her beauty, sophistication, and power wrapped up in a tight, dark-skinned package remained completely inaccessible to Teri.

"Maybe it's just an excuse for her to get you alone," Mitch teased from the cubicle next to Teri. She ignored the grin plastered across his bland, fat face. Her fellow accountant snickered as she passed by, emphasizing his amusement at her predicament. She left him with a kick in the shins to highlight her appreciation of his sense of humor.

For an hour, Teri sat in Karen's mahogany-rich office, trying to rein in her wayward thoughts and focus on her boss's directions. When the door swung open and T.J. Santos, chief programmer from Network Operations, strolled in, Teri felt a wave of envy. Of all the office personnel, T.J. seemed the only one capable of eliciting a smile from Karen. T.J.'s brown eyes sparkled as she sauntered in and sat on Karen's polished desk.

"Forget your password again?" she asked, addressing her question to Karen but giving Teri a wink.

"Well if you didn't insist on making me change it every two months, this wouldn't happen." A smile pulled at Karen's full lips.

What Teri wouldn't give to be the one who could make Karen smile like that. Teri sat in her chair, all but ignored now that T.J. was in the room. She watched as T.J. took over Karen's seat and began tapping at the keyboard. Karen hovered over T.J.'s shoulder, leaning close enough that Teri felt certain Karen's full breasts must be pushing against T.J.'s sweatshirt-clad back. Not that T.J. took any notice of Karen's obvious attentions. The two of them had broken up over a year ago. No one knew the full details, but Teri was certain Karen hadn't been the one to end the relationship.

A moment later, Teri was summarily dismissed. She shut the heavy oak doors as she left, her cheeks burning more from envy than embarrassment. She sank into her creaking chair in her gray cubicle and doodled in the margins around the notes she'd taken in Karen's office. When she heard the oak doors open again, she peeked around the corner of her cubicle. It was only T.J. coming out. Teri rolled her chair back to her computer and tried to pull up the Fiestan file. When the custom accounting program locked up, she cursed and banged the side of the monitor for good measure.

"I don't think that's a documented procedure for accessing my program."

Teri turned to see T.J. leaning against the cubicle doorway. Teri smiled up at T.J., in spite of her frustrations. "Maybe you can make it work more reliably, then," she said, waving her hand at the computer monitor.

T.J. let out a melodramatic sigh. "How does this department function when I'm not around?"

Teri folded her arms across her chest. "So did you fix everything for Karen?"

Some of the sparkle left T.J.'s eyes as she answered. "She's the only person I'd recommend just write down the dang password somewhere. She forgets it at least once a quarter."

"Come on, you know she does it on purpose."

T.J. shrugged. "Not much I can do about that."

"How could you ever have let her go?" Teri asked, barely above a whisper.

"You have a thing for her, eh? Well, I can't give you unbiased advice, but looks aren't everything."

Teri made a show of studying T.J.'s appearance. T.J.'s teal sweatshirt, baggy black jeans, and boots hid any hint of what shape she might have underneath, but Teri knew better, having seen T.J. compete in the company's sand volleyball tournament. She ended her mock study at T.J.'s face, amazed to see a blush through her deeply tanned features.

"Speaking of looks, when are you going to start wearing something that isn't two or three sizes too big?" Teri teased.

"When you start picking my clothes out for me."

Teri rolled her eyes. "Can you fix this thing or are you just here to bother the boss?"

T.J. swiveled Teri's chair, placing her before the misbehaving software. She leaned over Teri and pointed to the screen. "First off, you can't run the program from Internet Explorer. It's only Netscape compatible."

"I can't close the browser," Teri complained.

Teri watched as T.J.'s light-brown fingers danced across her keyboard. T.J.'s wavy, short, brown hair brushed against Teri's cheek as she worked. Teri inhaled her faintly sweet scent as T.J. shut down the browser from some special menu and opened the accounting program properly.

"There you go," T.J. said as she stood upright.

Teri turned to face her. "What perfume are you wearing? It smells really good on you."

"Nothing," T.J. stammered. "Maybe it's my shampoo."

Teri nodded. "Maybe."

The oak doors swung open again, breaking the awkward silence. Teri tried to catch a glimpse of Karen's receding form but she couldn't see around T.J. When she looked up at her face, she saw a hint of sadness in the other woman's eyes, but T.J. just gave her a smile and went on her way. Teri sat, drumming her fingers on her notepad, wondering if she could slip back into her earlier fantasy before it was time for lunch.

With the lights out, and wrapped under a thick blanket, Teri silently wished for a way into Karen's heart before she drifted off to sleep in her dark bedroom. Her dreams were filled with mundane activities and the occasional elusive cameo appearance of Karen. She woke sometime before dawn and shuffled into the bathroom, barely opening her eyes enough to see by the scattered rays of moonlight that filtered through her blinds. A minute later, she stumbled back to bed and sank her head down on the pillow. The unexpected sensation of another's weight on her bed caused her eyes to fly open. There was a vaguely visible image of a small person sitting on the opposite edge of her bed.

"What the hell?" she hollered, pushing away from the figure until she fell out of bed and landed in a clump on the floor.

"Sorry," said a raspy voice that sounded like its owner had smoked a few too many cigarettes. "Guess I should have knocked first or something."

Teri's hands frantically searched the wall behind her until she found and flicked on the light switch. What she saw before her now made even less sense than the sudden appearance of somebody in her bedroom. "Who are you? How did you get in here?" Teri asked.

A tiny woman sat with her legs folded over the edge of Teri's bed, chewing on a toothpick. Her black work boots dangled at least a foot and a half from the carpet. In fact, the boots, well-worn jeans, and red flannel shirt all matched in a miniature construction-worker chic way. What didn't match was the pair of slowly undulating, translucent wings that sprouted from the woman's back.

"*What* are you?" Teri asked, keeping herself plastered to the wall, as far away from the creature as possible.

The tiny woman grabbed the toothpick out of her mouth and flicked it across the room toward the trash can. It missed. "I'm Trixie, your fairy godmother," she rasped.

"Excuse me?"

"Fairy godmother. Don't you recognize the wings?" She gave an extra-fast flutter of her wings, raising herself off the bed by a foot, and then let herself float back down.

"Fairy godmother," Teri repeated.

"Yep. You did make a wish, you know."

"And you're here to grant it?" Teri rubbed the sleep out of her eyes. "Look, pixie..."

"No, fairy godmother. Pixies aren't nearly as cute as I am."

"Right. Okay, Dixie..."

The fairy stood up on the bed, little hands irately placed on tiny hips. "Not Dixie, Trixie."

"Trixie. The lesbian fairy godmother," Teri repeated. "God, what did I eat last night?" She shuffled over to her bedroom door and opened it.

"Where are you going?" Trixie asked.

"To get a cup of coffee," Teri answered.

"Aren't you going to ask me to grant your wish?" Trixie hollered as Teri continued down the dark hallway to the kitchen.

"I don't talk to hallucinations!" Teri shouted back.

"I'm not a..."

Whatever the fairy said was blocked out when Teri slammed shut the door between the bedroom and bathroom area and the rest of her apartment. She flicked on the kitchen light and

groaned when she saw that it was only five o'clock in the morning. Turning on her coffeemaker, she stared at it while it dripped
out the dark elixir that would return her to sanity. Ten minutes
later, when she finished her coffee, she squared her shoulders
and braved the trip back to her bedroom. To her relief, she saw
no sign of her hallucination then, or as she showered and prepared for work.

Teri grumbled at Mitch when he gave a poor impression of a heart
attack at the sight of her showing up to work on time that morning. She had a dull headache forming between her eyes and was in
no mood for the lame comedy of a balding, overweight accountant. By lunchtime, she had managed to tick off Mitch, Karen,
and the UPS delivery girl with her short temper. Teri pushed her
way into the ladies' room and scanned the stalls. Four different
sets of shoes were visible beneath the row of doors. That left only
the handicapped stall. With a grunt, Teri pulled the wide stall
door open, stepped in, and slid the lock closed. When she turned
around, a tiny squeak escaped her lips.

"Can't you leave me alone?" she asked in a fierce whisper.

Trixie hovered rather disturbingly over the open toilet.
"Look, you're the one who wanted a wish. I have your wish,"
Trixie said.

"Shhh. Do you have to talk so loudly?"

Trixie tried to shrug but it messed with the rhythm of her
fluttering fairy wings, threatening to upend her into the toilet.
"No one but you can hear."

"Oh," Teri said, letting her voice return to normal.

"So are you going to use your wish or what? I haven't got all
day you know."

"If I make my wish, you'll go away?"

Trixie nodded.

"Okay. I'm sure Freud would have something to say about humoring hallucinations, but here goes. I wish Karen wanted me."

"*Wanted you?*" Trixie asked. "You want to be more specific?"

Teri sighed. "Fine. I wish Karen wanted me with a burning sexual passion."

Trixie pulled a tiny wand out from the folds of her flannel shirt. She waved it three times, repeating some gibberish that Teri assumed was fairy-speak. Or maybe just severe indigestion. Then the fairy disappeared with a small pop. Teri blinked, somewhat disheartened that she didn't feel any differently. She stumbled out of the bathroom stall, forgetting the original reason for her visit.

She looked up to see three faces staring at her from the line of sinks. Their eyes turned away as each woman silently hurried out of the restroom. Teri cursed. Trixie the pixie or whatever she was had failed to mention that everyone could hear Teri's side of the conversation. She leaned against the mock-marble counter, wondering how she could face her coworkers when she stepped out of the ladies' room. She had no delusions: gossip of her impending mental breakdown would be the top conversation piece around the office for the next week or more.

The ladies' room door swung open and T.J. walked in, much to Teri's relief. "Oh, there you are," T.J. said. "Karen's looking for you."

Teri swallowed hard. "And you heard that I was in here?"

T.J. gave her a puzzled look. "Um, no. I had to, you know..." She nodded toward the empty toilet stalls.

"Oh, sorry."

T.J. gave her a shy smile and disappeared into a stall. Teri smoothed invisible wrinkles out of her off-white blouse and then marched out of the restroom to face her fate. She studied each face that she passed in the hall on her way to Karen's office, but saw no sign that the gossip tree had gotten to work yet. She knocked on Karen's double doors and waited until she heard the other woman's voice before entering.

"Please shut the doors behind you," Karen said, not looking up from her paperwork. "And have a seat on the sofa."

Teri sank down on the leather sofa that was usually reserved for important clients. Is this how Karen fired people? Make them comfortable, and then give them the axe? When Karen stood up and walked around the desk to join her on the sofa, Teri was certain she was about to be given the boot.

"We don't get the chance to talk much, do we?" Karen asked, as she sat next to Teri.

Teri felt Karen's warm thigh brush against hers and could do nothing to stop the flush that raced across her cheeks. "No," she squeaked. "We don't talk much."

Karen rested her arm along the back of the sofa, her fingers just touching the back of Teri's neck. Those fingers traced a line of electric thrills as they roamed through Teri's short hair. She barely breathed while Karen leaned closer, brushing her lips against Teri's cheek.

"Is this okay?" Karen asked, her voice low and sultry.

Teri's mind couldn't come up with an answer with Karen's breasts pressed against her and her long, elegant fingers working at the buttons on Teri's blouse. A soft moan escaped her lips when a warm hand cupped her breast. Karen pulled her head closer and kissed her, covering any other sounds.

"Touch me," Karen demanded as she pulled out of their passionate kiss.

Teri lifted a trembling hand and held it just inches from the silky blouse that covered Karen's full breasts. She could see the hardened nipple pushing against bra and blouse and wanted to feel that nipple between her fingers, between her lips. But something held her back, something in the back of her mind telling her this was not the way she wanted it.

Teri looked up in horror as the oak doors swung open. She pushed against Karen, who kept her wrapped in a lover's embrace.

"Karen, did you finish with those backup...?"

Teri's eyes met T.J.'s and for an instant, she thought she saw a flash of anger. Embarrassed, Teri pushed harder and managed to slip out of Karen's grasp.

Karen turned, finally acknowledging T.J.'s presence. "Can't you see I'm busy?"

Teri stared at Karen, amazed at the angry tone she'd leveled at her ex-lover.

"I'll come back later." T.J.'s expression was a study in indifference.

"That's okay," Teri said, backing away from Karen. "I should get back to work." She slipped past T.J. and managed to button her blouse before hiding in her cubicle. Her heart pounded and her face burned, but not from the anticipated arousal at Karen's touch. Shame colored her cheeks as she recognized the emptiness of her boss's attraction. Her pulse had barely regained its normal pace when a warm, dark hand slid down the opening of her blouse and pushed its way into her bra.

"Come back to my office," Karen purred. "I'll lock the door this time."

Teri ignored the throb of desire she felt as she inhaled Karen's perfume. "No, this isn't real."

Karen nibbled her earlobe. "It's all real, baby."

When Teri pushed her chair back, Karen stepped toward her office, anticipating Teri's compliance. Instead, Teri sidled along the edge of her cube and scurried away. She heard Karen's voice as the other woman followed her, calling out in intimate detail how she felt about Teri's firm backside. Heads popped out of cubicles as Teri gave up all sense of propriety and ran full out for the ladies' room, the only room that she knew of with a lock. Why they provided a lock on the ladies' room remained a mystery, but it worked in Teri's favor today. She managed to make it into the restroom and lock the door behind her.

Karen's voice called at her from beyond the locked door, pleading for Teri and promising delectable treats of sexual satisfaction if she would only let her in. Teri braced herself against the locked door and scrambled to remember her fairy godmother's name.

"Pixie!" she called. "Dixie? Trixie?"

A pop and a flutter of wings announced Trixie's arrival. She sat atop the sink counter finishing off what looked for all the world like a miniature hotdog with mustard and sauerkraut.

"You hollered?" Trixie rasped between mouthfuls.

Teri looked across at the scratchy-voiced fairy. "Do you smoke?" she asked.

"No, why?"

"Never mind," Teri said, exasperated. "You've got to stop Karen."

Trixie crumpled the paper napkin that held the remnants of her hotdog and tossed it toward the bin. She missed. "Can't do that," she said, brushing crumbs off her jeans.

"What do you mean, you can't?" Teri shouted. "I can't leave this bathroom till you do something. Can't you hear her?"

Trixie made a show of leaning a pointy ear toward the door. "Sounds desperate. Just what you wanted."

"No, it's not."

"Sure it is."

"No." Teri took a breath to break the cycle of their insane

standoff. "Maybe it was, but reality is not what I dreamed it would be."

"Sometimes it bites when dreams come true." Trixie stood on the counter. "Anyway, if you're done with me, I have a fifty-year-old grandmother of three who needs a taste of what she's been missing all these years, and a pair of teenagers who need a nudge in the right direction."

"You can't leave me like this," Teri pleaded. "Can't you stop her?"

Trixie sighed. "I told you, I can't. It's against the fairy god-mother code to revoke a wish. I could lose my wings for that."

Teri shut her eyes and whimpered as Karen's fists started pounding on the door behind her. "There's got to be something you can do!"

"Sorry. Only you can end this wish."

"How do I break the spell?" Teri's eyes darted to Trixie, a faint echo of hope in her voice.

"Easy," Trixie said, flapping her wings until she was hovering in the middle of the restroom. "Get a kiss from someone you like, who likes you for who you really are, and the spell on Karen will dissolve."

"So if someone I like kisses me, it breaks the spell. But how can I find…?"

Trixie disappeared before Teri had finished her question. Teri slumped to the floor, ducking her head in her hands. "How can I find someone to kiss me who actually likes me?" she asked the space the pixie had previously occupied.

The sound of a flushing toilet shocked her into standing again. Her heart thudded as her face paled. Who was locked in the bathroom with her? She saw a pair of boots inside the far toilet stall. When the stall door opened, the boots led up to a pair of black jeans and an oversized teal sweatshirt.

"T.J.," she said.

T.J. smiled at her as she washed her hands.

"How much of that did you hear?" Teri asked.

T.J. leaned against the wall next to her, listening to the promises of passion with which Karen continued to serenade them. "I should be insulted that she's offering to show you all the sex games I taught her," she said.

Teri looked into T.J.'s laughing brown eyes and chuckled. "Sorry about that. I don't know how to stop her."

T.J.'s expression turned serious. "I do."

Teri's gaze drifted from T.J.'s dark eyes to the tongue that flicked out to moisten her red lips. She blinked once as her mind fought to comprehend what her heart already knew. T.J. lifted her hands to hold Teri's face as she leaned in and placed impossibly soft lips on Teri's. Teri let go of the door and wrapped her arms around T.J.'s waist, pulling her closer as their kiss deepened. She felt the pressure of T.J.'s tongue requesting entrance and opened her lips in response. As their tongues danced together, a ripple of desire coursed through her body.

T.J. trembled in her arms as they pulled apart to catch their breath. The pounding and pleading outside the restroom door had stopped, but neither of them paid much attention. Teri thought she heard the raspy chuckle of a miniature fairy, but she pushed the notion out of her mind when she felt T.J. pull her in for another long kiss.

THE ATTIC

K. I. Thompson

Jean surveyed the attic with a doleful eye. It looked as though a cyclone had run through just this section of her otherwise neat home. Dreading the thought of parting with the keepsakes of her past, she had allowed them to accumulate over the years until she had to face the consequences. What she initially thought would be a few hours' work now had the look of an almost insurmountable task.

"Oh, well," she exhaled on a soft breath. "You've got to start somewhere."

Attacking the project methodically, she began at twelve o'clock and worked clockwise. Anything that was trash she tossed into a large black plastic bag; anything that could be donated she placed in a cardboard box; and what she couldn't make up her mind to keep or not was left in place. After an hour of dusty, sweaty work, she uncovered her old phonograph and record collection. She nearly squealed with pleasure. Fanning through the pile of old albums, she selected a Glenn Miller record and placed it on the spindle. She plugged the frayed cord into a wall socket and the sound of "In the Mood" scratched softly from the speaker. She smiled warmly at the rush of memories —swinging to the sound of big bands in the local dance halls and ballrooms.

"Enough dillydallying!" She shook herself from her reverie.

A large stack of clothes commanded her attention, and Jean plowed through it with determination. When she reached the bottom, she discovered a box containing an old welder's mask, a memento of her days at the Kaiser shipyards in Oakland. She held it reverently, fingering the straps and running the tips of her fingers over the cool metal. How many times had she complained of its heaviness, of the sweat that streamed down her forehead and into her eyes while she worked? She gently placed it back in the box and closed the lid. After hesitating a moment, she put it in the plastic bag. *I don't need to hang on to that old thing anymore*, she thought.

As she collected a set of old dishes and placed them in the box, a packet of papers tied together by a faded pink ribbon tumbled to the floor. Leaning over a precarious stack of magazines, Jean retrieved the packet and perused the contents. When it dawned on her what the papers represented, she slowly sat on a nearby chair that tilted slightly when one leg wobbled dangerously.

Selecting a yellowed envelope, she carefully slid it from its place in the stack and glanced at the postmark, *Pearl Harbor, 0800, 7 12 41.* For a long while, she sat holding the letter. Images and memories came crashing in on her, disorienting her until she was completely immersed in them.

"Jean! I got it! I got my orders! Jean, where are you?"

"I'm up here," she replied, walking down the attic steps into the hallway.

"Hawaii, Jean! Can you imagine? Balmy nights on a tropical island, walks along a moonlit beach..."

"While I'm stuck here in the Bay Area..."

She was happy for her of course; her enthusiasm was contagious. But she couldn't help feeling a twinge of jealousy. They had just begun a life together, and to have this major change occur so early on in their relationship made her uneasy. She was afraid that the excitement of a new job in an exotic location might lead Emma to disdain such a provincial life in California.

"Oh, honey, I'm sorry." Emma kissed Jean softly on the lips. "But we both knew what being in the Navy meant."

"I know, sweetheart, I know." Jean returned the kiss again. "I'd only hoped you would at least be in the same town as me. Hawaii is...well, it's just so far away."

"But think of the wonderful reunions we'll have." Emma wiggled her eyebrows suggestively. "And in time I can put in for a transfer. And Hawaii is closer than some of the other places I could have been stationed. It's going to be okay, I promise."

Jean made an effort to smile and shook her head in agreement. But it wasn't very convincing, and she knew it.

"Baby, what is it? What are you worried about?" Emma grasped Jean's hand.

"It's nothing, really," She made a greater effort at convincing Emma, if not herself. She reached out, enveloping her in a protective hug; the collective warmth of their two bodies surged through her veins. All that mattered was here and now. There would be many more tomorrows.

"Hmm, Hawaii, huh? You're right. I guess it could've been worse. You'll have to promise to send me some pineapples. I absolutely love fresh pineapple."

Emma ran her hands down Jean's arms, then her hips and around to her back. She leaned forward and kissed her long and deep.

"Sweetie, I'll send you all the pineapples you can eat. But right now there's something I need you to do."
With that, they turned and walked toward their bedroom.
"Wait!" Jean pulled away and walked to the phonograph. She placed a Glenn Miller album on the spindle. Grinning, she grasped Jean's hand again. "A little 'In the Mood' music."

Jean's hands trembled as she removed the letter and began to read. The ink on the pages was nearly transparent with age, while one quarter of a sheet hung by a thread from its crease, evidence of constant handling.

December 6, 1941

My darling Jean,
I've been working nonstop with virtually no break since I first set foot on this island. My first year of nursing in the Navy is certainly more than I bargained for! I haven't had one minute to myself to explore this beautiful place. But things are looking up! I have a day off tomorrow, lucky me.
I was finally ordered to my quarters a half an hour ago by Dr. Anderson. I think he saw me nod off on my feet. I was never so embarrassed in my life! I'm lying in bed, but sleep won't come. I keep thinking about how we parted when I got my orders—and the uncertainty on your face. I finally turned on the bedside lamp and began this letter to you.
I love you. I know you know that, but I just needed to tell you again. I need you so much! If I could hold you in my arms right now I could make everything all right. I do know that my love for you will never change. I'm as sure of that as I am of your love. Oh how I wish I could look into your eyes right now and show you!

Sweetheart, if anything should happen to me, I want you to know I will always be with you. Wherever you are, whenever you feel the gentle breeze caress your cheek, it is my touch, and when a light summer rain falls, the drops that find their way to you are my tears telling you how much I miss you. And you will never be alone, for when you walk down the road outside our home, I am walking beside you.

The joys we have shared in our brief time together fill and complete me. I would miss you with all my heart, but the peace I would have knowing you continued on with your life would give me rest. This you must do. And when you think of me, remember all the good that we had, and forgive me for all the times that we quarreled. How silly they all seem now! I promise that when next we are together, I will never utter another disagreeable word to you as long as I live!

It's almost one o'clock and I'm finally beginning to feel tired. Don't forget to send Aunt Martha the extra pineapples I sent you. She loves them so. But tell her not to give any to Zelda! That poor cat has enough gastrointestinal problems without that.

I will write again sometime this week whenever I get a moment to myself. I read your letters over and over again, and wait anxiously for your next delivery. I think of you always and love you with all my heart. I will post this in the morning on my way to the beach and hopefully it will find its way to you quickly.

I love you,
Emma

Dropping the letter to her lap, she stared into space, conjuring up the image of a young, smiling Emma as she departed to what should have been a tropical paradise.

"Jean! Jean! You're supposed to be cleaning out…"

Jean looked up from the letter, tears welling in her eyes, momentarily blurring her vision. She blinked rapidly, the image of a twenty-one-year-old nurse in uniform fading from her mind.

"Honey! What's wrong?"

Without a word, she handed the letter to her partner, watching as she began to read. When she finished, Emma looked up at her with the depth of feeling that comes only from a lifetime spent together.

"I can't believe you kept this," Emma whispered in awe. She put her hands around Jean's shoulders and gently pulled her up out of the chair. "And after all this time, I still mean every word of it."

They kissed warmly—a kiss that reached out through the years from the past to the present—both knowing that it also promised whatever future remained ahead of them. When they broke apart, a large grin spread quickly across Jean's face. Taking hold of Emma's hand, she raised it high and spun her around several times before catching her abruptly in her arms.

"Madame, would you care to dance?"

"I thought you'd never ask," Emma said breathlessly.

To the strains of Glenn Miller they danced, each as sure of the other's next step as she was of her own. There was no guessing, no uncertainty as to what lay ahead. Whatever came their way, whatever events might be thrown across their path, they knew with certainty they would face them together.

DREAMTIME

Fiona Zedde

Twelve years after Alva left the island, I still dreamed of her. Those dreams were heady and ecstatic, fed by her ambiguously worded letters that gave teasing glimpses of what her American life was like. She told me of the first boy she kissed—she didn't like it—then the first girl who wasn't me, and after that the first time she let someone else touch her in the hidden places I'd always treasured. I never told her that for me there was no one—no man, no woman—who could take her place in my heart or in my bed. Over the years, the tone of her letters changed. I became an observer of her desires, no longer the object of them. She put distance between us. Eventually, my dreams were all I had.

Those dreams were plain, no disguised agendas, no twined meanings. In the twilight hours her touch immolated me. It roved with ease over my skin, setting each nerve ending alight; she licked my breasts, belly, and hips until I arched off the bed, gasping. Many nights I woke with Alva's name on my lips, my fingers buried between my damp thighs, and the phantom smell of her draped over me like silk.

Weeks ago I awoke a few minutes past three a.m., restless. Unable to sleep, I madly scribbled my feelings in a letter to her. At morning's first light I dropped it in the mail. Afterward, I felt like I had broken some unspoken rule. Alva never responded. The dreams kept coming, and the world itself seemed to be conspiring to press all of its concupiscence on me. Everywhere I looked, people were falling in love and making love. It was in their soft, sighing smiles, entwined hands, playful touches, and ripe laughter as they walked past me in the streets. I even noticed the flush-red hibiscus blossoms with their sticky yellow pistils and moist, inviting insides open to hummingbirds and bees alike. I missed her. I needed her. Then I found out she was coming.

What the gossips said was that she had been banished back to the island, for lying with American girls. Her mother thought that life back in Jamaica with her father would straighten Alva out. But wasn't she a grown woman, twenty-six, with income of her own like me?

My sisters brought me word that she was coming back, watching my face to see what would show. Did they see my relief? The relaxing of the tension that slid into my body twelve years ago when she flew away from me? I didn't understand then, but I do now. She got the prized passport and the sponsorship of her mother. I didn't, so I had to stay. No amount of crying or bloodied wrists could change that. At fourteen what did we know about love anyway? But I thought I loved her, thought I would die without her near me. I wondered what she thought now.

The first day that I knew she was mine, Alva and I had left school to play in the park and on the beach nearby. We picked up sweet-fleshed plums from under the trees that grew on the path to the water. Under the incandescent heat of the afternoon sun, she shyly pressed the fruit to my mouth and I bit. The temptation of her was too strong to resist, so I went willingly with her under the canopy of sea grapes where she touched me and rewarded my affections with warm, fruit-flavored kisses. After that, we dreamt together. We planned to leave Morant Bay for Kingston, get jobs in the city, and live in a house with plants and a kitchen full of food. We were happy. Then her mother came from New York and took her away from me.

The years apart had passed slowly. With my job at the bank in town I was able to afford my own small place. In it, I luxuriated in the aloneness I'd always craved as a child while crushed in one house between my parents and six siblings. My new home was tiny, four rooms and a little verandah from where I could watch the world go by. Here, no one could see how miserable Alva's absence made me. I wallowed in that misery, played our old songs and walked the length and width of my house, tearing open the old shoebox to press her old letters to my face and drown in my memories.

And now she was here. In her father's house, less than a mile down the road. I scrubbed myself in the bath, washed, oiled, and braided my hair, and put on fresh underwear. Then I went to her. The house was filled with people, all curious to see what Alva looked like now, to see if she'd brought something foreign for them. Cousins, friends from basic school, near strangers who walked by her father's yard every day and waved good evening as they passed. They all surrounded her, laughing, begging, entranced.

She was perfect. Slim and tall with her hair straightened and tucked up in little troughs that rode on her narrow shoulders. Skin the soft, teeth-tempting shade of figs and that lush, kissable mouth with the top and bottom lips that were perfect replicas of each other. Not even American MTV could have prepared me for such beauty. Her brown eyes were still quick and laughing, but I didn't recognize the hardness around her mouth, the way her hands were still unless she was reaching for something. Those hands of hers used to say so much, chasing the air as she talked, lying open and receptive, pressing against my skin. I hung back, waiting to see if she would notice me, or even realize who I was. I knew I had changed. I was softer, rounder. All my teenaged slimness had disappeared under years of chocolates and bread and fried fish. My mother said I had become another kind of beautiful. My sisters just said I was fat.

In my dreams of our reunion, Alva had stopped everything for me, brushed all other beggars aside to give coin in the currency of my choosing. But she never looked up, never noticed me standing there with my heart's cup held out. After a half an hour I stumbled away, holding my tears until I was walking down the dust-tracked lane where the sun sparkled green and gold on the foliage. The tears fell freely then. Though rich from the bounty of her new life, Alva had nothing to give me.

That night I made dinner for myself—peeled cassava, yam, and ripe plantains and dropped them in the boiling water. With each movement of the knife I kept seeing her face the last time we were together, the tears that limned its loveliness, the way she had clutched her lip between her teeth as I hovered over her, loving her and crying too. The time for tears was over. I had my life here and she had hers far away. Calalloo and saltfish simmered on the stove, releasing its rich flavors into the kitchen. My thoughts of her burned.

I heard a knock at my door. Of course, it was her. She immediately became the most exquisite thing in my house.

"I got your letter." Alva closed the door behind her and locked it. "I thought you didn't...you couldn't...anymore."

"I never stopped," I said.

A nervous smile came and went on her face. "I missed you."

The words were clumsy on her lips, but welcome. Alva was not as poised as she seemed, and perhaps my palms were not so wet. She lurched forward suddenly and touched me. I flinched, but she was gentle, tracing the bones of my hand with her delicate fingers before reaching for more, shaping my arm, my cheeks, the new roundness of my belly.

"You're gorgeous," she said.

All she'd ever meant to me came rushing back a hundredfold, crashing over my senses until I staggered against her, kissing her. I drowned in the taste of her on my tongue, the silk of her skin against mine. It was too much. I pulled my hand, my self, away, but she followed. Ah, her eyes... I melted, moved toward her, this stranger with the American voice. She caught me up, pressed her cool palms against my cheeks.

"I missed you," she said again.

Kisses like soursop ice cream melted over me, opened me. Alva was greedy. With her hands and silent mouth she told me what her letters did not, of her hunger for me, her thirst that our twelve-year absence had not dulled. My teeth pierced her lip; she gasped into my mouth and tugged at my dress, determined in her gentleness. Her fingers plucked at my nipples, raked them to hardness.

On the stove, the calalloo bubbled and boiled, threatening to spill over. The strength in her pretty hands had always surprised me. They lifted me, threw me on my grandmother's old table. It was sturdy under my weight, solidly straddling the floor as she pushed my thighs open. Her fingers parted the moist hairs under my panties, then slid home.

"I'm sorry I made you wait," Alva said.

The fullness of her inside me felt so good that it hurt. Breath boiled in my throat. Soft, needful noises bubbled up in my chest and flooded out of my mouth as I held her close, not quite believing she was there. Her coconut-scented hair brushed my face, and I clenched my thighs around her.

"I should have come back sooner," she breathed. "But I was afraid."

The fingers inside me began to move. In twelve years of lonely nights I had dreamed of this, of her hands on me, the voluptuous wet of her mouth against mine. In a fever, I clutched at her shoulders. My nipples scraped against her shirt, sending electric heat burning its way through my body. She pushed into me, her breath coming in loud gasps as the table slammed against the wall and my dangling legs jerked in the air. Sweat churned to the surface of my skin, my insides tightened and swelled, and my breasts tingled. I grasped at her one last time.

My moans sang out in the tiny kitchen as I twitched and shuddered in orgasm. Alva kissed my mouth and slowly withdrew her fingers. She licked them while I watched, limp, from the table. The muscles in my thighs trembled.

"You've always been so effortless," she murmured. "I forgot that too." With quick, impatient motions she shrugged out of her clothes and tossed them in a pile on the floor. Almost as an afterthought, she twisted away briefly to turn off the stove. My dinner was already ruined. "Show me your room."

I laid Alva out on my bed and feasted my eyes on the newness of her. The clipped and neat pubic hair, her flat belly and the diamond-studded post threaded through her navel. Her fingers were manicured, cut close and polished a strangely alluring green. I kissed the backs of her hands, then her palms. My smell on her pulled a response, visceral and immediate, from deep in my belly. She smiled up at me from the rumpled sheets, all wet mouth and slumberous eyes. Oh, I had missed this; her pliant, pleasure-seeking body under my hands, allowing me to do whatever I wanted.

Her skin smelled of a recent bath and baby powder and sweat. It yielded under my teeth and she moaned softly, arching her neck, widening her thighs. She whispered my name and asked for what she wanted. I slid my fingers against her slick wetness and she groaned, moving her hips against the sheets. The sound of my name on her lips sweetened the air again. I laughed with the pleasure of it and bent my head. She was a stranger to me, someone I had to relearn. I savored the lesson, cupping her soft hips as I charted the delicate geography of her forest and wetlands with my tongue. Hot sensation coursed through my body and pushed my hips against the bed in time to her groaning movements. Alva shuddered against my mouth, whimpering against the sheets as her body undulated and clutched, empty of everything except my love.

I knew she was not staying. How could she? Even now, her body under mine felt transitory, already in flight. Alva shifted until she was the one looking down at me, eyes tracing my face as if to memorize its every curve.

"Are you staying?" I asked.

"No." Her fingers settled on my belly. "But I want you to come with me."

I shook my head. Pain blossomed on my tongue from the fierce pressure of my teeth.

"We can't live here," she said, lacing our fingers together. "Not like this. Not like I want it to be. Come with me."

I closed my eyes. After twelve years, she had finally made my dreams real. How could I give that up? Already my skin clawed itself at the thought of leaving hers. I turned to her in the small bed, the bed I had bought for us, with one word on my lips.

"Where?"

BRIGHT, BLOWSY POPPIES

Maggie Kinsella

Jo sees the new arrival approaching from a long way off. Her caravan occupies a site on the edge of the campground—a deliberate choice, so that she's looking at French cows and hayfields rather than at the other campers. She has an unobstructed view of the narrow, winding lane that leads to the rural campground, and so she can chart the approach of the lone figure. There is nothing else for her to do, so she sits with her glass of *vin de pays* and watches the countryside settle into the evening. As the person gets closer, Jo can make out a striding, rolling gait, and a bulky rucksack on his or her back. A long-distance hiker, she guesses, coming in to spend the night, barely ahead of the threatening rain clouds.

She sips her glass of wine, wrapping herself in self-imposed solitude. Around her, the campground surges with life; children play on the swings, their parents call to each other in happy holiday tones, and in one corner a group of Scouts sings hymns. She could wander over and join one of these groups, if she wanted. She knows many are regulars who come every year to Alsace. As she and Frankie used to come. In years past, they would have joined one of the laughing groups, shared a glass of wine, conversed in their schoolgirl French. But that was then, and this is now, and Frankie is gone, and Jo is alone.

It's a surprise when Alain, the camp host, approaches with the lone hiker a pace or two behind. Jo can see now that the hiker is a woman—a girl really—with a long ash-blonde braid hanging loosely over one shoulder. She wears khaki shorts, sturdy boots; has sun-browned skin and a wide smile. She must be English, thinks Jo, and Alain needs her to translate.

"Bonjour, Jo, *ça-va?"* Alain greets her and indicates the new arrival. *"Cette fille est Anglaise.* Please can you translate?"

"Oui, of course," says Jo, and turns to the girl. "You want to camp the night?"

"I could hug you," the girl replies. "I don't think I've spoken English for a week! But yes, one, maybe two nights. It depends if it rains tomorrow." The flat vowels and a twang mark her as American.

Quickly, Jo translates the necessary details, and the American nods her thanks. Jo watches Alain lead her off to fill in the forms the French government requires. As the American girl's braid swings around the corner, Jo pours herself another glass of wine.

The chair beside her is empty, as it has been all week. She's here by herself, a tribute to her Frankie, a rare and true love, a lost love. Every year, she and Frankie had hitched up their aging caravan to the equally old Land Rover, left their horses in the tender care of the neighbor's teenage daughter, and driven from Sussex through the lanes of England to the ferry and over to France. Here they had sat for two weeks in the clear French sunlight, topping up their farmers' tans, rambling the footpaths, and talking and making love with equal fervor.

This is where Jo first told Frankie she loved her. This is where Frankie first told Jo about the leukemia that finally killed her.

Eight years they had together; eight years training horses for the show jumping circuit, eight years of hard graft, and eight years of love and laughter. Eight holidays at this rural French campground.

Jo finishes her wine. What else is there to do? She goes inside the caravan to find another bottle, and when she returns, the American is setting up her ridiculously tiny tent next to her.

Right then, she hates Alain. This year, sensitive to her solitude, he has only sent campers to that space if it's the last one in the whole damn campground. But here, in the quiet midweek, this oh-too-pretty, oh-too-young one is pitching her tent where Frankie and Jo used to kiss in the long grass, in the cow parsley, in the fragile, blown poppies.

"Hi," the American calls. "I think your friend took pity on me. He gave me this spot, next to the only English person here. I hope you don't mind."

Wordlessly, Jo shakes her head. For the next hour, she watches the girl fight a losing battle with the weather. The dark, charcoal clouds roll in thickly as she pitches her silly little tent. Jo sits underneath the caravan's awning as the first fat, dark drops of rain fall, and watches her try to heat a tin of something on a spluttering camp stove. The girl must sense her reticence as after the first greeting she keeps her back turned toward Jo.

Jo nurses her third glass of wine and watches the shoulders of the girl's fleece darken as the rain falls in a steadily increasing downpour. She closes her eyes. Whether she likes it or not, she will have a visitor. Frankie would never have sat and watched someone toil in the rain.

Before she can change her mind and retreat into the bottle, she strides over and taps the girl on the shoulder. It's soggy under her fingers, and the blonde braid drips a steady stream of water into the small pan she holds.

"You can't stay out here," Jo says. "Come and cook in my van and get dry. We can talk English."

The girl grins up at her, through a forelock of rain-sleeked hair. "I thought you'd never offer."

The caravan seems too small with another person in it, another person who isn't Frankie.

"I'm Allie," the girl says. "American, but I guess you figured that."

Jo holds out her hand, introduces herself. There's a tingle of awareness as their hands touch, a frisson of something she hasn't felt since Frankie died. No, she thinks, it's too soon, and doubtless Allie has a boyfriend. There are no lesbian vibes from this girl.

She sits at the small table and watches Allie heat her meal on the caravan's stove. She's having cassoulet, a gourmet French dish, but this one's from a tin. Over a glass of wine, they exchange snippets of their lives, the sort of edited highlights that strangers share.

Allie's from a small town in Oregon. Not Portland, she says, that's very exciting and liberal. Where she lives is a fruit-growing town, out on the plains to the east, where the people are as planted as the cherry trees.

"Every year I go somewhere new," she says, between forkfuls of haricot beans. "Last year it was Chile, the year before Thailand. This year, I wanted to see some of Europe. So, I caught a plane to Paris, took a bus to the furthest point I could, and started hitching. Then I found one of the *radonnees*, and started walking. I'm loving it."

Jo catches the resonance of Frankie in her words; Frankie and she did exactly that, striding away from their rural campsite in the mornings, walking the fields and the pathways, with careless disregard for rules and rights of way.

"I used to do that," says Jo, "with Frankie, my partner."

The words, once said, can't be retracted.

Allie shovels beans. "Where's Frankie now? Did you leave him at home?"

Jo scarcely notices her use of "him." The lump in her throat swells again, as it does whenever anyone mentions Frankie. "No," she says stiffly. "Frankie died ten months ago. We used to visit this campsite every year. That's why I'm here."

Allie stops eating, stretches out a hand, touches her arm. "I'm sorry. I know that doesn't mean much, you must hear it all the time, but it's all I know how to say."

Jo pours wine into her glass with a suddenly shaking hand. "Thank you. I should be used to it, but I'm not."

"He must have been young—you don't look more than twenty-five."

"I'm thirty-two." Jo tries a wobbly grin. "And it was leukemia. Frankie was twenty-eight."

The numbers seem so final somehow when she voices them. Their ages shouldn't matter; why should it be more tragic simply because Frankie was so young? She waits for Allie to say there's plenty of time, she'll find someone else, but Allie is silent, her food forgotten in front of her.

Outside, the rain is still streaming down, obscuring the far side of the campsite in the downpour. But the van is too crowded now that Frankie's ghost has been raised between them. Jo rises and, glass in hand, goes to sit outside, underneath the awning.

A few heartbeats and then the young woman sinks into the chair next to her.

"I'm sorry," Allie says, quietly. "I didn't mean to upset you."

"It's okay. No one normally mentions Frankie. It's as if she never existed. As if she's not supposed to matter, since we couldn't be married. I'm supposed to march off into the rest of my life without a backward glance."

"She?" Allie is still, sitting quietly in her seat, placid as the depths of a meandering stream. "I'm sorry. When you said Frankie, I assumed…" She shakes her head. "I should have been paying better attention."

Jo waits for the shutters to fall over Allie's expressive face. A rural Oregon girl probably feels uncomfortable around people who are different. Jo's read the stories of hate in small-town America.

The silence stretches. "It's okay," says Jo finally. "You don't have to stay to be polite. You can finish your wine and go back to your tent—"

Allie cuts her off. "It's not that. Really, it's not. I was trying to gauge if you wanted to talk about her. I guess direct is best, less misunderstandings." She leans forward, cradling her glass between both hands. "Please, tell me about Frankie."

Instead of answering, Jo stares off into the rain. In front of her, the field runs wild where Alain and his mower don't go. Poppies stud the long grass, their heads bowed over with the rain. Frankie loved those poppies; loved their bright, blowsy heads; loved that they grew unhindered and wild.

"We met at a horse trials," says Jo. "Frankie was competing on a mare she'd been schooling for someone. I was there, looking for promising young horses to buy—I'd already started buying horses and bringing them on and reselling them. She tried to interest me in the mare, but I could see what Frankie was trying to hide. The horse was a dud, and it was only Frankie's skill that got her around the course. I told Frankie that, and she laughed, agreed, and invited me out for a drink to see if she could change my mind. A week later, she came and found me in Sussex, saying she'd found a good youngster I might be interested in."

Jo's lips twist. "We fell in love with that horse and with each other. Frankie was only twenty; I thought it couldn't last. She'd never had a serious relationship before. But it did."

"What happened to the horse?" Allie asks.

"He's quite a star on the American circuit."

Jo rises, goes inside the caravan and brings out a bowl of cherries. Placing it on the table between them, she gestures for Allie to help herself.

The rain has eased to a steady drizzle as the dusk steals in. Allie's little tent stands forlornly on the edge of the long grass. Grass seeds and flower petals cling to its gray sides. Jo is silent for a few minutes, then Frankie's life, that brief and glorious life, is brought out into the twilight a sentence at a time for the stranger's ears. She tells the small things, the things she remembers best, not merely cataloguing dates and facts. How Frankie ate tartar sauce on lasagna, and toasted peanut-butter-and-tomato sandwiches for breakfast. The small indented scar on her foot where she'd stuck a pitchfork through it. How she had a habit of putting dandy brushes on the windowsill, so that the stable cat always knocked them into the feed bin. The strong skinny roll-ups she smoked. How she refused to walk under ladders, once climbing out of the window when a ladder blocked the doorway.

"When she died," Jo says, "people who knew very well what we were to each other were offering condolences and saying it would be hard for me to find as good a business partner. As if that were all she had been. They're kind people, they meant well, but it was like they wanted to make our relationship into something more conventional in retrospect."

"So that they knew how to behave?" suggests Allie.

"Yes, I think so. But they couldn't just *see*..." Her face crumples in on itself, and she wills herself not to cry in front of this compassionate stranger. She gropes for a tissue, but of course, there isn't one. She wipes her face on her sleeve.

"They couldn't see how the denial hurt you."

"Exactly." Jo sniffs slightly, feels the embarrassment that her grief always brings. To cover it, she turns the conversation. "When do you go back to Oregon?"

"Next week." Allie makes a moue of disappointment. "I like it here. College doesn't seem so appealing right now. Maybe I need to pick grapes in France, teach English in Japan, train horses in England!"

Jo smiles. "You'll find something different. Do you have a boyfriend?"

"No. Too busy with other things." Allie buries her face in her wineglass, sniffs, tastes, and savors. "Nice wine."

"It's plonk. *Vin de pays.* Less than a euro a bottle."

"Guess I better knock wine taster off my list of prospective careers then." Allie stretches out a hand, puts it over Jo's where it rests on the side of the chair. "I should go to bed. The rain has eased a little. I'll stay dry now."

She stands and hesitates. Jo takes the hint and rises to see her off.

"Thanks for the loan of your roof, and the wine."

Allie moves forward, embraces Jo in a spontaneous hug. Briefly, her lips brush Jo's cheek, and once again, Jo feels that undeniable tingle. Attraction, a moment of knowledge, and she wants to turn her face into Allie's kiss, transform it into something more. Briefly, Frankie's presence mutes and fades, and her fingers ease their stranglehold on Jo's heart.

But Allie withdraws, her hands sliding slowly away from Jo's shoulders.

A straight woman. Right.

Allie leaves, and Jo watches her trim backside as she crawls into the little tent.

In the morning, Jo rises late. Too much wine, and the sound of the rain drumming on the roof of her caravan kept her in bed past her normal seven o'clock. Through the van's window, she sees a flattened patch of grass where Allie's tent had stood. She's gone. Jo quashes her stupid feeling of loss. Allie didn't even say good-bye.

When she exits the caravan, coffee in hand, she spots a note wedged into the window frame. Her name is written on it in a bold, flamboyant hand. Unfolding it, she realizes it's from Allie.

Thank you for the wine, shelter, and company, the note says. *It was much appreciated. I hope you enjoy the rest of your vacation.* It's signed simply, *Allie.*

Jo twists the note in her hand, and thinks of those few moments last night, when Frankie faded into a corner. Only briefly, but in those scant seconds, the hollow pit of grief in Jo's belly was gone, replaced by shared laughter, warmth, and conversation. For a flickering moment, she thinks about dating again.

The note is scrunched, but Jo sees more writing on the back. Curious, she enters the van and spreads it out on the small bench, smoothing over the sheet with a careful hand.

P.S., she reads. *Maybe I shouldn't tell you this, but you were way off course when you asked if I had a boyfriend. I've never had one—only girlfriends. I didn't mention it, because I didn't want you to think I was hitting on you. I enjoyed our evening, Jo, and I like you, maybe more than I should. Here's my email address if you feel like staying in touch. I'll be traveling again next summer. Maybe you'd like someone to help you with the horses for a while?*

Jo stares at it for long moments, until the bold, black writing blurs on the page. With a steady hand, she wipes away the moisture in her eyes, and then carefully folds the paper and puts it in her diary.

"Would you mind, Frankie?" she whispers to the air.

Going outside, she stands on the flattened patch of grass where Allie's tent used to be. Birdsong threads the air, and a light breeze is blowing. She can hear children playing on the swings at the far end of the campground, but over here there's only her and Frankie and the French morning, which is suddenly so full of hope.

Frankie's bright, blowsy poppies tremble in the light breeze, then are still.

CHANCES ARE, OR MURPHY WAS AN OPTIMIST

Saggio Amante

*M*urphy *was a fucking optimist,* Talley thought as she glanced at her watch for what seemed like the hundredth time. Traffic to the airport was gridlocked. Her flight was due to leave within the hour, and there she sat in a cab at a dead stop in an endless line of traffic.

Truth be told, the whole trip had sucked. First, there was the temporary loss of her luggage, which meant she had no suitable clothes for the meeting at which she was the featured speaker.

And then there was the mix-up in room reservations…no record of hers, even though they had been made three months ago and she had the confirmation number. The list went on and on. She hadn't even had time to check out the local talent. The trip wasn't a total loss, however. There had been time for her to sneak in a visit to her favorite shop to pick up some of the latest toys and replace a few worn-out ones. She smiled as she thought about breaking them in.

The cab inched forward slowly, and Talley felt her impatience rising. She tapped her fingers against the armrest.

"What's the holdup?"

"Looks like a fender bender up ahead," the cabbie groused.

"Just my luck. How far are we from the airport?"

"About five minutes if this mess ever clears up."

"Listen, there's an extra fifty in it if you get me there in time for my flight."

"When's your flight?"

Talley looked at her watch again. "Fifty-eight minutes, thirty seconds from right now."

"You got it, lady." The cabbie carefully inched her cab across three lanes until she reached the lane nearest a sidewalk. Then, in a move worthy of a Grand Prix driver, she flew up over the curb and turned down a side alley. "We'll just have to take an alternate route."

Talley leaned back in her seat and closed her eyes. Maybe there was hope after all.

"So what brought you to Medford?"

"Publishing conference." Talley kept her answer short and her eyes closed, hoping the cabbie would concentrate on driving instead of conversation. No such luck. Murphy struck again.

"You a publisher?"

"No."

"What then?"

"Writer."

"Oh, yeah?"

Talley couldn't miss the excitement in the cabbie's voice. *Oh, no. Here it comes.*

"I'm a writer too."

Of course you are. Talley groaned inwardly as she waited for the cabbie to continue.

Surprisingly, the woman didn't tout her talents. Instead she asked, "So, what's your name? Are you anybody I might've heard of?"

Talley laughed. "I don't know. My name is Talley Edwards. I'm…"

"Oh, my god. I thought you looked familiar. Talley Edwards? I love you!" the cabbie enthused, turning to look at Talley. "Well, I don't exactly *love* you. I mean, I don't know you. But I bet I own everything you've ever written. I love your work."

"Shit! Watch out!" Talley screamed as the driver narrowly missed a black sedan pulling onto the highway.

"Gotcha covered. Sorry." The cabbie averted her eyes and stared straight ahead.

"Just keep your eyes on the road, please. I'd like to get to the airport on time and in one piece." She looked into the rearview mirror as she spoke.

The driver glanced into the mirror at the same time, locking onto Talley's eyes then quickly looking away in embarrassment.

Gorgeous eyes, Talley thought. *If only she didn't talk so much.*

Talley leaned back against the car seat again. They rode in silence for a short distance.

"So what do you write?" *I can't believe I just asked that*, Talley thought, berating herself for restarting the conversation, until her own mantra for success crowded out that thought: *Be kind to your fans.*

"Nothing like you. Just poetry." The driver's tone was soft, almost apologetic. "I mean, I know there's not much of a market out there for poetry but…well…I just have a passion for it."

"Good for you." Talley's voice was warm with sincerity.

"You're into poetry?"

" 'The crown of literature is poetry. It is its end and aim. It is the sublimest activity of the human mind. It is the achievement of beauty and delicacy. The writer of prose can only step aside when the poet passes.' "

"Maugham?" the driver asked.

"Yes, Maugham."

"I'm impressed."

"Don't be. You'd be surprised how many people like poetry... even the ones who wouldn't admit it publicly. But that really doesn't matter, does it? Follow your passion. It won't lead you wrong."

"I will. Thank you. You're very kind."

"So, what's your name?"

"Andrea."

"Andrea what?"

"Brazeale."

"Well, Andrea Brazeale, it's nice to meet you. I look forward to reading your book when it's published."

The lights of the airport came into view, and Talley remained quiet as Andrea negotiated her cab through the airport traffic, pulling up in front of the TransAir terminal.

Talley looked at her watch. The ride had only taken ten minutes; she had just over forty-five minutes until boarding, and she prayed it would be long enough for her to make it through the security process.

The two women exited the cab at the same time, and Talley waited as Andrea removed her bag and laptop from the trunk. She pulled the fare from her wallet and added another fifty dollars. "Thanks. You made an otherwise miserable day bearable," she said, flashing a dimpled smile at Andrea.

"Keep it," the cabbie said, handing the extra fifty back to Talley.

"Take it, please. You earned it," Talley responded. "It's the least I can do."

"No, there's something else I'd rather you did." Andrea looked terrified and hopeful at the same time.

Talley hesitated, wondering if she was going to have to reject a pass. Not that she wouldn't have enjoyed it. She certainly was horny enough. And the cabbie wasn't bad…not bad at all, but Talley had a plane to catch.

Talley took a deep breath. "What is it, then?"

Andrea reached into the front seat of the cab and pulled out a tattered journal. "Read these. Let me know what you think." She grabbed a pen, scribbled her name and address on the inside cover, and held the book out to Talley.

Christ, a fifty-dollar tip would have been a lot easier. Talley smiled. "Of course, I'll be happy to read them." She took the journal and grabbed her bag and computer.

Check-in was easier than expected, and Talley attributed that to the fact that many of the passengers were probably still tied up in the traffic jam on their way to the airport. She headed to the security checkpoint and dropped her laptop and small suitcase on the conveyor belt. Just as she stepped through the gate to retrieve them on the other side, she heard the sound…a dull buzzing at first, and then a full-fledged symphony as her bag began to vibrate.

The security guards went on high alert the moment they heard the sound. Two of them grabbed Talley and shoved her against the wall as they unholstered their pistols.

The bag on the conveyor belt began vibrating harder and continued to shake as it moved through.

"That your bag, lady?" one of the guards asked gruffly. The other put her hand in the center of Talley's back and held her up against the wall.

"Wait. Wait. You have this all wrong," Talley protested. "It's not what you think." *Shit! I knew I should have removed the damn batteries.* Her cheek was against the wall, but she could see out of the corner of her eye as her bag came to a halt under the X-ray machine.

The red began to creep up Talley's neck and into her face as she watched the first guard look at the picture on the X-ray machine and then call the other guards over one by one. The laughter began slowly then erupted as the guards recognized what they were looking at. The conveyor belt started again, and Talley wanted to melt into the floor as she watched a guard open the bag and hold up the first item, which buzzed rapidly in her hand.

"It's okay, Tip. Let her go."

The guard holding her against the wall stepped back, and Talley turned to look at another chuckling guard standing by the conveyor belt.

"And this would be?" the guard said, looking at Talley with undisguised amusement.

Talley took a deep breath and responded in a serious tone. "That would be an electrical device consisting of a vibrating conductor interrupting a current."

"Say what?" The guard holding the vibrator looked quizzically at her counterpart.

"Looks like a pocket rocket to me," the second guard said.

"So, are you one of our satisfied customers?" Talley asked, looking at the woman who had correctly identified the vibrator.

The other guards laughed uproariously.

"Look," Talley said with all the aplomb she could muster. "I work for Consumer Laboratories. We test products to see if they meet manufacturing standards. Now can we please shut those off?"

Talley smiled sweetly at the guards who were looking at her in disbelief. "Hey, it's a job, and it pays well."

After a few seconds of uncomfortable silence interrupted only by the monotonous buzzing of the toys, one of the security guards turned them off and threw them back in Talley's bag. "Ya might wanna remove the batteries next time," she said gruffly.

Talley closed the suitcase and grabbed it off the conveyor belt. "Thanks. Watch for my article in *Consumer Reports*," she called over her shoulder as she started toward the boarding concourse.

"Talley! Talley! Ms. Edwards!"

Talley stopped dead in her tracks. 'What now?'

She turned toward the sound and saw Andrea racing toward the checkpoint swinging a gym bag over her head.

Oh, crap! I can't believe I forgot...

The thought barely had time to race through Talley's mind. The scene played out in slow motion as she watched Andrea trip, then fly through the air, the gym bag flung out ahead of her. The bag arched in the air, and it and Andrea hit the concourse floor at the same time with a sickening thud.

Talley raced back through security toward the fallen woman. "Andrea, are you all right?" she asked, kneeling beside the fallen cabdriver.

"Andy." The cabbie looked up at her with a dazed expression. "What?"

"Andy. My friends call me Andy." A hint of amusement joined the embarrassment in the cabbie's eyes as she started to sit up. Then dizziness seemed to overcome her. "Oh," she gasped weakly as she fell back.

Talley dropped her bags and sat down beside the cabbie, gently lifting Andrea's head onto her lap.

"Can we get some water here?" Talley yelled at the guards who stood aimlessly by watching the scene playing out before them.

When no one moved, Talley yelled, "Snap out of it. Stop

gawking. We need some water here, and a cold cloth if you can find one."

The tallest of the guards nodded and headed rapidly toward the closest restaurant. She returned in a few minutes with a wet towel and a glass of water. She knelt by the two women on the floor and placed the wet towel against Andrea's head.

Talley helped Andrea sit up a bit and cradled her in one arm. "Here." She tipped the cup so that Andrea could sip some water.

The cabbie looked up gratefully. "Thanks."

"Are you okay? Do you need a doctor?"

"I'll be fine. Give me a minute."

"Take all the time you need." Talley smiled down at the dark-haired woman in her arms. "You're going to have some goose egg tomorrow."

"Nah, it's nothing. Go on. I'll be all right. You'll miss your plane."

Talley thought about it for a moment but stayed put. "To hell with it. There'll be another one."

"Too bad," Andrea muttered.

"What?"

"Too bad there'll be another plane."

"Feeling better, are we?"

"I'm sorry. That was rude of me." Andrea moved her body away from Talley's and started to rise.

"Wait!" Talley pulled Andrea back against her. "If you try to get up too quickly, you'll probably get dizzy again. Relax, rest a minute."

"You're right. Just let me catch my breath." Andrea relaxed into Talley.

The two women sat on the concourse floor oblivious to the small crowd that had begun to surround them.

The guard stood and began to move the crowd away. "Okay,

folks. It's all over. Give the lady some air. Move it along."

Then the guard looked down at Andrea. "Lady, maybe the airport doctor should check you out."

"I'm fine. I don't need a doctor. But thank you."

"All right, then. But I really think you—"

Talley glared at the guard. "She said no. Just drop it."

The guard glared back at Talley. "I'll be right over there if you need me," she said.

"So, where were we?" Talley asked with a smile. "Ah, yes. You write poetry."

Andrea blushed. "This is a heck of a time to be talking about that. Besides, I can't believe I was so pushy. Or so clumsy for that matter." She flashed another embarrassed grin at Talley.

"Well, look on the bright side. You've certainly caught my attention. So, are you ready to get up now?" Talley said, rising and grasping the other woman's hand to help her up.

Andrea nodded, and stood up slowly, holding on to Talley's hand. "Thanks. You really have missed your plane, you know."

"I know. Like I said, there'll be another one."

"Well, let's go check on it, then."

"No. I'll get a room and check from the hotel. This was the last flight out tonight for my destination."

Andrea was quiet for a moment, apparently weighing her next words carefully. "I'll drive you to the hotel. Uh, then can I buy you coffee or dinner? I mean it's the least I can do after..."

"You know, I think that would be lovely. But I'll buy. After all, I'm the cause of that lump on your head."

"But..."

"No buts. Let's go. I'm buying!"

Talley picked up her suitcase in one hand and reached down with the other to pick up her computer and the gym bag.

"Here. Let me help you." Andrea started to take the gym bag from Talley's hand.

"No, I've got it."

"Let me."

It wasn't a struggle, really. Talley pulled one way; Andrea pulled the other; and inexplicably, the bag opened, spilling its contents onto the floor— blouses, stockings, lingerie—and in the middle of it all was one firm, curved, object looking very much like...

"What's this?" Andrea asked innocently as she held the flesh-colored thing in the air. "It looks like a...oh, my god!" Andrea stood there holding the object in her hand like a baseball bat. "This is a...it's a...oh, my god."

"Jeez, Andy, get a grip! It's only a dildo," Talley croaked, wresting the offending piece from Andrea's tight grasp. "At least it doesn't vibrate."

"What?"

"Never mind. I'll tell you later."

Talley stuffed the clothes and the dildo back in the gym bag. "Let's get out of here."

"You've had one hell of a day, haven't you?" Andrea could hardly contain her mirth.

"You don't know the half of it," Talley sighed.

If Murphy will just fuck off, chances are it's going to get a lot better soon, Talley thought as she watched Andrea's callipygian butt swinging ahead of her down the concourse toward the terminal exit.

A lot better.

UNDER THE SKIN

Lisa Figueroa

My girlfriend, Salfina, and I went to Rosarito Beach for a vacation as well as a celebration of our one year of living together. It was a milestone for each of us; she had never been faithful to any woman before me, and I hadn't been able to tolerate a roommate before her. For me, previous live-in lovers had meant too many borrowed clothes and a myriad of shared feelings. My past girlfriends had been femmes like me, and we had had such an overwhelming need to understand one another's femininity that the last thing I wanted from a relationship now was any kind of mutual sensibility.

Sal being butch made everything easier. I liked to think of our relationship as two complementary halves coming together into a greater, more fulfilling whole, a sort of lesbian yin and yang. I have to admit, our opposite femme/butch outlooks resulted in spectacular sex. But to better illuminate the differences between us, I longed to return to the sandy shore and turquoise waves where we had fallen in love, while Sal looked forward to two-for-one fish tacos and an endless quantity of cheap beer. I suppose being opposites did have its drawbacks.

We checked into a hotel with cute little bungalows along the beach. Ours was the farthest from the main hotel, and all the windows had been left open. Gentle breezes and sounds of breaking waves greeted us as we entered, making it easy to imagine us alone on an island happening by chance upon a deserted refuge, especially since the room had a rustic charm with few amenities. Sal noticed immediately that something was missing.

"Hey, where's the TV set?" She walked around the room and even checked the bathroom.

I didn't recall her asking about a television the first time we'd been there. We hadn't been interested in anything but each other. "There isn't one, remember? No TV, no radio, no phone. I guess we'll have to entertain ourselves," I said with a meaningful wriggle of my eyebrows.

Sal flopped dramatically on the bed. "God, I'm tired. The drive wore me out," she said, placing her hands behind her head as she looked up at the ceiling.

I lay next to her and mirrored her position, pretending the same interest in peeling stucco as our elbows brushed against each other. Side by side our bodies were another illustration of how we were different yet alike in the most essential way. Sal has a beautifully classic Latina body—voluptuous curves, with a flat backside and generous breasts I adore. Her gorgeous, fleshy body, its feminine attributes in direct contrast with her butch outlook, is a combination I find irresistible. I, on the other hand, have what might be considered the antithesis of a typical Latina body, too-slim arms and legs and a small, insignificant chest. However, my best feature, according to Sal, is my "J. Lo" ass. It's round and pops like a full-blown kernel of sweet kettle corn.

I heard Sal sigh and wondered if she was tired or just bored. Bored with me? "Let's check out the beach. You can take a nap there," I offered.

Sal nodded as if remembering where we were. "Okay."

We changed into our bathing suits: a new pink bikini with matching sarong for me, while Sal opted for shorts and tank top. Before we left, she grasped me around the waist and buried her face in my neck.

"I love you, Adela," she said, hugging me too tightly.

"I love you, too."

Her fervor caught me off guard, but I returned it eagerly. I caressed the back of her head and squeezed her shoulder as my fingers traced the almost imperceptible lines of a distinctive scorpion tattoo, like a blind woman reading Braille. I closed my eyes as I thought about what the colorful shape disguised, about the letters hidden beneath the curved line of tail. Sal moved away from my exploration, breaking contact.

At the beach, surfers took advantage of afternoon swells, two elderly women lounged under an umbrella, and a couple with three small children were building a lopsided sandcastle. The elderly women looked over at us as we spread a blanket near the water, and I glanced back at them wondering if they were sisters or friends. Perhaps they were thinking the same thing about us. I smoothed sunscreen down my legs and arms, careful not to miss any areas, struggling to reach my back.

"Here. Let me help," Sal said, taking the tube from me.

She poured lotion into her palms, then stroked it onto my shoulders, working her way down to my hips. Her strong hands felt good, and I smiled until I felt her lips on my neck.

"Cut it out," I said, pulling away from her. The woman with children frowned at us before turning to her husband.

"What?" Sal said innocently, ignoring my look while working

lotion into her own arms and shoulders.

"This isn't the time or place. There are kids around."

"Hey, it was just a kiss. Lighten up."

She stretched out on her stomach, and I reached down contritely to touch her thigh but hesitated. Part of me knew I was being silly, but another part, a section that seemed to be located in the small of my back, resisted being outed against my will. Was Sal honestly being affectionate or was she putting our relationship on display out of defiance, like she did with those tattoos she was so proud of? I gazed at her other tattoo, an Aztec symbol of peace, exposed just above her waist. If I stared long enough, I could almost make out the name it concealed. There were two tattoos, and two exes who had been significant enough for her to etch their names in her body. Mistakes, she had explained so simply. She also said the secondary tattoos, to cover the first ones, had hurt much more because the artist needed to go in deeper, past the wounds of the original ink. Still, the new tattoos could not entirely obliterate the old ones.

In passionate moments, especially when we made love, I liked to believe Sal's body was mine and mine hers, each of us blending into the other like two shades of the same color forming something brighter, but those tattoos were areas that remained elusive to me, as if scar tissue had created a barrier I couldn't penetrate, no matter how hard I tried. Sal just didn't understand; once she promised to put my name on her body, but I talked her out of it. Sharing space with other names didn't appeal to me no matter how much they were camouflaged.

As the heat of the sun blazed and shimmered across the sand, I studied the waves washing over the shore. Instead of filling me with peace and contentment, they made me hot and restless. I wiped sweat from my forehead, stood up to wrap my sarong around my waist, and walked to the water's edge. The foamy

surges formed a pool that bathed my feet and calves in cool-
ness as I splashed around like a child, moving steadily down
the shore.

After a while, I turned back to check my distance from Sal,
who sat watching me. Waves were tumbling wider and rougher
between us, as if pushing us apart, and for once I wasn't sure if it
mattered or not. She raised her hand and as I began to lift mine
in response, I halted mid-gesture, noticing an old man pushing
his cart full of beer and ice in front of her. When I saw him handing her several bottles, I turned and continued on my way.

I reached the pier in a few minutes. There were more vendors
and open-air shops selling fresh fish and local crafts. I strolled to
the end of the boardwalk, past fishermen casting lines, to where
more tourists gathered, families and tanned slim men without
shirts moving about in rowdy groups. Two young women with
shaved heads walked by holding hands, unconcerned that several people stared at them, myself included. For a moment, I
yearned for their symmetry and casual disregard for what anyone thought. I wondered if it was bravery or indifference.

Sometimes Sal was too insistent on showing affection in public. I preferred a little more discretion, something my previous
femme girlfriends had understood, but which Sal interpreted as
fear. Perhaps it was apprehension, but although I didn't hide our
relationship, I didn't feel the need to display it boldly. I knew I
let her down, but it was different for Sal who'd been out since
she was thirteen and didn't give a damn what people thought. I
admired that attitude and appreciated how she had never lied to
me about who she was, or more importantly, her past. She willingly told me about the two women, the "mistakes" she regret-
ted permanently honoring with tattoos, and how her infidelities
had destroyed those relationships, and damaged her as well.

Sal was different now, older and wiser, and she knew love

meant more than a simple tattoo. Much more. But why did I keep thinking about them? Just what did I expect her to do about them? Maybe they were resilient pieces of Sal, parts of the puzzle that shaped the woman she was, the woman I loved. The urge to return to Sal hit me unexpectedly, like a spritz of sea air. I left the pier, retracing my steps in the sand. Nearing our spot, I saw she wasn't alone. Sitting with her on the blanket was another woman, a local I assumed, dressed in a traditional Mexican dress, with lovely skin as dark as an avocado seed. They were deep in conversation, and at one point I saw Sal touch her ankle. Neither looked up as I approached.

"What's going on?" I shouted, rushing up and shoving Sal away from the other woman.

My actions surprised both of us. I ended up on Sal's lap as she held on to my wrists trying to gain leverage without hurting me. She finally maneuvered me onto my back, her face so close to mine that I thought for one crazy second she was going to kiss me.

"Nothing's going on! We were just talking about tattoos. She has a pretty one on her ankle that her brother created. He has a studio, and I told her I've been thinking of having your name tattooed on my body."

The local woman watched us warily, and the family and elderly women were staring at us too. "Okay, okay. Get off me," I said. Sal released me and I sat brushing off sand as she stood.

"Here, señorita. My card. Come see us if you're still interested." The woman handed Sal a business card and, without saying good-bye to me, walked away in the direction I had just come from.

I noticed two bottles of beer and opened one, guzzling the cool liquid while Sal stood staring out at the crashing waves. Her shoulders were stiff and her arms folded.

"I'm sorry, Sal."

She slowly dropped down beside me. Neither of us spoke for a long while. Then finally she said, "You really think I'd cheat on you?"

I took a thirsty swallow of beer, the burning aftertaste lingering in my throat. "It's just...I saw you two together and..."

"Oh, I see. You go off without saying a word and I'm the one not to be trusted."

"How was I supposed to know you were talking about tattoos?"

"Shouldn't we trust each other?" she said.

Of course she had a point there. Now I was both miserable *and* feeling guilty that Rosarito Beach didn't have the same magic for us as before. I also hated the jealousy that lingered, cascading through my body. "You're right," I told her, then took the woman's card from her hand and studied it. The advertisement alone was a small work of art with its beautiful native Mexican images.

"I want to tattoo your name on me. I promise it's the last one I'll ever want. I've never wanted anything so badly."

I gazed at the card until the lines began to blur. "You already know how I feel about that."

Sal's plump mouth became a thin hard line. "I don't really need your permission."

"I guess you don't." I handed her the card, making sure our hands didn't touch.

Sal took a deep breath. "Please, *mi amor*. Don't you know I'd cut those other tattoos out of my body if it'd make you happy? They're just designs now. They're nothing. The names no longer exist."

"Yes, but why do I keep seeing them?"

"You see what you want to, but look under the skin, past the ink and flesh and bone to where my soul is linked to yours. Can't you see that? I only want to be with you. You, Adela. You're my *otra mitad*, my true other half."

She was achingly sweet and sincere in her appeal. I'd never seen her this vulnerable, and I realized I'd been missing it. I did see we were joined and that I wanted it to be forever. She leaned in for a kiss, and for once without caring what other people thought, I met her lips with mine. It was a brief moment but packed with emotion. Sal smiled and stood, reaching out for me in a courtly gesture. I shyly raised my hand to hers, and she swooped me up and into her arms. We gathered our belongings quickly, and holding on to each other, we made our way back to the bungalow, to our own private island.

SIVONYA

Teresa Lamai

*L*owell, *Massachusetts, 1915*

General Prudence gazes out my window and wipes her forehead. Her Salvation Army uniform is dark with sweat.

"Miss Shea," she sighs, "you're an example to the others." She reaches to rub at the greasy brown windowpane but thinks better of it. Her gloved hand fumbles its way to her purse. She draws out four silver dollars—I hear their sweet clink—and lays three of them near my washstand.

Each Sunday, General Prudence visits the boarding houses for us mill girls. Now that her brother owns the mills, she's made it her mission to keep us all contented, sober, and safe from moral turpitude.

"Your kind influence is so helpful," I murmur. She turns then, grinning proudly.

She has the distinctive smell of a charity lady, as if she bathed in camphor before coming to our neighborhood. When she steps nearer I squeak, "Thanks again for the lovely book." I glance at the title, *My Second Reader*.

There's the crow of a rooster and we both glance outside. Barefoot children race among the swags of sooty laundry. They cover their mouths and bite their lips as they play; the landlady's sons will beat them if they make noise before noon.

Sometimes the silence plumps and expands all around me, as if I were being suffocated in mattresses. I won't cry out, although I feel the scream like a very hot bullet, just in the back of my throat.

The general shudders and closes her purse. "Well, lord knows you need something useful to do on your Sundays off...."

Three fucking dollars. Stingy cunt.

The sky is pus-colored, the humid air almost unbreathable. The streets are grim, dusty—crowded but silent. As I walk downtown, hundreds of exhausted women swarm around me; most of them work in the mills. They carry day-old bread or morphine-drugged babies. All I can hear is the slither of skirts, the furtive slap of worn-out shoes.

Moving soothes me, reminds me I have two legs beneath my skirt. Under my breath, I can't help singing one of Sivonya's songs. I close my fists tight; lately I find myself stretching my fingers before me whenever I think of her, as if I wanted to draw her shape out of the hateful empty air.

Red-eyed policemen stand at every corner, waiting for a fight or demonstration to break out. One of them spits at my feet.

Ten yards from him, there's the entrance to the nickelodeon —closed today—and beside it, down the stairs, is a heavy black door with three milk bottles on its stoop. I open the door and push aside a heavy curtain.

"Peg!"

"I have them, Sasha."

But before he takes my sheaf of papers, Sasha kisses both my cheeks and leads me into the crowd. The basement is lit with old-fashioned oil lamps covered in Chinese shades. I squint to make out faces.

Someone puts a glass into my hand and I take two swigs. Pernod absinthe. It goes through me like a flame.

"How've you been?" Here's John's face, gleaming like chocolate in the half-light. He punches my shoulder with exaggerated gentleness and I smile.

Sasha sits and pores over my papers, thanking me floridly. I didn't really do much. He translated the leaflets from Russian into English. All I did was edit them. John knows someone with a printing press, and I'll bring a hundred copies to the mill on Monday. If the foreman knew what we mill girls could hide in our skirts, he'd make us all wear trousers.

Sasha is gesturing for me, but I can't bear another of his earnest speeches.

"So where's the gramophone?" I snap. "It's like a morgue in here."

More people come through the passageway. There are complaints, kisses, shrieks of laughter. I drop my three dollars in our jar, pour myself another Pernod, and stumble to the gramophone. I paw through the records: "Turkey Trot," "Grizzly Bear," "Women and Cocaine." And "The Internationale," which I hide at the bottom of the stack.

Someone's saying my name, but all I want now is the darkness, and the flaming absinthe, and Sivonya's voice.

> *Stay home with me baby, stay close by*
> *The snow's already three feet high*
> *Don't leave me here to ache and cry*
> *I'll bake you a sweet apricot pie*

The record's already scratched, but Sivonya's voice makes everyone go silent. I stand before the Victrola and sway, closing my eyes. *Apricot pie,* that was my damn line. I want to be annoyed, but a memory surfaces in my mind: a February blizzard, Sivonya sprawling naked and laughing on my bed, her skin gold and crimson in the firelight. She held my gaze and let her slender thighs fall open. Her cunt a perfect blushing apricot. My mouth flooded with saliva and I fell to my knees.

My face is wet, but I keep dancing. Other dancers surround me now. We're all singing along with Sivonya. No wonder this music is banned—it's distilled pleasure, and we're so thirsty we soak it in through our skin. It fills my blood with sweetness; it fills my head with wicked rushing dreams. I want to take off my gritty old clothes and do something shocking; I want to end it all tonight so that I never see another colorless Lowell dawn. I feel like a fish that's been taken from the sea to be kept alive in a pail of fetid water.

The record crackles as Sivonya wails the next refrain. I remember her flushed round cheeks, her tilting mouth. My eyes are still shut tight and I reach before me, imagining her shape. Sometimes, drunk and swaying to her music, I feel her so intensely I think she must have died somewhere in Europe and her spirit's come to torment me.

A small hand slips into mine and then I'm seeing Sivonya's face. Her cheeks are thinner, and there's a scar at her temple. Her eyes are darker, hard and luminous as obsidian. When the lamplight flares, her lashes flutter.

Someone bumps her and she spills her drink on my shirt.

"Oh," she says, and the spell breaks. She lifts her eyes to mine and I back away.

Of course I've rehearsed this moment in my fantasies. I've imagined slapping her; I've imagined clutching her knees and

sobbing; I've imagined giving her a blithe greeting, then saunter-
ing off to dance with a stranger.

Instead I stand gaping.

She speaks first. "I couldn't risk writing you." Her accent is
thicker. "I—I sent you money from Calais."

She steps closer. Her black hair is shorter, cut almost to her
chin. I've only ever seen such short hair on girls who've been in
prison.

Someone puts on another record, a rollicking song from New
Orleans. Sivonya touches my chin and her fingers are hot as a
brand. I want to slap her hand away, but I'm paralyzed.

"A year," I stutter. The music roars around us. "Sivonya."
With my next breath I'm sobbing. "I come home one night to a
note on our kitchen table. And then you're gone a year! A fucking year! I thought I'd die, I thought you'd died."

I turn away, but she grabs my wrist and pulls me through
the kitchen, into the larder that's crowded with books and pow-
dered milk. She lights the kerosene lamp. Her hands are frail and
small, like the skeletons of birds.

I'm pulling her to me. Her head nestles under my chin, her
arms circle my waist. I feel hot for an instant, then terribly cold,
as if my heart has stopped.

"I had to," she whispers. She huffs against my shirt, and
I spread my hands over her heaving shoulders, her poor bare
neck. "I had to, Peg, the resistance needed me. I told you I'd
have to go."

"What did you do?" I touch her face. It's so much more
delicate than I remember. Her skin is pallid and fine, with trembling arteries. I can't stop touching her cheeks. Chills run up
my arms.

"I was in Belgrade, then Prague. I brought money to the resistance." Even here, she glances around in a panic. "They bought

guns. Then I was among the émigrés in Paris. I performed in a café *chantant* in Montmartre and I relayed messages. If I sang of a red bird, then the next meeting would be at my flat. A green bird meant we'd meet at the Lycée. If I sang of a blackbird, it meant we were being watched and we would lie low for six weeks."

Her face gives off light, a pale summer moon. I imagine biting her, wrapping my fists in her thick hair. Instead I lean in and put my mouth over hers. She's still trying to talk; she jerks away from me, but I can't let her go. Someone has put on another record, a Spanish voice full of incomprehensible longing.

I clutch her shoulders. I kiss her again, till she stops shaking, till she goes still. Then everything's silent and slow and tinged with silver, as if we'd been plunged underwater.

We're half-fallen. Somehow she's braced against the wall, sliding downward till she rests on the floor. I crouch before her, pulling her blouse open. My hands shake and one button flies into the corner.

She never wears corsets or chemises; she's warm and sleek as a weasel. Her nipples are dark as little figs. When I hold her breasts she moves her shoulders and cries out sharply. I cup her jaw and she turns to bite my fingertips. I nuzzle her throat, breathing in her scent, the scent of wide green rivers and wheat. She kicks under me, shuffling till her skirt is bunched around her waist. I open her drawers and suddenly there's the scent of the sea—the scent of cliffs, of dark endless waves, of escape.

She stretches out under me. I grasp her thighs so tightly she flinches and squeaks. Her cunt looks swollen and painfully raw; my own stings as if it's been slapped. I fit my mouth over her labia and I feel her melt, like the softest sand just at the edge of the water.

My thumb grazes over her clitoris and my tongue reaches

deep inside her. She twists beneath me but my touch is light. I trace slow circles over her insistent skin. I'll never let her come— I can't bear for this moment to end, for her to dissolve and ebb away from me again, for her scent to fade from my skin and hair.

But she presses against me and comes violently, thrashing, her hands scrabbling over the dirty floor. When I lie on top of her and fit my thigh between her legs, she comes again, crying out like someone wounded. I cover her mouth.

If she were wounded, she could never leave....

Then I'm coming, shocking myself, grabbing her neck so tightly that her black eyes widen with fear. I mustn't hurt her, I mustn't.

"Don't leave me," I'm saying, "again." I can't stop saying it. "Don't leave me again." Lust and fury rush up and down my spine. She holds my face, but I can already feel her slipping away. "Don't, don't, don't..."

I sob in her arms for a long time. She holds me, rocks me; she doesn't realize I'm crying from rage.

Outside, someone's put on another of her records, and her voice bathes everyone in sweet warmth. Her lips rest on my ear. She's whispering: "Come with me this time. Come with me."

I pull away and sit up, heart racing. I think she can't mean it, but she rises to her knees and grabs my wrists.

"I'll keep you safe as I can," she hisses. "It's pretty rough. I'll understand if you don't—"

I stand and move away from her; I put my back at the door. Then, as if the floor tilted suddenly, I'm stepping toward her, falling into her arms.

"I'll come, Sivonya."

I say it two more times before she seems to hear me.

ALL YOU CAN THINK ABOUT

Rachel Rosenberg

You feel light-years less cool than this place deserves, with the striped gray and cherry-red walls, the '90s trip-hop playing from the speakers, the chipped secondhand coffee mugs, and the tables that are old school desks. But that's just a problem you've been having in general since you first moved to the city, amidst the lights and drama and businessmen and women hurrying along, the people asking each other, "What kind of artist are *you?*" at parties, the homeless people bumming change in the subways.

There's one café that's your favorite. Some days it's all too easy to finish reading entire books sitting at a table in back, lost in foreign lives and lands. Although the café is usually busy, it's never packed. It makes you miss being a student. Probably that's what the envious pang is about anyway, as you glance at the obvious students around you, each of them drowning in academia. Most are dressed similarly in a sort of artist-kid uniform: wool hats and fuzzy sweaters with argyle patterns or stripes. They talk about the Importance of Art in serious tones, as though their conversations are essential to the continuation of the species. Or there are the students who pour over books on serious subjects, math and science; preppy-looking kids talking *at* each other instead of *to* each other in their Barbie-and-Ken way of speaking. What is it with preppy girls having squeaky voices? It's comforting to you to be around these students, sitting and people-watching and smirking into the blank pages of your notebook.

The walls of the café are decorated with paintings—two per wall, always a series by a local, struggling, friend-of-the-owner artist. The paintings change on a weekly basis, as New York has no shortage of struggling artists with well-meaning friends. The low lighting makes you feel warm-headed so you lean forward and press your cheek into your palm, staring out of one of the big side windows into the snow-covered streets, watching the people going home after work carrying bags of groceries, hidden behind hats and mittens, scarves, and big coats.

Terra had been the one to bring you there, two weeks after you'd started dating. She'd met you at an especially windy street corner, and her cheeks were red with cold. The plan had been to catch a movie, but she'd shown up and immediately asked, "How into the movie idea are you?"

You were supposed to see *Mulholland Drive* together, and actually you *were* pretty into it. But she had her hair tied up in the cutest pigtails in the world, tiny pigtail buns that made her look like an anime character, and her eyes looked so bright and excited.

"Pretty good, but I can be dissuaded."

She took your mitten-clad hand with her own, and the two mitten-hands pressing together looked so sweet that she could have led you anywhere without argument. She'd brought you to the café and excitedly gone to sit down right away, running her hands along the desk tables and saying, "Isn't this great? It's so comfortable. I spend hours here." She stood up again and, looking sheepish, added, "I want to spend hours here with you."

Many afternoons and evenings were spent reading quietly together or talking, some with each of you working separately. You work at a local DIY fashion magazine that barely pays, and most of the articles you've written have been done in this café. Both of you know the staff by name, and some of their personal lives. Too many cigarettes have been smoked standing outside, watching people as they bustle around you.

Even now, after the separation, everywhere else seems lacking. So you sit at a table in the back, trying to write your article, sipping from your dollar-twenty-five Diet Coke. Your best friend, busy with his new candy-coated blissful boy-love, was supposed to meet you and his lateness is distracting. It was his idea to meet here, as the Boyfriend works two blocks away at a used video and CD shop on Bleecker Street. But here you are, waiting, five minutes past the time when Davis should have arrived. He's always at least fifteen minutes late, so you discounted that right away, but it's now been an extra five, which is utterly out of character.

Last week, the two of you had plans to go to CBGB's, and then without warning he brought the Boy with him, a skinny kid with highlighter-yellow hair wearing a tie and tight-fitting old jeans who talked about the raw emotion of punk rock until you wanted to vomit on his shiny clean sneakers. Davis ate that shit up, though. By the end of the night you had spoken seven words total to him. And those had been squeezed in quickly between his and the Boy's make-out sessions. You went to the bathroom to cry and ended up distracted by all the messages

written on the stall walls, incredibly deep thoughts such as: I
HEART BOYS, I CRAVE BOYS, BUT DON'T LET THEM DESTROY YOU,
and MARCY WUZ HERE '04. It was difficult to be sad in a room
that smelled of spilled beer and people's bowel movements, but
hey. You tried.

Your friends aren't helping matters much: They ask (over
and over and *over* again) how Terra-and-Tuck could possibly
have broken up after three years. Like the two of you were char-
acters on a sitcom and they loved to follow your *oh-so-wacky*
exploits (See them make tea for guests! Hear the stories of the
questions they get asked by strangers! Watch them kiss—isn't
it sweet?), and now they have to turn off the program and find
something else to do. When it first got around that you'd moved
out, people were full of opinions on what this tremendous decision was doing to *them*. But but but, you thought. What about
you? What about your near-catatonic state of sorrow and par-
tial denial? But.

All you can think about is Terra. You start articles you can't
finish, dial phone numbers you hang up on, read books you need
to skip to the last page of. You eat tuna sandwiches and takeout.
At night, you imagine being rescued from Davis's sock-strewn
apartment. You imagine her hands curling around your arms,
pulling you close, imprinting your body with their need. Once,
when you had the flu and couldn't sleep from fever, she sang
"Dream a Little Dream of Me" to you until the lull of her voice
let you drift. Since you've been away from her, the song keeps
reentering your head.

You've been sleeping on Davis's couch for three weeks, alone
in the apartment since he's unable to be parted from the ever-
present Boy. He tries to be supportive when he actually emerges
from his euphoric daze, but those moments are few. Mostly it's
just you poring through old photo albums, page after crinkling

page of the two of you smiling, making weird faces, kissing, cuddling, eating Chinese food with chopsticks, lying in grass, leaning against stop signs and traffic lights. Or sometimes, for an exciting change of pace, you watch television blankly and wonder if the crime will be solved by the end of the hour.

Terra called, a week and a half into the break, wanting to know how you were doing. It sounded rehearsed: "Oh, hello, Tuck. How are you?" She was soft-spoken and extra polite, like you were acquaintances making small talk, or coworkers exchanging shifts.

You traded sentences like baseball cards, meeting her news with some of equal value. You talked briefly about an article that was nearly finished; she told you they were going to start another run of the musical she'd been doing. Made you wistful, remembering watching her rehearse her dance number, you on the sofa pretending to write an article but sneaking glances in her direction.

You do what you have to do in order to remain distracted, walking around the West Village and buying old diner art from hipster shops, standing outside in the snow and watching it drift through the light from streetlamps, spending hours in Strand Book Store until you get dizzy from reading book title after book title.

Books remind you of Terra: you find yourself picking up novels you know are her favorites and reading the back, flipping through and scanning sections. Music reminds you of Terra: you download her favorite songs on Davis's computer and pretend she's just in another room. Movies remind you of Terra: you see them by yourself and remember watching films on the sofa with your head in her lap or her head against your shoulder and her legs crossed beneath her body. Being in the city reminds you of Terra. You grew up in Rockland County surrounded by trees and silence and no sidewalks. You used to visit the city with your friends and each time the atmosphere was breathtaking, lights everywhere and constant noise and movement.

Unlike you, Terra was always a city girl, having grown up in a tiny Hell's Kitchen apartment with cracked plaster walls. When she was younger, she had lived with her dad. She had fickle interests and could never figure out what exactly she wanted to do to get out of there. So she started with a religion major, switched to social work, then briefly entertained thoughts of doing art professionally before making a final switch to theater.

You met her on the Sunday just after you had decided you'd live your life alone. She had a class with Davis and he used to talk about her, raving about how everything she said in class came out so eloquently. As you are terrible at public speaking and not at all intellectual, you hated hearing about this perfect girl.

One day he brought her over to his place to work on an oral for the class; you didn't know and went by to visit him. She was sitting cross-legged on his counter when you came in; he was on the phone with a guy he'd recently started seeing. Terra's hair was pink at the time, slightly dreaded, and she looked at you with a barely-there smile. He stayed on the phone for an hour—later explaining he'd wanted to give the two of you time to talk and that he had forced a very awkward, overlong conversation with a boy he barely knew on your behalf.

You and Terra chatted, going outside and sitting in the sunlight on Davis's steps. She wore faded blue jeans and new-looking Vans, still their original color, and was eating a green apple. The crunch of it kept drawing your attention to her mouth.

For a week and three days, the two of you kind of, sort of, pseudo-dated. She told stories about her ex-girlfriends, but you'd never had a real one before. Finally, chain-smoking and avoiding her eyes, you admitted to crushlike feelings and asked her on a real date. She stared for a moment, gazing through the haze of your cigarette, then nodded.

"Yeah," she had said, and grinned. Three weeks later, you were spending four days a week at her place. Two weeks after that, you started paying rent. It was a small cramped one-room apartment in Brooklyn, an area that had been dangerous thirty years ago but was now full of artists and students. It was her job to unpack and do dishes, yours to decorate.

In the café, sipping from the two white straws placed carefully in the soda can, you flip through a design magazine's article on lofts. You want to be the kind of girl who lives in a place like that: self-sufficient and inspired, in an unaffordable old warehouse in SoHo with a single brick wall and the rest painted coral. There would be seashells glued around the large window frames, postcards sent by friends in faraway places in a collage on the kitchen wall, a coffee table pasted with pictures cut out from magazines, mismatched—

"Tuck?"

Your name, her voice. It has always sounded just like your name was waiting for this person to pronounce it. Which doesn't mean you wanted to hear it uttered from her lips right now, but of *course* this would happen, of-fucking-course; you knew it would, because life sucks that way. Slowly you raise your head to find the most sweet-sad girl in the universe before you, shifting nervously, looking somewhat pained, clutching a mug so that her knuckles match its white porcelain surface. Your stomach feels stretched, aching slightly.

Things between you went downhill fast, so fast that at seven months she was already complaining she needed more alone time. You got resentful, clingy. She was stressed she couldn't find an acting job and very up front about it, often saying you were irritating. You started crying a lot, almost every day. You never remembered to call after having promised to; she would go for days without speaking more than monosyllabically to you. She tore up things you had written her and left them in a pile by the computer so that you'd be sure to notice. She spent more and more time working on her plays, often coming home after you were already in bed. She'd stumble into the apartment sometimes and it would wake you, and when her body filled the bed the smell of alcohol accompanied it.

You packed up everything she had ever given you and hid it all because it reminded you of how drastically things had changed. Nearly three years into the relationship, she had suggested the two of you take a break, not necessarily permanent, but just to see if you'd be happier apart—which angered you because you didn't *want* to find out that you were happier apart and the anger made you tell her you "would fucking love to" and pack up your things.

You had expected this at some point, except, really, you sort of didn't. "Hey." Until the breakup, the longest you two had been separated for was a week when she'd gone with friends to Boston for a wedding but you'd had a deadline to meet. It had been a week of phone calls and emails, and letters she hid around the apartment for you to find while she was away.

Tapping painted nails against the surface of the table, you fight the urge to tug on the slightly pointed ends of your pixie haircut.

The chair feels impossibly uncomfortable. Terra seems to be hiding behind her brightly dyed red hair and underneath a way-too-big-for-her black sweater. Now she's pulled her sleeves down so the knuckles are hidden and only her thumbs are visible through the holes in her sleeves.

"Well," she says, struggling to find something else to say.

Some guy a few tables away is singing a campy old show tune to his friend, his voice scratchy-loud. He's wearing a pink wool scarf and the clear glass mug in front of him seems to contain a red-colored tea. His voice sounds like raindrops.

Terra's voice brings you back: "Bye, Tuck."

You look down and find her feet turned slightly inward, left shoe pressing slightly against the side of the right one. Her same old Vans, gray with dirt and extra scuffed around the toes. The knot in your stomach tightens. You remember when those Vans were still new. You remember her kicking off the shoes while stumbling, kiss-busy, into the bedroom, and how one of them went flying and it took forever to find it later on.

"Would you like to sit?" you ask, thinking *Fuckshit. What are you doing?* The occasional phone call was one thing; face-to-face interaction was unacceptable. *Too much pressure not to be horrible. Remain nice. Remain casual.*

"Yeah, sure." Her voice sounds hesitant, understandably. The breakup had been semi-explosive, coming after weeks, maybe even months of constant fighting. Her asthma had been acting up from stress and cold, and you couldn't write more than ten consecutive words. Nights were hard to get through, both of you turning away and shifting.

She sits, the chair scraping against the floor as she pulls it back, and you flash back to a million moments like this. The two of you in countless coffee shops. Your Diet Cokes or black coffees. Her chamomile tea with milk. The ever-present ashtray filled with cigarette butts. Teasing voices. Stolen glances. Hands held across tabletops. Knees touching. Quick kisses. Long kisses. Promises of kisses.

"How have you been?" she asks.

"Good. Well, not really. Quite bad, actually."

You realize you should never be allowed to speak again, then roll your eyes at your own ridiculous honesty before continuing with, "But okay despite that, I guess. How about you and Mazzy?"

Her eyes brighten at the mention of her pet, her mouth turning up into a smile. "She's always sitting in the laundry hamper looking upset." Terra laughs then shrugs her shoulders.

You fight back a sigh. It's strange and sad and makes the pain in your stomach deepen, not knowing what's been going on in her life for the past three weeks. Not knowing about Mazzy, the only cat you will ever remotely love, a prissy plus-sized feline prone to scratching and hiding.

Still, she looks like the same girl despite the distance. The scent of her chamomile tea is so familiar because she drank it every night to relax. "She purrs for you, waiting by the door." Terra takes a sip of tea before continuing, "Been busy, classes are neverending. I've been meaning to call you again, see how things are."

"Me too," you say, though you were meaning no such thing. The phone, with its endless dial tone and intimidating rings, has never been your favorite form of communication.

"The apartment seems so empty, you know, sans Tuck."

"Quieter, I suppose," you say and wince. Not the right thing to say, certainly. Trying again: "I quit smoking."

She presses her lips together tightly, a thin line. The brief happiness from the mention of Mazzy is gone, and she looks exhausted, even with her eyelids dusted by a thin layer of violet glitter. Her voice is like a lullaby, soft and slightly husky. "After I'm gone and wouldn't have to smell it anyway?"

She sounds hurt and that makes sense, since she spent the better part of two years pleading for you to quit. Her father smoked constantly and she grew up smelling like someone else's cigarettes. The walls of their apartment were yellow with nicotine, and she'd developed asthma at thirteen because of it.

He started smoking outside, but occasionally she'd come home after school and he'd be depressed about something. She knew because the air would hang heavy with the smell. She spent a lot of time sitting on the curb outside of her apartment building, at friends' houses, in cafés. You tried to quit for her when you were together, but it was too hard. Instead the rule had been that you would smoke outside but sometimes you would do it inside the apartment when you were upset with her.

You smoked too much that first week of the breakup and then became obsessed with the idea that if you sacrificed something maybe she'd find you again. *In case she comes back,* was the thought that finally gave you the willpower to give it up. And you did, and here she is. So maybe.

You glance at the door and finally there's Davis. He's spotted Terra and knows what to do. Your eyes meet and he raises his eyebrows at you questioningly. He's wearing a black corduroy coat you don't recognize. *Nice fit.* You stare at him a minute and shake your head slightly. He nods and mouths something you don't follow at all. You glance at Terra, who has returned her gaze to her hands. Since she's oblivious, you give him a grin. He leaves and you return your attentions to the girl across from you. Her downcast, hunched-over posture gives you a good look at the familiar freckles that dot her cheeks. You used to press kisses into them while breathing in her lavender scent.

Terra looks up at you, blinks, leans forward in her chair. "I miss you."

You wonder what the bed feels like with only one person sleeping in it after so long, and you start to feel this could be the beginning of a beautiful reconciliation. You hope so, because in your loft fantasy Terra lives there too and the coral walls were always meant as a compromise, what with her favorite color being pink and yours being red.

Everyone is so loud—in competing voices a group of friends sitting on the couch by the window discuss their latest art shows and performances. Terra doesn't seem to notice them. She continues, her voice steady, "We broke up to see if that was what we needed, but I'm not any happier."

You scratch a blunt nail against the soda can in front of you, making a barely audible scraping sound, and then say, "Yeah." You want to say, *I miss you too.* You want to say, *Every day my mind is full of you and my heart feels empty.* You want to say, *Without you, I don't feel like I'm living.* But the words are jumbled together in a big pile and lodged in your throat.

All you can manage is: "Maybe we could, kind of...hang out again. Kinda sorta pseudo-date. Work on fixing things so we don't need to live apart permanently."

She bites down gently on her lower lip and looks down at the table. You follow her gaze, taking note of the crumbs left by someone else.

To the table, she says, "You can still stay the night once in a while, right?" You don't answer right away, because her eyes fix on you again as her soft, small hand covers yours.

Her lips turn up into a smile as she leans across the table and presses a brief kiss to your lips, and there's her taste of raspberry lip gloss—*your* raspberry lip gloss, which you'd obviously forgotten when leaving—and fragrance of the peach-scented shampoo you remember vividly. She stares into your eyes, raises one eyebrow sweetly. "Is my clever ruse to distract you from saying no working?"

"Oh, yes," you say, shifting in your chair and moving forward to kiss her again.

THE PETRIFIED GIRL

Katherine Sparrow

'd been living with Betty for a month, ever since she'd seen me spare-changing outside the Food Conspiracy and taken me in, in the same way she kept a special eye out for all the broken animals. She'd helped out a gimp coyote and in the springtime she had a whole row of nesting boxes for abandoned chicks. She had picked out Ranger from all the other dogs at the pound due to his having three legs and a piss problem. Hell, one time she found a flat copperhead on the interstate and spent a whole evening hunting off the road, looking for eggs. Found 'em, too. Old people got to do something, and I guess it made her happy enough. Besides, she was all alone, five years widowed, pictures of her wife, Ellen, on every mantle in the house.

Betty was an old butch, close to eighty, and I was a young one, just getting started. We got on all right, except when she tried to get into my business. Mostly she just let me be, but I was thinking of moving on, maybe hitching up north. I always get an itch to move on. Besides, Tucson was too hot in summer.

It was so hot, way up into the hundred and tens, that the only refuge was Betty's pool. We stayed out there the whole hot afternoon, and when the sun went down it didn't even get all that much cooler. Neither of us had a stitch of clothes on as we lay half-submerged on twin yellow plastic floats. It was good to be naked with Betty. I could look over at her and see all the things a body could survive. She had that old desert skin that bore a million wrinkles and just hung off her. It made me feel like maybe I could survive in this world too. Betty kept our cups of Jim Beam and Mountain Dew full all afternoon and into the night, 'cause as she said, it was too hot not to drink. On about midnight, the hot air was just starting to feel bearable again, but neither of us was keen on getting out.

"Tell me about leaving home," she said. She'd been trying to get me to talk all day.

"Had to get going. That's all."

"Your parents know where you are? How old are you, Cassie?"

"How old are *you*, Betty?"

"Old enough to get twice the respect you give me."

"Then tell me what it used to be like being a butch." Get her to talk about herself, so she'd lay off me. Old people love talking about themselves.

"It was harder back then. Illegal. They could take you in just for dancing with another woman. All of it was different." She shrugged and made ripples in the water with her fingers. "Had to be stronger, fight more for it. But we knew who we were. Not like y'all today."

"I know who I am."

"Sure you do, pup."

Out past the pool I heard a rustling; sounded like something big.

"What's that?"

"Could be about anything." She stared up at the night sky, and there was something sly in her voice. "Why don't you go take a look?"

"No. It could hurt me."

"Not unless you spook it, scaredy cat."

I left her floating and grabbed a towel to wrap around me as I went out past the adobe gate into the desert. Something was moving around behind a whole bunch of prickly pears. I walked in an arc around the cacti to get on the other side of it without getting too close. There was a whole gang of peccaries snorting around on the ground—and something bigger, too. The something got up and I saw it was a girl. She stood all frozen in her body as her head turned toward me, caught on me.

"What're you doing?" I asked and took a step toward her, ready for anything. If she wanted a fight, I'd fight. The little pigs raised their ugly tusked heads toward me. There was enough of a moon out that I could see her in a general sort of way. She had long dreadlocks, fuzzy and thick as rattlers. Plenty of them, too. She dressed like any crusty in a large T-shirt and torn-up jeans. She was scrawny but thick about the middle. I felt stupid standing in front of her in a towel, but hell, she was the one rooting around in the cacti.

"What're you doing?"

She stood there all frozen like I hadn't said anything. Then a firefly lit up near her, then another, and another, all around her head, making a bug halo around her face. I forgot about all the rest of her as soon as I saw that face. Desert-dark and round, with dark eyebrows and a hawk's nose. A small worried mouth with fat lips. Eyes so big they could have taken in the whole world in one glance, but here they were fixed on me. And everywhere, all over her, was pain—as though God had only used the pain paint to make her face. I looked down, feeling funny about looking at her, like I was staring at something naked. Not just naked, but like all the skin had been peeled off. I looked back up and saw she was running up the hill toward the arroyo. Barefoot and fast over the hot desert sand.

"You see something out there? Peccary or deer?" Betty asked when I came back, a little too casually, like maybe she knew exactly what I had seen. She was out of the pool and standing on the patio wrapped in her tatty blue bathrobe.

"Saw something. You know what?"

Betty didn't answer me, so I kept quiet too. We stared at each other with our hands on our hips, and it got to be a bit of a challenge—two dogs eyeing each other up.

I won.

Betty spoke haltingly. "What'd she look like?"

"Weird. My age, or thereabouts. White probably, hard to tell. Desert-burned, maybe a little Arab in her. Hell of a face."

Betty nodded her head. "Like a tortured saint."

I nodded. Like she said, the girl looked real impressive. "Yeah."

"She'd be on about seven months now."

"She was wearing baggy clothes. You think she's knocked up?"

Betty nodded. I liked the girl a little bit less. Anyone who got caught like that was just plain stupid.

"Who is she?"

"She used to show up here around summertime, but I haven't seen her for a long time. There was a story a while back about a wild girl up in the petrified forest so I expect she travels between there and here. I've never known anyone else to see her around here." Betty looked at me all angrily, just like the time I'd stolen money from her wallet. She called Ranger to her and went to bed, leaving me to wonder how she knew the girl was knocked up.

The next night, Betty made up a whole plate of lasagna and salad and put it out near the chunks of chuck she set out for the lame coyote, but higher up, so no animals could get into it.

"Don't she got a home to feed her?" I asked.

"You leave her alone. She's doing just fine."

The next day wasn't quite so hot, so I sat out sweating in the dark and watched the stars poke out as I waited for her. I'd been looking forward to seeing her all day, not much else to do at Betty's. She came and took that plate of food and shoved it down her mouth like she hadn't eaten in days. It was dark enough that I couldn't see much of her, but I liked what I saw. There was something raw to her. When she was finished she ran off barefoot again. How she avoided all the desert stickers, I don't know. I gave her some distance, then jogged behind her until I couldn't see her anymore and had to stop, heart racing hard. She was faster than me, even with that fat belly. She headed up toward Sweetwater Reserve. I've been homeless before, but in the desert? It didn't make much sense. All around me were some noisy chirruping insects and a night bird hooting away. I thought about her, wondered about her, as I took my time walking home.

On Tuesdays, Betty drives her old Suburban up the road to the Sonoran Desert Museum where she teaches tourists about cacti. I'd been waiting all week for her to go, because I just knew she wouldn't approve of what I was planning. Halfway out the door, Ranger already curled up inside her car and panting, Betty turned and gave me a level look. "It's too hot to go out in the desert during the day."

"I know it."

She shook her head. "Look in my room before you go, fool girl."

She had set out flowing white pants and a shirt, and a fine

leather cowgirl hat. I put them all on and swaggered up and down in front of her mirror. The hat hid most of my sheared-off hair and made my face look even tougher. Any girl looking at me would have been quite pleased with the image. Betty also left me a whole backpack filled with water bottles. It was too heavy, so I emptied all but two of them out.

Standing out in the driveway before I left, I spat, found some wood to touch, then spun around three times and made my wish. Wouldn't help, I suspected, but it wouldn't hurt, neither. *Let me find her,* I asked, to no one in particular.

I walked over the rise above Betty's house and down into the arroyo, orange rock and white dust everywhere, little spots of green where a plant had the audacity to think that it could survive here. An arroyo, Betty had explained, was a small canyon that turned into a river when the rains came. Hard to imagine rain on a day like today. The sun just baked the rocks, shone so high in the sky that there wasn't any shade anywhere. I had to squint just to keep my eyes open. A flat rattlesnake lay out on a rock, expired in mid slither, by the look of him. Survival was for the tough. Lines of sweat ran down my face and arms, not getting very far before they dried up.

I drank through a bottle of water as I trudged alone, moving past the million-dollar houses up beyond Betty's to where there was only me and the cacti. I climbed out of the arroyo and walked up a big hill that stood out above everything else on the edge of the Sweetwater Preserve. It was only me and the saguaros here, no one else dumb enough to be out walking at midday.

Saguaros, the ones that look like funny men with both their arms raised and Humpty Dumpty heads. There was a whole patch of them I passed by that were deformed. Their arms grew all corkscrewed and then dropped off leaving black holes where they had been sticking out. With every step I took up the hill, I felt the sun sucking on my energy. A horny toad stuck its old leather-head out from between two rocks, cocked it, then scooted back and away. I wished I could crawl back with him and find some shade.

At the top of the hill I could see all of Sweetwater and the haze of Tucson that stretched up into the sky, sitting on the earth like a predator. I looked in every direction, but didn't see that ragged girl anywhere. No sign of her. All I found was a used condom and a pair of panties tied up on a spiny bush. I started on my second water, just meaning to take a sip, but swallowed all of it before I remembered it was all I had. I noticed my arms were shaky and I wasn't sweating anymore. The sun was getting to me, making me feel fuzzy. Heat waves rose off the ground in shimmers, and I felt them moving through me.

"Hello!" I yelled out, then said it again. "Hello!"

I sat down to rest and then lay myself out on the sand. It was burning hot, but it felt good to be still, and once I was there it felt hard to even think about getting up.

Someone poured water into my mouth. I started coughing and opened my eyes. It was her.

"Drink."

I did, even though it had a funk to it, like it had been sitting around for a long time.

"Come on. You can't stay out in the heat." She helped me up, then walked in front of me slowly, checking that I was following. She led me this way and that until we came to a big rock that hid a blue tarp tied to four saguaros. She had another tarp on the ground and a red sleeping bag with white fuzz that stuck out along one edge of it. There were also a whole bunch of water jugs and a pile of white stones and pink cactus fruit along one edge of the tarp. Nothing fancy, but kind of homey and normal. I had half-expected to find her nestled up to a barrel cactus.

"Who are you?" I asked, pleased that she was talking to me and that I had found her, even though I felt nauseous and shaky in my body.

"Mayda."

"What kind of name's that? I like it. Mayda, I'm Cassie."

She sat down under the tarp and gestured me toward her. It was still hot, but better underneath it. She grabbed one of the water jugs and poured some into a plastic cup. I took it from her and sat down.

"Why you live up here?"

Mayda turned and looked at me, maybe a foot between us. She was hard to look at in the daytime, all that pain with no shadows to hide it. It was like Betty said, a saint's face. Something crawled in her hair.

A class-A scorpion worked its way up her scalp. Three inches long, yellow bodied, gray backed, scuttling up in between her thick dreads.

I pointed at it and whispered, "Careful."

Before I could say anything else, she reached up and grabbed it, cupped it in her hand like it was something precious, and set it down on the sand. "That little old spider can't hurt me. Nothing can." She smiled without anything funny on the other side of it.

"You can always be hurt more," I told her.

She lay down on her sleeping bag and faced away from me. "Let them try, let them try," she said as though she was talking to herself.

It was five times too hot to touch her, but I lay down beside her and reached for her anyway. Hell, why else had I come all the way up here? Been too long since I'd been with a girl. I hooked my knees behind hers, and put my arm over her, let it rest on her big belly.

"This okay?" I asked.

She stiffened all over at first, but then nodded her head and pushed herself back against me. I ran my hand over her belly, taut as a balloon, getting ready to burst.

"What you got in there?"

"Twins. It's always twins. I'm a twin too. Trouble always comes in twos." She had a way of talking like she was far away from me.

"I always wanted a twin sister. Someone to understand me."

"My sister hates me." Mayda rubbed her neck.

"Known a few like that," I said, nodding my head. "Who's the father?"

She didn't answer.

"Don't you know?"

"I was raped in my sister's house," she said flatly, like it was just the facts.

"I'll beat him up. Hunt him down, if you want me to."

She laughed, her belly constricting under my hand. A hollow sound as dry as the desert. "He's not around anymore. I'm the only one left, but thank you, Cassie."

"When are you due? You got a plan for them yet?"

"They'll come out at summer's end, when the rains come."

Under my hand something kicked. "She's going to be a little soccer player."

"He." There was no uncertainty in her. No delight, either. "I dream about them every night, tearing me up, over and over."

I didn't know what to say to her, so I lay beside her, sort of scared, but my hand had ideas all its own. It crawled up her belly and wandered over her big boobs, soft flesh spilling out all over the place.

"This still okay?"

She nodded again. I found a raised ridge of flesh just below the neckline of her T-shirt, and Mayda got tense all over again. I pulled down the cloth some and raised my head to look at it. An inch-thick scar ran across her neck, in front and back. It made a complete circle like someone had tried to cut her head off. I felt the urge to find the man who had done it to her, and cut him back, but I just held her instead. I guess she had plenty of reason for being alone up here. We stayed curled up on each other, and I didn't even try anything else. She slept some, and I looked at the stones next to the fruit. They were shells and branches that had long ago been petrified and frozen into stone. Sometimes you found things like that in the desert, and it was strange to think they had survived without changing at all for thousands of years. The whole world changing around them, but them just sitting out in the desert, stuck as stone.

It got dark out and we walked back down to Betty's. A plate of food sat out for Mayda, like always, and she scarfed it down. Like always.

"You can come in. Take a shower. Take a swim, at the least."

She stood just in front of me, we were the same height. Pain, pain, pain, but beauty, too. She turned and ran up into the desert, an owl hooting and swooping in the sky above her. I stood outside thinking; not ready to see Betty, to see anyone else, yet. I just wanted to think about her. Not like Mayda was the first girl to catch my eye, but she was special. Then again, I always thought that about girls, at first.

There had been Mandy, the mud-biker in Moab. Red-dirt belly and arms. Grease tattoos all over her calves. A wild scent to her like the dry Utah wind.

Amy in Forks, who wore that sweet little pink diner uniform that got me to all kinds of imaginings. She was crazy about condiments, liked to put them on everything, just everything.

Claire in Santa Cruz, who had piercings in the craziest places and a round baby face. She could dance all night at the Blue and go home not even smelling of cigarettes. She had long hair that got everywhere, even my teeth, like weak pieces of floss. After I left her, I kept finding her hair on me for a whole week. I always got that itch to go about the time they got serious and wanted to talk about everything.

They were so important to me when I was with them, but now I couldn't hardly remember any of their faces. I knew that was what would happen with Mayda. I would fall under her girl spell for a while and let her make me feel all kinds of funny on the inside. For a while. Except...there was something different about her. Like maybe I could be with her for a real long time and never get to truly knowing her.

I went inside and Betty was sitting out on her tan leather sofa, waiting up for me. She sipped on one of her drinks and looked me up and down, her blue eyes sharp against her old leather skin. "You found her."

"That's my own business."

"Careful of her, Cassie."

"I don't need an old mother hen watching me. I'm not a kid."

"Not far from one, either. I went out looking for her, once, but I never found her." She gave me an angry look and I could tell she was a little drunk. "What do you have that I don't?" she asked, as though she was my age and we were competing for the same girl.

"She helped me out when I got thirsty, that's all."

Betty laughed and some of the tension between us went away. "Should of tried that, didn't even think of it." She had a plate of food for me set out next to a big coffee-table book—one of her leather-bound goddess ones—and a bottle of bourbon.

"Sit. Let's talk," she ordered.

I did, and set about eating almost as fast as Mayda. I didn't want to talk to Betty. Hell, she was starting to get as bad as one of my girlfriends.

Betty sucked on her drink and stared up at the ceiling. "My daddy died young. My mother never wanted to hear about anything I wanted to tell her. She never met Ellen, wouldn't answer the door if I brought her around. She called us filth. Family can hurt you, Cassie."

I nodded my head, not wanting to think about mine, but to keep my head out in the desert with Mayda.

"You seen her scars?"

"One of them."

Betty rubbed her own neck. "My mama was nothing compared to what that girl's family was like. They weren't good to her, none of them. No one can make you hurt like family. That's why we need to stick together, make our own kind of kinship."

Mayda and I took to each other like bees to honey. More often than not I hiked up into the desert to find her. Betty always watched me go, and I couldn't tell what she was thinking about, or what she thought of Mayda. She just ran her rawboned hands through her short white hair and seemed...worried or thoughtful, one or the other.

Mayda didn't talk much, which I appreciated. We got to know each other through silence. At first I was worried she would start in on me with all kinds of talking—telling me all the bad things that had been done to her, wanting me to tell her the same, but she didn't. She was real quiet all the time.

I didn't even know at first if she liked me or just put up with me, but once we started kissing, I knew it was good. I wasn't sure if I could lust after a pregnant girl, but it turned out I didn't have any problem doing just that. It was good between us out in the desert, all those long hot days with the heat making our bodies slippery, and no one around to hear any of the animal noises we made. I caught sight of snakes and lizards watching us from time to time, but I didn't mind. The bigger Mayda's belly got, the more I couldn't think about anything else but her.

One night we walked down to Betty's, both of us exhausted. Mayda ate and ran off, but I didn't mind. There were lots of weird parts about her, but hell, everyone's weird on the inside. The sky was a sick color overhead, as though it had eaten something rotten, and the air felt heavy. It was the first time in weeks that there were any clouds in the sky at all.

Inside was a plate of food for me, and more of Betty's goddess books piled up on each other. I flipped through them and looked at the pictures as I ate, my mind a mile away up underneath a blue tarp, worshipping a girl goddess all my own.

"Wouldn't hurt you to read something, instead of just looking at all those pictures of naked women," Betty said, sneaking up behind me. "You might learn something important."

"I don't believe in spiritual shit."

Betty came around the couch and sat down next to me. She looked ragged and skinny. I felt bad, like maybe she was sick and I hadn't even noticed. Not that it was my job to take care of her.

"You okay?"

"There's been something I've been meaning to talk to you about but don't really have the words for, so how am I supposed to say it?"

The sky grumbled outside.

"I don't know. Don't say it, if you don't want to." I didn't like her tone. I didn't like how serious it sounded. She frowned and poured us two drinks—half whiskey, half sour mix—into big plastic cups.

"I've been seeing that girl of yours for a long time." She paused and took a long sip. "Since I was young. Before Ellen."

"You mean her mother. Or some girl who looked like her."

"No. Exactly her. Every year she shows up just the same, pregnant and forlorn, then she disappears when the rain comes. She's been stuck out there, doing the same thing over and over. Stuck like stone."

"That's crazy. Why're you saying that? You jealous of what we got between us?" I started to get up, but Betty grabbed on to my forearm.

"I decided a long time ago that she must be a ghost. She'd never talk to me, or let me get near her. But then you showed up and started touching her, so I started looking around for other explanations. I don't know why she's out in our part of the desert. Maybe there's a lot of girls like her, wandering out in the lonely places of the world. Hurt is what keeps her alive. I'm sure of it, Cassie. She's not like a normal woman."

I tried to pull away from her, but the old goat was stronger than she looked. She grabbed on to one of her books marked with a dozen yellow Post-its. She showed me a picture of an ugly woman with beetles covering her body, another with snakes for hair, and another with horns.

Bullshit. "Stop talking crazy, Betty."

"All these goddesses started out powerful, Cassie, but bad things happened to all of them. Horrible things that make you sick to read about. Your girl is trapped in it, she can't escape. It just keeps happening to her, over and over."

It started raining outside. Hard. I rubbed my belly, so different from Mayda's.

"Sound familiar?" Betty looked at me like she expected me to believe all that crap.

"No."

"It won't matter what you believe, Cassie. You'll see. The rains are starting. There'll be nothing left of her by morning. Then, next year on the hottest day of summer, she'll show up and nothing will have changed."

"No! I love her!" The words made me feel a little sick the second after I said them. I'd never said that about a girl, ever.

"Sure you do, pup. She's your Petrified Girl, all hurt and stuck, so you'll never have to show her who you really are."

"Get off the crazy bus, Betty!" She was just trying to ruin something good. I pulled my arm free and ran out of her house. I was drenched before I'd gone five steps. Mayda was caught out in the rain, and it wouldn't be good for her.

The rain fell so hard it stung my skin, and I couldn't see more than five feet in front of me. By the time I got to the arroyo, it was already running high with water and too full to cross. I ran alongside it, all the way up to Sweetwater. The rain just kept coming down and it was hard to even believe this was the desert. The water got wilder in the arroyo, until it was as angry a river as I'd ever seen.

"Mayda!" I yelled across it, even though I couldn't see much of anything on the other side. Maybe she hadn't crossed over before the rains started.

Lightning flashed silver bright and I saw her on the other side of the river, clutching her belly as it spasmed under her hands. She stared, helpless and scared, across the water at me. Into me.

"Mayda!" An instant later I couldn't see anything again.

I heard her scream, or maybe it was the river between us. Another flash of lightning lit the world for an instant. She was gone.

I yelled out to her all night long, even when it got so cold I couldn't stand up for all my shivering. The rain just kept falling down on me until I felt like there wouldn't be anything left of me but a puddle come morning. Just as the sky began to lighten in the east, the rains stopped. Around me were all kinds of new desert sounds. Frogs croaking. Dragonflies and hummingbirds buzzing through the air. Everything around me seemed alive. "Mayda! You okay?" I had no hope I would hear anything back, and I didn't. Betty's stupid idea that she was gone was stuck in my head. "Mayda!"

Around the time the sun came burning up over the horizon the water was just low enough to get across. I grabbed on to a long branch that had lodged itself across the arroyo and lowered myself into the cold brown water. The water grabbed at my legs and the branch was not as sturdy as I would have liked. It took about forever to get to the far side, where I swung my leg up over the rim of the canyon and hauled myself out.

"Mayda?"

A black snake with red diamonds down his back lay out on a rock and raised his head to look at me.

"Mayda, where are you?" I yelled and walked, pushing away the thought that she was gone. I looked in every direction, but there was nothing to see.

"Mayda?"

"Cassie."

Her voice was weak but not far off. I found her behind a big rock. She was nestled in sunshine with two little white things sucking at her boobs. She was naked and had blood streaked all over her belly and thighs, but still she looked real beautiful. Not far from her was a bloody mass of afterbirth, drying out in the sun.

The light made a kind of halo around her, and she looked like something holy. She smiled at me and there wasn't any pain in it, only happiness. It scared me a little.

"You all right?"

She nodded her head and looked down at the two small faces

staring up at her as they pulled on her nipples. I knelt down in front of her and looked at the babies. They were perfect. Nothing bad had happened to them yet.

Nothing ever would, either, I silently promised to both of them, then felt like crying for no good reason at all.

"Girls," she said, then looked up at me. "Twin girls. After all this time, something changed. I don't even know what I should call them." She laughed, real pretty-like.

I put my face down close to their two faces. "This one's got my nose and this one has my eyes," I joked, but part of me felt real serious about it. They stared back at me, something ancient in those brand-new faces, something wise, like out of Betty's books. Little twin goddesses.

"We'll get you home soon as the water goes down. Betty'll cook us up something good. She'll be glad to meet her little granddaughters," I said, then looked at Mayda to see if it was all right if Betty and I could be part of all this.

"Family," Mayda echoed, and the word was no longer a wound inside her.

THE LOVE BOAT

Aunt Fanny

My twin sister is straighter than a guided missile, and just as dedicated to target. I, on the other hand, have been interested in girls since the day we turned twelve and Betty Jane McAllister slept over. Pam and I turned thirty last month, and to celebrate we each took time off from work and booked a ten-day cruise to the Mexican Riviera. I wanted Olivia Cruises. She wanted Royal Caribbean. We settled for a straight line that looked gay friendly in the brochures. And here we are.

We're redheads, and not the copper-penny kind. Our hair is actually a collection of many different colors, mostly a deep chestnut red. Our noses are straight but tilted up at the tip. Our eyes are a rich green, with flecks of gold. There's a dimple in our chins, and two more on our cheeks. When we were teens, we were asked if we'd like to model. Pam said yes, I said no. It was a deal-breaker without the twin angle. She's never really forgiven me for that.

I always wear my hair butch short and, for the cruise, I packed men's clothing—mostly jeans and T-shirts. Pam, on the

other hand, is a devoted "Love Boat" fan and took the opportunity to design an incredible wardrobe. "You look like Ginger
from 'Gilligan's Island,' " I quip, on our first day at sea.
Pam looks me up and down disapprovingly. "Better that than
Popeye the Sailor Man," she says scornfully. I laugh at her.
She gestures to what she's wearing. "Now *this* is couture,"
she says. I take her word for it since she's a New York City fashion designer. It's ten in the morning, and she's in a short little
tennis skirt and formfitting white tank, with an emerald-green
angora sweater knotted around her shoulders. Her leather tennis shoes are spotless, and her green ankle socks have white lace
edges. A brand-new tennis racket swings easily from her hand.
Her hair looks perfect. She wears it in a crisply cut long page-
boy, with girlish bangs across her forehead. It accents our bone
structure, she says.

"Pam, you're a hoot," I say good-naturedly. It's trippy
enough being twins, but to be identical except for this butch-
femme thing? It's like looking into a mirror from "The Twilight
Zone." "I'm going for a swim."

She pointedly examines my slender frame, obviously disap-
proving of my swim trunks and sleeveless black muscle shirt. I
grin at her cheekily and say, "Hey, a woman's got to advertise,"
and strike a homegirl pose.

"What would they say if they could see you like that back at
Smythe, Milton, and Ford?" she clucks, referring to the advertis-
ing firm I'm part owner of.

"They'd say, 'Just like Pat,' and we'd go over the next project. My work speaks for itself." I say this a little too sharply.

"Well, don't be late for dinner," she warns. "And it wouldn't
hurt you to wear a dress. I designed one specifically with you
in mind."

"Never," I growl, swinging one of the cruise line's towels

over my shoulder and heading for the door. I glare at her. "I appreciate your effort, but you just don't get it. I like the way I look and the way my clothes feel on me. Isn't that what you're always talking about? The clothes should suit the person?"

I hold her gaze and she nods reluctantly.

I turn on my sunniest smile. "But I did pack some nice clothes, so don't worry that I'll disgrace you tonight." I wink at her as I close the door behind me.

I spend the morning swimming and working out. It feels great not to sit in front of a drawing board. My body appreciates the exercise. Afterward I head for the buffet lunch that's being served on the lido deck.

I spot Pam, seated at a table with a man. He looks about our age. I wave at her and she smiles vaguely in my direction, then deliberately turns away. I know why she didn't wave back. It's the twin thing. Too many men get wrapped up in the idea of two identical women to ever see Pam as an individual. I take a distant table so I'm in no danger of being seen by Mr. Man.

I examine the eye candy all around me. Tall, short, slender, plump; blondes, brunettes, and redheads—a banquet of women. I make eye contact with several and flirt leisurely for an hour or so. Then it's off to the tennis courts.

A pretty blonde sees me and asks if I'd like to play. I agree, readily. She's really stacked and wears a fire-red tennis dress. Her legs are long, tan, and exquisitely shaped. Full hips and breasts strain against the bright fabric. Her lips are full, raised in a smile. Blue eyes twinkle when I finally reach them. She's amused by my frank appraisal.

"Like what you see, big boy?" she coos, then gives me a credible Mae West wink. Contact.

We play a few games, and I have to work to beat her. She's in great shape, and I love the way that shape moves across the court. After our match, I ask her to have a drink with me. We take a table near the pool.

"What would you like?" I ask as I motion for a waiter.

"A Dyke Drama, please," she says as she crosses those beautiful legs. She sees the confusion on my face and adds, "Bloody Mary with a twist, hold the stalk, on the rocks."

I snort at her cleverness and order the drink per her instructions. The waiter winks at me and says, "A Mama Drama, right?" My laugh booms across the bar.

The blonde grins seductively.

"So what's your name, lovely lady?" I ask her.

"Constance Clairmore," she says, "Connie." She extends her hand toward me.

"Well, Connie, I'm Pat Milton." We shake hands as our drinks arrive.

"You want to try it?" she asks, holding out her drink to me.

"Been there, done that," I answer with a wry smile. "I've had enough dyke drama to last a lifetime."

"We'll see." She grins as she tosses away the straw. "I've got to warn you," she says, laying a slender hand on my arm, "I come with some complicated baggage." She sips at her drink.

"Don't we all?" I say, thinking about Pam but giving nothing away.

There's plenty of time to tell Connie I'm a twin. Women like the idea a little too much sometimes. I shift the focus back to her, knowing how erotic that can be for attention-starved women. I casually place my hand over hers and squeeze gently. "What's your complicated baggage?"

She opens like a flower in spring, her incredible blue eyes dancing at my invitation. She blushes charmingly and looks down at the table. I'm captivated. She turns her palm over and we're holding hands.

"I'm married," she says flat out. "To a jealous man." She waits to judge my reaction.

I flinch.

She frowns slightly and says, "It's not working out. I've already filed for divorce, but we booked this cruise a year ago and it's nonrefundable. We decided we could be adult about it." She shrugs eloquently. "So he's traveling with me, and that's my situation at the moment."

Those big eyes look up from under dark-fringed lashes, and it dawns on me that we're out on a ship in the middle of the ocean. Great for romance and privacy. Horrible for suspicion, outrage, and reactionary violence. Like I said, been there, done that. Not at sea exactly, but somewhere I couldn't run from. I tense up. "I don't know, Connie," I say cautiously. "That seems a lot more like a stumbling block than baggage." I grin at her, but it's clear I'm backing off. She pulls her hand from mine, and I miss it.

"I understand, Pat," she says, looking disappointed. I quickly reconsider. I need more information.

"Tell me about him," I say. I take her hand back and hold it. She smiles.

"He's a great guy," she says, which surprises me. I expect to hear what a bastard he is. I frown.

"Then what's the problem?"

"I like women," she says simply. "That kind of leaves him out."

"Do you cheat on him?" I ask, my voice squeaking.

"All the time and he hates it. But it's the only reason we've lasted as long as we have," she says boldly, no longer caring if I approve or not. "I thought I was bi when we met, and then convinced myself I could live without women. I found out the first year that wasn't going to happen. When Simon discovered me with a lover one night, he was furious, said he didn't understand what he was doing wrong. He isn't doing anything wrong. It's just not what turns me on." She's been looking at the table, but now she flashes me a tiger's grin, her eyes lighting up. "We made an agreement. I get laid once in a while, and he tries to handle it." She squeezes my hand, and I squeeze back. "It's not fair to him, I know. I make him miserable. We were best friends before we got married. We should have left it that way."

"How long has this been going on?" I ask weakly.

"Eight years," Connie laughs. "Too long. It's time for me to leave the straight life. I want to meet a nice woman and settle down." Her voice sounds like the chiming of a church bell. "I keep telling him he's wasting time on me and that he should get on with the rest of his life." She's gorgeous, relaxed now that her story's out. Her perky breasts rise and fall under her red tennis dress. She sips her Dyke Drama.

A couple of guys pass by, and I hear one of them say, "Damned dykes." So original. We ignore them.

"So Simon knows you're on this cruise to..." I pause, not sure how to phrase it.

"Get laid? Oh, yeah," she coos with a seductive smile. Well, that's clear. "We had a big scene about it this morning as we were boarding. I was really honest with him. He finally seemed to get it, so I sent him out looking for a good time as soon as I could. He has his room and I have mine." She winks. I wink back.

"Would you like to meet me after dinner?" I ask. "We can take a tour of the ship together."

"Sounds great. We're at the first seating. How about you?"

"I'm at the second," I say with a shrug. "But the Love Boat never closes. We'll find something to do." We agree and part ways. I watch her pert bottom sway as she walks off. Yum.

I'm humming in the shower when Pam turns up in our room. "You sound happy," she sings out, sounding just like me. Many of her words are my thoughts.

"You too," I laugh. "Was that Mr. Right Now I saw you with?" I towel off and step out from the shower. I pull on a pair of clean boxer shorts, then a sports bra. Pam wrinkles her nose but keeps smiling.

"Oh, yes," she sighs. "He's a handsome lawyer with a good sense of humor, and no children. In fact, he's perfect, except for one thing." She starts stripping to take her shower. "Simon's married."

I let my head fall forward on my chest in disbelief. I stare at her with stunned eyes identical to hers. "Simon Clairmore?"

"You know him?" she asks, heading for the bathroom.

I quickly fill her in.

"You're kidding," she says. "You're dating the wife and I'm dating the husband?"

"Seems that way," I tell her, as I pull on my best slacks. Twin coincidences happen, but this is really weird. "Connie doesn't know I'm a twin."

"Neither does Simon," she calls from the shower. "I just told him I was here with my sister."

"Will he think 'kinky threesome'?" I ask, fastening the buttons on my black silk shirt.

For several minutes there's no answer, just the sound of the running water, then she answers as if I'd just spoken. "I told you he's nice." Pam looks thoughtful as she steps out of the shower and towels herself off. Pleased, she adds, "He likes me for me, just the way I am." She grins at me, happier than I've ever seen her. "He's so sweet. We talked all afternoon. He may be more than Mr. Right Now. He just might be Mr. Right."

"A married man?" I start to ask, then make a wry face. "Kettle, you're black, says Pot." I laugh. Pam raises her eyebrows then joins me, our giggles rising. I know she's feeling naughty, because I am.

I nod at her. "Go for it."

Simon does sound like a nice guy. Even the woman divorcing him says so. Maybe this will work out for Pam. I tend to believe no man is good enough for her, but whether that's a sister thing, twin thing, or butch thing, I don't know.

"Hey," I say as she quickly throws on the least spectacular of her outfits. "Where are you going?"

"I scheduled a facial before dinner. You might try one sometime. We have sensitive skin, you know."

"Yeah, yeah," I say, waving her out. "Whatever." I grin at my reflection in the mirror, admiring my sharply tailored evening suit. "You have time, I guess," I say, looking pointedly at my watch.

While Pam's off getting her facial, I spend a few minutes scouting the ship for likely make-out spots on the tour I've planned for Connie. I see the Clairmores going in to the first dinner seating, and when Connie glances my way, I wave. She waves back, a wide grin lighting her face as she takes in my outfit. *I know how to dress to impress*, I think as I wink at her.

Simon is staring straight ahead and doesn't seem to notice how fabulous she looks in a pale blue gown that drapes just over her breasts. When she turns back to join him as they enter the dining salon, I notice her dress plunges down her back, stopping just where the swell of her ass begins. My heart skips a beat. Connie is one hot mama.

I go back to the room to pick up Pam. I'm surprised to hear her still putzing around in the bathroom, shocked when she emerges with her face swollen and red. It looks like a sunburn gone wild. "What the hell happened to you?" I ask her.

"Oh, Pat!" she cries, throwing herself into my arms. I give her a squeeze and pull her back to assess the damage. "I'm allergic to avocados! I didn't know that!"

"Well, you should," I tell her sharply. "I ate one when we were ten and nearly died. Have you called the ship's doctor?"

"He came to the beauty salon and gave me this." Pam holds out a tube of ointment. "He says it should go away by tomorrow, but that's too late!" She wails loudly and collapses into my arms.

"Why?" I demand, suddenly worried. "Why is it too late?"

"My first date with Simon is after dinner," she moans.

"So?"

"So I can't meet him looking like this!" Pam breaks into loud sobs and throws herself on her bed. Such drama.

"If he's Mr. Right, he'll understand," I offer, sitting beside her. The bitter part is, I know just how she feels. It's a twin thing.

"Not on the first date!" I hear my own voice wail from under a pillow. "I can't miss it, but I can't keep it!"

I hate to see Pam cry. We often feel the same way, but we react totally differently. I would just bull it through, but she wouldn't. I feel sorry for her. "Oh, honey," I soothe, patting her back. She's wearing only a bra and panties, but they're red lace, trimmed in black. Her lucky set. "It's okay."

"It'll never be okay," she cries, even kicking her bare feet a little. Then she looks up at me with that look. The one that says, *You owe me, and I'll do the same for you one day*. I shake my head, knowing what's coming.

"You be me tonight, and I'll be you," she says. "You'd still go on your date if this happened to you. Let's just pretend it did."

"Oh, no. I've got plans of my own."

"I know, and I won't do anything to let you down," Pam cries, her blotchy skin puffing into lines of hope. "Please, Pat?" she begs.

"You're not gay!"

"And you're not straight!" she counters. "But we both want each other to be happy, don't we?" Fresh tears brim in her eyes. "We'll just help set ourselves up for knockout dinner dates tomorrow. C'mon, Pat!" she urged. "You know I'd do it for you!"

"Oh, yeah?" I tell her. "Then how about you cut your hair to match mine for tonight?" I know this'll stop her. My hair is two inches long.

To my surprise she agrees. "I want this so much I'm willing to wear a wig for the rest of the cruise, if you're willing to wear one tonight."

Well, that sets me back. Pam has never had short hair, and if she's willing to go that far, well, I have to take this seriously. But I'm no fool. "Let's go to the salon right now," I say. To my amazement she opens my suitcase and pulls out a pair of jeans and T-shirt. She quickly puts them on, then leads the way out of the cabin and down two flights of stairs.

Ten minutes later her puffy face glares back at me from the mirror, watching miserably as her long red locks hit the floor, and the stylist seems more upset than she does. I'm glaring back at them both as acrylic nails are being cemented to my fingers, and painted. This Simon had better be worth it.

Pam runs a hand over her scalp. "Why do you have to wear it so short?" she pouts. "It's going to take forever to grow out again!"

She turns to scan the assortment of wigs lining a wall in back. "If I'm going to wear this wig for months, it's got to be good," she says. Apparently none of them are suitable. "It's got to match our color," she tells the stylist. The woman disappears in back and emerges with three wigs. One is a short football helmet, another a mass of long curls, and the third a perfect French twist. I point to the football helmet.

"Oh, no," Pam grins at me. "You're supposed to look like

me, not like you dressed up to be me." She points to the French twist. "We'll take that one," she says to the stylist who winks at her knowingly.

When we get back to the stateroom, I help her change into my evening clothes. With her face free of makeup, her hair short, and wearing my clothes, Pam's my spitting image. Except for the nasty rash, but that should disappear by tomorrow.

Now it's my turn. I go to the closet where Pam's hung her array of gowns and poke through them. I find a plain navy-blue sheath in the back and pull it out.

"Oh, no," Pam says again. "That's the one I designed for you to wear on this cruise. *I'd* never wear it to a formal dinner." She pushes through the closet and finds what she wants, a low-cut, forest-green sequined gown with a flowing skirt. I stare at it in horror then look at my twin already looking like me at my best, and shrug. In for a dime, in for a dollar. "And you've got to wear my underwear," Pam says pointedly. "Boxer lines are definitely not my style." She giggles, clearly loving this.

I put on the black bra and panties she hands me, then Pam helps me into the dress. I've never worn anything like it, and it's surprisingly comfortable. Kind of like a heavy cloud hugging my body and swinging from my hips. The bra's got to go, though, and Pam agrees. The plunging neckline accentuates our large breasts, something I usually take pains to conceal. Next come the makeup and wig.

Some minutes later I look in the mirror. I grin at her—uh, my—reflection. I have to admit, I look hot. I'd go for me, if the other me wasn't my sister. I smile at Pam and she smiles back. She is me; I am her. I hear the "Twilight Zone" music in my head, quickly followed by the theme from *Psycho*. "Freaky," we both say at the same time.

Pam fastens a bracelet on my wrist and pushes rings on my

fingers. The earrings are a problem, because my ears aren't pierced. "I cut my hair for you," she says, her voice quivering. She touches the short tufts ruefully.

Ah, what the hell. We call the jewelry store, and fifteen minutes later I have two diamond studs in my ears. Pam pays for them, and a matching pair for herself. She slips them into her ears, knowing I'll have to explain them some way tomorrow.

"They hurt," I complain, rubbing antibiotic on my ears.

"One must take pains to be beautiful," she says to me piously.

We leave our cabin when the dinner bell sounds. I remind Pam to offer me her arm just the way I always do for her. I take it just the way she always does. I practice walking in high heels, learning to sway my hips from side to side.

"Not so much," whispers Pat, laughing. "Let your walk do it. Don't force it. Our hips are wide enough that a little goes a long way." She watches my ass for a few steps then pronounces me ready. We enter the dining salon.

My sister coaches me through dinner, reminding me to touch up my lipstick when we finish. For the first time in my life I see my face reflected in a compact, but it isn't my face anyway. *I am Pam. I am Pam,* I keep reminding myself. *I am Pam.*

I head for the bar where she's supposed to meet Simon. Pam heads for Connie Clairmore's cabin to pick her up. "Good luck," we wish each other as we part.

Simon is holding a table, and I join him. He stops me as I'm about to take a seat, grabs my hand, and holds me still. "Let me look at you," he commands. "Turn around."

I feel like a goose, but I do as he says, turning for his appreciation. I wouldn't even do this for a lover, but I'll do it for Pam. I want her to be happy. But I'm gonna grill this Simon like a swordfish.

"You're beautiful, Pam," he says. "Thank you for joining me."

I smile at him and sit down. "What would you like to drink?"

I'm tempted to ask for a Dyke Drama, but Pam would be furious, so I order a martini, dry. I can't stand them, but she thinks they're elegant. The dumb wig itches, and I catch myself scratching it. I force my hands to the table. "Tell me about your wife," I say, smiling indulgently at him. How he describes her will tell me volumes.

"Connie is wonderful," he says with a wide, honest smile. His voice is strong but subdued. I bet he makes quite an impact in a courtroom. "She's beautiful, smart, great company. Everything a man could want in a wife."

"Sounds like you love her. So why are you cheating on her?"

"It's over," he answers. "She told me to go find someone new. She's got a date of her own tonight."

"It doesn't bother you to see her with someone else?" I say innocently, distracted by the flash of my red fingernails.

Simon smiles and takes one of my hands in his. "Connie's a wonderful woman," he says, "and a lesbian." He smiles into my eyes. "Yeah, it bothers me to see her with women, but it makes her happy. And I want her to be happy." He's looking at me strangely, and I realize I'm scratching the wig again with my free hand. I drop it but then worry that I've dislodged the thing. I fish out Pam's compact and surreptitiously straighten it, pretending to check my makeup. I've got to be a better Pam.

"So," I say teasingly, leaning in to give him a glimpse of cleavage, "when will the divorce be final?"

"How'd you know about the divorce?" His eyes drink in my breasts.

Whoops! "You mentioned it earlier. Don't you want to be available?" I say in a hurry, directing the attention back at him. Men expect that.

Simon smiles at me and leans in. I'm afraid he's going to kiss me, but he just whispers, "I didn't, until I met you." I pull back, feeling a blush rise on my cheeks. Good for Pam, bad for me. I draw the line at kissing a man.

"We'll see how things go." I sip at the martini and trying not to make a face. Simon grins and nods toward the dance floor.

"Shall we?" he asks.

I take his hand and rise. This is one thing I know how to do. Pam and I have practiced dancing since our first junior-high sock hop. Simon and I cross to the dance floor. His large hands feel strange on me, but we start moving together.

Quickly I learn that leading is easy, following is difficult. Everything I usually do, I'm doing backward. And in high heels, which are torture devices worthy of the twelfth century. I look up and see Pam grinning at me from across the room. She's at a table with Connie, whose back is to the dance floor, and she's holding a bottle of beer—Becks. I drink Sam Adams. Close enough.

Connie reaches over to finger Pam's earlobe and the diamond stud glittering there. Such a lovely, lively woman. I would catch that hand and kiss it. Her blonde hair is swept up, showing her lovely neck to perfection, leading the eye down an expanse of smooth skin to her saucy, barely covered bottom. I hope Pam is being as charming as possible.

"I'd like to see you again," says Simon as we return to our table.

My opening.

"Would you like to have dinner together tomorrow night?" I ask. "My sister will trade places with you, if you like, and you can join me at the late seating." That'll leave me to dine with Connie at the early seating. I smile at him, trying for "winsome." Not easily accomplished when your feet hurt, your eyes are half-closed by heavy eyelashes, and your scalp is itchy with sweat. I gotta say, it's no snap being Pam.

"That's a lovely suggestion," he answers.

Then I ask him about his law practice, and he talks away for a long while. It's actually pretty restful not to have to direct the conversation. I watch Pam and Connie surreptitiously.

Things seem to be going well. Pam's blotches are paling, but I notice she's blushing. It's really hard on her to have her face be less than perfect. I see her reach up and run her fingers through her hair once in a while, as if wondering where it's all gone. It makes me laugh, which luckily happens at the right time. Simon smiles at my appreciation of his wit.

"Tell me about yourself," he says.

Ten points for interest. But a long pause ensues as I consider what to say. I equivocate. "I'll tell you all about myself tomorrow night over dinner," I say with a smile. "Tell me about how you grew up." I try to pay attention so I can fill Pam in later; otherwise he'll wonder why she doesn't know these things.

I see Connie rise, and watch as Pam scrambles after her, heading for the dance floor. Uh-oh, she should have held Connie's chair for her. This ought to be interesting. My sister has never led in a dance. Never.

For a minute, they both stand there awkwardly. Then Pam takes my date in her arms and moves ploddingly, much less sure of herself than usual. I watch Connie's blue dress swirl around her ankles, its careful drapes accentuating her breasts and ass. I use my twin sense to imagine what Pam's hands must be feeling, warm at Connie's waist, enjoying the softness of her skin.

Simon gives me a somewhat puzzled expression, and I realize he's waiting for an answer to a question. I can't blow this for Pam. She's trying so hard for me. Maybe too hard. I see her pull Connie close. I long to be where I belong instead of here, building up some man's ego. But I focus, for Pam.

"I don't know," I offer. "It seems to me…" I hesitate, hoping he'll jump in, and he does.

"I know, I know," he says almost apologetically. "I probably should never have asked Connie to marry me in the first place, but we get along so well together. I thought we'd just be like the old couples I see around, you know, more friends than lovers."

"That shouldn't be enough," I advise. "There has to be more to a committed relationship than just friendship." I blink my eyes earnestly, the way Pam always does when lecturing me. "You have to be lovers, too, and partners. If any one of the three is missing, the relationship is doomed." I smile at him, snatching my hand down before it scratches something. Out of the corner of my eye, I see that the dance has ended. Pam and Connie stand chatting, waiting for the next to begin. The dance floor empties around them.

Two young men approach them aggressively. One reaches out and rubs Pam's new haircut condescendingly. I can't hear what they're saying, but I feel Pam's fear. At this point I would lead Connie away, and if confrontation was unavoidable, I'd stand in front of her. I've had to convince more than one guy that I didn't want his company, and I'm not afraid to hit a man. But Pam stands frozen.

One of the men reaches for Connie's arm, then pulls her toward him. I look around to see if someone's going to help. No one's doing anything, not the other dancers, or any of the ship's staff, but plenty are watching. The other guy reaches out and pushes Pam's shoulder. That's it. I'm up and moving across the room as fast as this stupid dress will let me.

"Hey!" Simon's voice calls, then I hear him come after me. I reach the scene first and shove the one who shoved Pam, while reaching out for Connie's arm and pulling her free of the other one. I push both women behind me.

"What the fuck?" snarls one guy. "Stay out of this lady," he warns me.

"Connie!" I hear Simon say, and see him looking quizzically from Pam to me.

"This is between us and the dykes, bitch," growls the other guy, the one who was holding Connie. He reaches back and takes a swing at me. I dodge. My wig falls off, and I kick it free of my feet.

"Pat?" asks Connie, also looking from me to Pam.

The other guy tries to get behind me, but I suddenly feel Simon there. He grins at me and places his back against mine. He's facing one bad guy. I'm facing the other.

"Pat?" asks Pam, looking at me.

"Get out of the way," I tell my sister. She's frightened but pulls Connie off the dance floor.

The two men advance at the same moment, and someone screams. The next thing I know a fist lands square on my nose, and I'm seeing stars. I swing out blindly and strike something hard. A punch lands on my ribs, and I hear another scream. It might be mine.

Soon enough a strong hand grips my arm and I'm being hustled out of the room. Simon and the other two men are also in custody. Pam hands me a napkin she grabs from a table and holds it to my nose. She doesn't want blood to stain her pretty dress. Connie trots along.

In the brig, Pam puts her rescued wig on. Connie's voluptuous body is nestled in my arms, dabbing at my nose. Simon looks at us then crosses to stand in front of Pam.

"So you're Pam?" he confirms.

"Yes, Simon," she sniffs. I flinch. I never cry. It looks absurd with her standing there in my evening suit.

"And you're…?" Simon looks at me.

I reach over and shake his hand. "Pat, Pam's twin sister," I say. "And Connie's date for tonight." That makes him pause, his head tipped to one side. It *is* a lot to absorb.

"Why the charade?" Connie demands, but I keep quiet. This was Pam's idea, let her explain it. "Is this how twins get their jollies?"

"It's my fault," Pam says. "It's just because I'm so vain, and I didn't want Simon to see my rash." She blushes deeply, making it worse. "I like you too much," she tells him, with tears in her eyes. "I couldn't let our first date be ruined because of the way I look."

"Simon doesn't judge on looks," assures Connie. "He's all about substance." The married couple grin at each other with sincere warmth as the guard comes to open the door. The ship's captain enters our cell. We take turns telling our story, which soon has him scratching his bald head in confusion.

"A waiter says the two men started it," he finally announces. "A case of too much to drink and too little respect for women. They're cooling off as our guests tonight in the brig. You're free to go," he tells us. "I'm very sorry about what happened."

"I want a drink," Connie says as we're leaving. I grin.

"That sounds good," says Simon, taking Pam's arm. But I intervene.

"Let us change clothes," I say. "Then we'll join you as ourselves."

"Good idea," says Connie, looking from one to the other of us. "I thought it was odd you didn't know how to lead in a dance," she says to Pam, then turns to me. "And diamond earrings? That really surprised me. You're obviously such a butch."

"Not obvious at all, until she starts punching," laughs Simon. "But I think that spectacular dress will suit you better," he says to Pam with a wink. He leads his wife off to the bar, and my sister and I head for our room.

We exchange clothes. My nose is puffy but fortunately unbroken. Pam and I break into laughter as we leave our room and head off to meet our dates.

"I could never be butch," says Pam.

"And I could never be femme. I like being who I am."

"And I like being me."

We spend a pleasant hour together at the bar getting to know the Clairmores. I like them both. But I have plans, so I take Connie off to one of the secluded nooks I'd scouted out earlier. She snuggles into my arms, and her breasts press against my shirt. I kiss her.

"Do you always protect your women that way?" she asks, gently stroking my bruised nose.

"Always."

"You know, there's no finer aphrodisiac in the world than being fought over," Connie coos then offers me her lips again. The stars above shine in her eyes, before she shuts them seductively. I claim my prize. She tastes like heaven.

We retire to her cabin, and I show her what a real butch can do. Kisses turn to touches. Touches turn to fire. Clothes slither to the floor. Her skin is smooth, her breasts and hips perfect. Her triangle of blond curls parts as I search out and find her ruby clit. I want to make her moan in my arms. Our fevered bodies writhe and thrash together on her bed. I leave no part of her untouched, unlicked, unloved.

Sometime in the early morning Connie decides to show me what she can do. She dons a sexy nightgown then takes it off for me slowly. Although I'm already familiar with her perfect body, her striptease turns me on like no one else has before. She's my passion, hunger, and longing personified. I pull her onto the bed with me, and she shows me something that makes my toes tingle. I like it so much we do it twice.

Round about dawn we both learn what lovers can do together. The sex becomes lovemaking. Touching becomes tender. Our kisses are filled with longing, much stronger than our satiated lust. We whisper secrets to each other. I think I'm in love.

I meet Pam back in our room in time for lunch. My twin's rash has all but disappeared. She's glowing, and there's a new gold necklace surrounding her throat, a heart charm dangling into her cleavage. "We stayed up all night, talking," she beams at me.

"Just talking?" I ask with a wink. She blushes. "No woman ever got a gold necklace from *me* just because of sparkling conversation."

"Simon's a wonderful man," she says, not telling me anything. I'm happy for her. I hope it works out. For both of us.

"What time does the jewelry store open?" I ask, looking at my watch and imagining a gold necklace gracing the sexy contours of Connie's beautiful throat.

"This is the Love Boat," my twin laughs at me. "It never closes."

MO'O AND THE WOMAN

Elspeth Potter

There's a story the people tell on Maui about a creature called "Mo'o." Mo'o means "lizard," but in this story it means a kind of demon, who looks like a voluptuous young woman. You see her on the beach at dawn or dusk. She's always naked and has long black hair and big breasts and hips. When you see her, she doesn't speak, but she beckons to you with her webbed fingers, and in the strange half-world between night and day you don't see anything wrong with going to her and touching her. Then she will jump on your back, *wham!* and ride you to her cave, where she rips off your clothes and licks you all over, getting the salt from your sweat. Her tongue is really long, like three to six feet. Her tongue is so long she can use it as a surf-board. That's what they say.

Of course you know these stories never have happy endings. If you can't escape, and no one ever has, she'll ride you to death, lashing you with her tongue so you'll fuck her on and on and on, in whatever way you can. They'll find your body rolling in the surf, green as grass from her spittle.

Some people say they've really seen her, Mo'o. There was a Japanese fisherman, a new immigrant, who said he accidentally trapped her in his net, but when he saw her tongue he screamed and passed out, and when he woke up she was gone. He didn't know anything about the stories people tell. He didn't speak any English yet. She's just what he saw. At least, that's what a friend at the senior center told me one time.

I always wanted to see her, just once. I'd had a boring life, you know? School, helping my parents with their store, getting thrown out when they caught me with a girl, roaming the world—well, the Islands, and Southern California for a year—working the tourists with card games and trinkets, maybe living with someone for a few months here, a few months there, just enough to keep me from noticing that, really, I had nothing. And now here I am, menopausal and gray and getting a bit fat around the middle, like a pineapple. I live in a little apartment complex with scrubby palms outside my window, watch TV, go to the senior center. And I swim. I can still swim. It's even *good* for old people. That's what my neighbor told me, the one who takes off her bikini on the roof so she won't have tan lines. I asked her if she knew about Mo'o, too, but she didn't.

I had dreams about Mo'o. I would wake up and wonder what she would do with a willing partner, if she would let her live. I wondered if that woman would get power or just pleasure beyond imagining. My dreams didn't say. I didn't really care. I just wanted something different. Something where I could say— well, I wouldn't really be able to say to anyone, or I'd find myself in a home getting fed with a spoon—but I wanted something. Something in my life no one else had.

Mo'o is sacred. Her and the ocean and the waves. Getting

taken by her would be like swimming into the morning surf and not making it back to shore, sacrificing yourself to the gods, the way they used to in the olden days. I started spending all my time hiking the beach looking for magic, looking for Mo'o. I slept out there for months, like I had done when I was a kid, only this time without the bottles and friends. But Mo'o never came. Finally I gave up, just gave up and went back to my tiny apartment, killing time at bingo and other events at the senior center. I felt stupid, you know?

Weird things happen to you when you get old. You start wondering what you were up to all that time, and what you're going to do with what time you have left.

So I took my bingo winnings and left Maui and got a job renting bikes on Jekyll Island, off the coast of Georgia, as far away as I could afford to get. I couldn't quite stand to leave the ocean behind, even though this is a different ocean, not so warm and blue, and the sand is harder and grayer and everyone seems to be either white or black, nothing else or in between, even the tourists. And it's hot. Too damn hot. Jekyll's far, far away from home.

I had sex a few times with the woman who runs the snowball stand down the path. She's younger than me—most people seem to be—but not so young I felt like some kind of lady chicken hawk. It was all right. Not like I'd imagined it being with Mo'o, but nice. It had been a very long time for me. Rhea told me that in the winter, she goes back to Savannah to live with her un-married sister, so when winter comes I'll be alone here with the caretakers and recluses. I could live with that.

Rhea talks slow and velvety like the sand seeping between your toes after a long golden morning back home on Maui. If things were different I might go to Savannah with her, come November.

"You aren't satisfied, are you?" she says, and "I could eat you out if you want. I like doing that." She says it like a slow curvy wave, and if I'd found her a long time ago, we might have lived a long and happy life together, just for that sexy voice. But she's not magic. I've made a mistake, coming here.

I go down to the beach at night when the water comes up high, high. I wish I had a surfboard or a boat so I could paddle out and float around in the twilight, waiting for her. Waiting for Mo'o to surge up out of the warm fishy ocean and stretch her warm salty body on the board with me, smelling of warm musky woman and fish. I want her. Why won't she come to me? I want to go home. She and home are the same thing.

I wade in water that slaps my ankles. I'm wearing a swimsuit, but there's nobody here to see the varicose veins on my legs and my sagging breasts and belly. They warn the tourists not to go on the beach after dark because of the water rising. I strip off my suit and flip it up on a rotting wood pylon half-covered by drifted sand. Little broken seashells press at my calluses as I trudge through the rising water wearing nothing but my shell necklace. The water slapping my knees is her bathing, soothing tongue.

It was like this: she never made any sound in my dreams, so I didn't know how to call her. I talked to her anyway. I think she liked it when I talked to her in the cave afterward. Her hair looked like seaweed but felt like worn cotton sheets that are so soft you can hardly feel them on your skin. Her tongue gently, oh so gently, curled around my clit and slithered up and down, around and around....

I would wake up and I would be leaking salt like the sea, both my cunt and my eyes.

Maybe she didn't mean to hurt people.

I dive into the sea, swimming as hard as I can. The oncoming wavelets beat at my genitals, bathing me, fluttering each tiny fold. I tread when the water gets deep enough and look at the magic shimmer surrounding me. From algae, they say, but maybe it's magic. I can see my hands in the green glow, see little fish under the surface. I hold my breath and pull myself under the surface, kicking hard, watching the colors of the water. Maybe Mo'o sees like this. The colors change when I go down deeper, and I want to see more, but then I need air. I break the surface, gasping and flinging droplets off my hair. My cunt aches with a pounding like the waves.

I don't need my hands to tread water. I reach down with one, then the other, touching myself gently and swirling around like her tongue. Is she there? Can I bring her to me? My fluids wash off or float away and I'm not very slick, but my own touch still feels incredible. I'm balanced perfectly at the edge of coming: I can tell I'm just going to glide in to shore, fast and smooth enough to take my breath away. The waves rock me and my hands speed up. I'm close. Waves slap my back, hard enough to sting. I'm too close to care. I try to freeze, make it last, but it's too late, too late, and I'm coming with the ocean.

I see double as I jerk and spasm with pleasure: moonlight reflecting off water, green haze over gray stone flecked with black, her hair making a curtain before my face.

Her hair. Black as the sky above, with streaks of white reflecting starlight and green algae. The stories don't tell you she's going gray. I can't see her face very well, but I know she's smiling. I hold out my hand to her.

Mo'o doesn't talk. The stories say that, but they don't say she makes other noises instead, whimpers and barks like a puppy. I know she's not an animal, though. I can see that in the gleam of her eyes, in the purposeful way she puts her webbed hands, scaly but soft, on me, under my neck and back until I'm floating in the sea.

I can't see her tongue, not really, just a gleam of green and a shine of reflecting dampness before it touches me, soft and searching, encircling and tasting, drinking the salt off my skin until I writhe and gasp; then her tongue is tasting me inside, and I never want it to end.

I open my eyes to the sun. I'm on the beach, my skin parched and my ass sore. The sun hurts my eyes. I don't know how I got to the beach. The sand feels deeper than it ought to. Then a surfboard glides in, missing me by a foot, and I recognize the guy whose mother runs bingo. I'm on Maui.

Did I ever leave? Was that brief vision real? If she was, why am I still alive? I don't feel powerful. I just feel alone.

Wasn't I good enough to give to the sea?

I don't ask anybody how I got here or what day it is, or if they remember me getting on a plane for Savannah a few months back. I know what would happen then. Senile, they'd say. Alzheimer's. Put the old lady in a home. Can't have old ladies talking about sex.

I don't talk to anybody. I sit in the sand and wait for the dusk. For Mo'o.

When it gets full dark, she comes.

IN THE HEART | OF EGYPT

Anne Laughlin |

My job at *Archeology Today* is wonderful in almost every way, but sometimes the amount of time I spend away from home seems punishing. I'm often gone for three months at a time, moving from one country to the next, reporting on dig sites, interviewing academics, unraveling the mysteries of both the ancient past and the modern politics that complicate the pure scientific process. After two months on the road I was enjoying a few days' rest in Cairo, staying at one of my favorite hotels and savoring a stretch of temperate weather. The only thing missing was someone to share the time with. These trips often became quite lonely.

As I settled in the hotel lobby lounge one afternoon, armed with the *Herald Tribune* and a fresh pot of tea, I glanced up to see a new arrival coming through the door. A bellman followed in her wake with several pieces of expensive luggage, but the woman herself was casually dressed. She wore light linen pants and a T-shirt, with a broad-brim hat hanging off a cord down her back and a backpack slung over her shoulder. She was stunning, with long, dark hair; bold features; tanned limbs; and a long, determined stride. I watched as she checked in quickly and headed toward the elevators, gone from sight and leaving several of the hotel staff hopping in her wake.

I let a few minutes pass before wandering to the reception desk and asking the clerk about the new guest. Predictably, I could get nothing out of him, but when the phone rang and he became distracted, I looked down at the charge slip still on the counter. The credit card belonged to Dr. Sandra Milthorne, with an address in New York City. I recognized the name at once. I was scheduled to interview Dr. Milthorne in two weeks when I returned to the dig site in Tel el-Armana. She was an expert on Egyptian miniature statuary and had been called in to assess some exciting finds at the dig. This would be an extremely handy reason for me to introduce myself to her, which I intended to do at the first opportunity.

That evening found me sitting in the same chair in the lobby lounge, sipping a cocktail and hoping Dr. Milthorne would come down to do the same. I glanced up from my notebook at each *ding* of the elevator bell, but I was well into my third drink before she appeared. Perhaps the cocktails had made me bold, but I am a journalist after all. It's not my way to wait for things to come to me. When it became clear Dr. Milthorne was headed toward the exit, I leaped to my feet and caught up with her on the other side of the revolving door.

"You're Sandra Milthorne, aren't you?" I asked. She was signaling the doorman for a cab and turned at the sound of her name.

"Yes. I'm sorry...have we been introduced?" She kept a cool look on her face, more wary of intrusion than curious who I was. I barreled on.

"No, we haven't yet, but I'm scheduled to interview you in a couple of weeks in Armana. I'm Bren Michaels with *Archeology Today.*" I stuck out my hand, which she took firmly but briefly. "I see. Well, I'll look forward to speaking with you then. If you'll excuse me, I'm expected elsewhere just now." She turned and nodded at the doorman, who whistled for one of the cabs lining the winding drive up to the hotel entrance.

"I was wondering if you'd care to have a meal together while we're here in Cairo. Nothing to do with the dig, nothing on the record. I'm traveling alone, you see."

"I'm afraid I'm very booked up these next few days. Perhaps while we're in Armana? Now, if you'll excuse me, I really must go." With that she climbed in the cab and was gone.

I'm not a fool. I can spot a brush-off when I see one. Dr. Milthorne apparently wasn't a very friendly person. Still, she had an amazing face. What would it be like to see those ice chips around her mouth and eyes melt into a smile? It would be pretty hot, that's what it would be.

I walked back into the lobby and was contemplating getting another drink when I heard my name called. I looked toward the elevators to see Mickey Gaines heading my way, her ever-present camera bag dangling from her shoulder. She threw an arm around me and gave me a quick hug.

"Hi, Mick," I said. "I didn't expect to see you until next week."

Mickey was a freelance photographer who often pulled the same assignments as I did for the magazine. We'd become good friends over the years, feeling the sort of camaraderie that comes with being in far-flung locations together, baring your souls over countless drinks in hotel bars, then sailing off in different directions, not knowing when or if you'll see each other again. I'd trust Mickey without question, yet I never thought about her much when she wasn't around. I was pretty sure she felt the same about me.

"Yeah, I know," she said. "I was in Jordan for a shoot, and I was supposed to head to Lebanon for something this week. But that got all fucked up because of the political situation, so I have to cool my heels here before I go up to Alexandria in a couple days."

I was really glad to see Mickey. We went off to get drunk and bitch about our rotten assignments, all the while knowing we were leading charmed lives and couldn't imagine doing anything else. I didn't think much more about Sandra Milthorne, except that every time someone walked into the bar I looked over to see who it was. And each time it wasn't her.

If you're a lesbian and you've been in Cairo enough times, you may have heard about the once-a-week lesbian night at a bar near the university. It's not advertised anywhere, and word of mouth isn't effective in a city where no one talks about being gay. But I twigged onto it during my last trip to Cairo when I ended up sharing a bed with another guest at my hotel, a museum curator who knew everything there was to know about the capital cities of the ancient world. I had kept the information she gave me safely filed away in my laptop, and Mickey and I headed over there the night following our drinking bout in the hotel bar. I was eager to see what a lesbian bar in Egypt would be like and equally eager to scout out possible companions for the evening.

I must have been expecting something along the lines of a student pub when I imagined where the lesbian night would take place. I almost gasped when we walked in to find something more along the lines of Rick's Café in *Casablanca*. The walls were beautifully painted, and decorated with tasteful sconces and European art. The tables were covered in white linen. The bar that ran along one wall was massive and made of glowing wood, with a tuxedo-clad woman cleaning glasses behind it. I immediately felt underdressed, and when I glanced at Mickey she was scrutinizing her own attire as well.

"Shit, I feel like I'm straight off the farm," Mickey said, trying to tuck in her shirt as surreptitiously as possible. Another tuxedo-clad woman approached us and asked if we'd like a table, but we shook our heads. We were barely dressed well enough for the bar. As we settled in with our drinks, Mickey chatted up the bartender, who filled us in on the place. Six nights of the week it was a restaurant and nightclub catering to gay men; the other night the owner rented out the space to a lesbian friend. A bandstand and dance floor occupied one end of the large table-filled room. Beyond that was another room furnished with more tables and lounge areas. I stared out into the main room as Mickey and the bartender continued their banter. A lot of women were seated at tables, some of them finishing up meals, some enjoying cocktails. A band started playing and dancers moved to the floor. I'd never seen anything like it in my entire lesbian life.

"Say, Mick. I'm going exploring, okay?"

Mickey gave me a quick wave before turning back to her butch buddy. I moved through the room, appreciating the generous amount of space between tables, imagining a time when elegant nightclubs like this were the norm. I made my way past the dance floor, pausing to admire the singer who had just taken the stage, backed by a Glenn Miller–style, all-female band. Cairo is a huge city, but I'd never guessed it would have a gay and lesbian culture diverse enough to include something so unique. I spent the next half hour or so watching the singer, wandering around, checking out the back room where women who all appeared to have dates were lounging, sipping drinks, and chatting. Prospects for companionship appeared slim, but I was highly entertained. That was often enough for me.

As I headed back to the bar, Mickey was coming toward me, a sour look on her face.

"What's up, Mick?"

She waved her arm as if swatting away a fly. "Oh, I just got blown off by some snooty woman at the bar. I thought I'd shove off and try to find a nice girl."

"Yeah, good luck with that. Everyone seems to have a date here. It's cool, though. Fun to look around."

Mickey snorted. "Museums are for looking around in, Bren. That's not why I come to a club." She nodded her head over to the bar. "And if you land in the jaws of Ms. Barracuda over there, don't say I didn't warn you."

"Duly noted. If I don't see you later I'll see you back at the hotel."

Mickey and I went our separate ways, with me heading to the bar, curious to see who had shot her down. You got it: Sandra Milthorne. She sure was making it difficult for me to like her, and yet when I looked at her I felt a rush of arousal. I didn't know her, didn't think she was a particularly nice person, and yet I felt strongly drawn to her.

I took a seat next to her at the bar and ordered a scotch from the wary bartender.

"This must be one of the many engagements you spoke of when I met you outside the hotel yesterday," I said.

Sandra looked at me with a slight frown. "Pardon me?"

"Are you responsible for upsetting my friend?" I asked.

"I'm sorry. I'm having a hard time following you."

"My friend Mickey was just at this bar, happy as a clam when I left her. Now she's left, clearly upset, and I see you sitting here. I'm guessing you said something that made her feel terrible. Am I wrong?"

Sandra took another sip of her wine and shrugged. "I wouldn't presume to know what your friend is feeling. All I know is she seemed to be interested in getting to know me better and I didn't share her enthusiasm."

"Well, I guess I should be grateful I only got a polite brush-off yesterday, rather than the full-scale takedown you must have given Mickey." I slurped up some scotch and tried to look pissed. Sandra sighed and started to gather her things.

"Your friend," she said, "was aggressive and ham-handed, and the last I heard it was a woman's right to choose who she spends her time with."

"Hmm." I couldn't argue with that. Mickey was known to hit on women in a fairly direct manner, but it wasn't like her to take a rejection badly. She was usually pretty good-natured about it. "What did you say to her exactly?"

"I may have mentioned something about her unusually un-subtle style."

"Mickey is a good person," I said, a little lamely. "You didn't need to make her feel bad."

Sandra took another sip of her wine. "Why don't I buy you a drink? I'll try to be nice."

"I find it telling that you have to *try* to be nice. That's like saying you're not a nice person by nature."

"I never claimed to be one. Nor am I sweet, gentle, or cute." Sandra smiled a little ruefully as she watched my face. "I see you don't disagree."

I took a healthy swig of scotch and tried to sound gruff. "Well, you are cute. I have to disagree with you there."

Sandra's sad smile turned into a genuine one. "Well, thank you. I'm curious, Miss... I'm sorry, I forgot your name."

"Of course you did. It's Bren."

"Bren. May I ask how you knew who I was when you saw me in the hotel lobby?"

I hesitated. I didn't want to give this woman an advantage by telling her I'd gotten the information by snooping around the reception desk. It made me sound like a stalker. "I'm a reporter," I said. "It's my business to know these things."

"Well, I'm impressed. *Archeology Today* hires very knowl-edgeable writers if you're any example. I know my area of ex-pertise is quite specialized." Sandra was fiddling with her cock-tail napkin and twirling her wineglass. Suddenly she seemed to have lost her composure.

"To tell you the truth, I only know of your specialty and qualifications because my editor supplied them to me. I'm not familiar with your work. I do know of another specialist in your field. Dr. Andrew Milthorne? Strange coincidence that the names are the same."

"Not particularly. Andy was my husband...but no longer."

"I'm glad."

"Glad?" As Sandra looked at me her face took on several ex-pressions in rapid succession. Hope, fear, confusion, pleasure.

"I mean," I said, "I'm glad you're no longer a married woman."

"Why?" she asked.

"We're sitting here in a lesbian bar in Cairo, which means you're either a lesbian or thinking about being one. The fact that you're not married any longer gives me hope that you're not just window-shopping or experimenting."

"I see." Sandra went back to looking uncomfortable and started to gather her things again.

"Did I say something to offend you? You're very hard to fig-ure out." I reached over to help her into her light jacket.

"Actually, no, you didn't offend me, unlike your friend

Mickey. I just think it's time I head back to the hotel. You're welcome to share a cab with me if you'd like. "

By the time we got back to the hotel I had decided it would take a combination psychologist and psychic to understand Dr. Sandra Milthorne. One moment I felt an icy comment pushing me away, the next I saw a warm smile pulling me in. In one exchange I heard an icy chill in her voice, in another I felt the charm of her laugh. She careened from arrogant to vulnerable in short order, then flashed back to arrogant again. Instead of wanting to run for the hills, I felt intrigued, unexpectedly protective, and aroused at the thought of breaking through her guard, giving her warmth and safety, giving her touch. She aroused any butch instincts I had, most of which I'd been unaware of until now. As the hotel elevator reached her floor I held the door open and asked if we'd be able to see each other again in Cairo.

"Bren, I just don't know. There's a lot going on with me. I'm not sure I'm ready to share any of it. "

I tried on an engaging smile. "Well, don't then. Let's just go out and have fun. That can't hurt, can it? "

"You wouldn't think so, would you? We'll see, okay? "

"When are you free tomorrow? We could just go to the Khan el-Kalili and wander around. That's harmless, isn't it? "

Was I sounding a little desperate? She gave me a relenting smile.

"All right. I wanted to go to the Khan this trip anyway. How about four at El-Fishawi? "

"Perfect. I'll see you there." I beamed as she left the elevator.

I hit the DOWN button and headed back to the hotel bar, guessing Mickey would be there if she hadn't found a girl at the nightclub. I found Ahal behind the bar, just as I did every time I came here. I climbed up on the stool nearest him and asked for a scotch. Then I asked him if he'd seen Mickey.

"Ah. Mickey came in looking very sad, but she just left looking very happy."

"Found a girl, huh?" I smiled at Ahal as he continued wiping down glasses.

"Yes. It didn't take her long this time. I was glad. She looked so defeated when she came in tonight. I'd never seen her like that."

"Well, apparently she got shot down pretty good when we were out earlier this evening." Ahal refreshed the drink sitting in front of me and waved away my money. "A woman who's staying here did the honors, as a matter of fact. Dr. Sandra Milthorne? You know her, Ahal?"

"Where did you see Dr. Milthorne?" Ahal stopped his polishing and waited for me to respond.

"We saw her at a nightclub. That's where she and Mickey had words."

"And you just returned from there with Dr. Milthorne?" He was frowning at me, and I started to feel a little defensive.

"Ahal, I did try to defend Mickey, but she's a big girl. And maybe she did come on too strong with this woman. She's an academic, for god's sake. She's probably a little more refined than the women Mickey's used to carrying away over her shoulder. Anyway, once you get past that haughtiness, there's a pretty vulnerable woman underneath."

I was surprised to see Ahal shudder slightly and turn to busy himself rearranging bottles in the well. He muttered something to himself, and I leaned over the bar trying to hear him. "Ahal, you're going to have to speak louder than that. I can't make out what you're saying."

"I'm just trying to say that I've seen Dr. Milthorne here many times over the years. Very, very complicated person, and capable of hurting you. I think Mickey was the fortunate one. If you have some interest in Dr. Milthorne I just pray you will be on your guard. All is not as it seems."

I sat back in my chair, my face a blank as I processed what he'd said. "Ahal, what are you telling me? You're making it sound like she's a spy. Or maybe a vampire. What's the story?"

Ahal started cashing out his register, and I looked around to see the few remaining patrons gathering their belongings. It was closing time. Ahal looked up at me again and said, "Just watch yourself, Miss Michaels. You're a nice girl and I don't want to see you get hurt."

That was all I was getting out of him, so I picked up my bag and headed off to my room. Of all the things Ahal could have said to me, none would have piqued my interest as much as what he did say. Now I was determined to crack the code of Sandra Milthorne. It was a challenge. But the truth was also that I wanted her to like me, I wanted her to let her guard down with me. I wanted to affect someone that guarded, knowing the gift of her trust would be precious. I went to bed trying to work out the best way to go about my mission.

The next day I made my way to Islamic Cairo and stepped through the fourteenth-century gate into the Khan el-Khalili. The medieval marketplace appeared unchanged from what it must have looked like centuries ago. Dense and multilayered, it made me think of a warren, its layout understood only by the rabbits inhabiting it. The famous café, El-Fishawi, was located near the main entrance to the market and was a convenient meeting place. If you were to meet someone at any other location in the Khan, you would need walkie-talkies and GPS equipment.

I approached the café a few minutes after four and saw Sandra sitting at a table, talking with a man who sat down to join her. The towel tucked into his waistband told me he was an employee of the café, and the way the two of them smiled at each other revealed they were old friends. I watched for a minute or two as Sandra leaned toward the man, touching his forearm, smiling, chatting, then throwing her head back and laughing out loud at something he said. My heart thudded. I felt it grow larger as I watched a relaxed and happy woman being herself with a trusted friend. I wanted to have her laugh like that with me. As I approached the table, Sandra saw me and leaned away from the man. He turned to look at me and rose from the table.

"You must be Miss Michaels," he said, bowing slightly and offering his hand. "I am Omar, proprietor of El-Fishawi and a friend of Dr. Milthorne. Please have a seat." He waved me into the chair he had vacated. I looked at Sandra and she smiled at me and then at Omar.

"Thank you, dear friend," she said. "We'll have that tea now before we go exploring. It's been so wonderful to see you." Sandra watched Omar kiss her hand then make his way to the kitchen. Then she turned to me, blushing slightly. "Omar," she said, as if it were a full sentence.

"Indeed," I replied. A waiter came up to us with a plate of *meze* and some tea, and we sat quietly while he fussed about. After the tea was poured and he had left, I said, "The secret is out now, I think."

Sandra raised her head quickly. "What do you mean?"

"Now I know you've been hiding a warm and charming woman behind that guarded exterior. I saw how you were with Omar. And then you shoved that girl back into hiding when I arrived, replaced by this careful, sort of nervous person. What's that about?"

"God, you are forward, aren't you?" Sandra looked a little annoyed, but it seemed like she also admired me for being so straightforward. "Let's just enjoy our tea and then explore the

Khan. Are you looking for anything special to buy today?"

I took her lead and let the straight talk die. We drank up our tea and headed into the marketplace, finding ourselves several layers deep within it before pausing to get our bearings. Sandra trotted out her fluent Arabic to get us directions to the spice stalls, without the usual runaround tourists receive. In the spice stalls the feeling of time travel is intensified. Great sacks of overflowing spices line the narrow pathways of the market, pathways made nearly impenetrable by the constant flow of people, handcarts, donkey carts, scooters, and, insanely, the occasional car. The spices are watched over by merchants in the tiniest stalls imaginable, and bargaining between customer and merchant is nonstop.

Beyond the rows and rows of spices, we came upon the perfume market. Here delicate aromas fought one another to become an innocuous scent wafting through the stalls. Tiny shops, some of them four by four feet, had shelves lining each wall and dozens of handcrafted perfume bottles lining each shelf. I stopped to purchase a few for my mother and sisters and Sandra stepped in to bargain in Arabic. I walked away with enough musk to last five lifetimes and ten perfume bottles, all for less than a couple of grande Frappuccinos. I felt guilty, but only for a moment. I watched as Sandra relaxed and enjoyed herself. In the textile market she examined an unbelievable number of fabric bolts before settling on a rich blue. I didn't understand how such an extended debate could lead to such an unassuming choice, but apparently this was the perfect blue for something she had in mind. Mostly what I saw was her having fun.

The afternoon drew to a close, and as it was Ramadan, most of the locals were preparing to head off to their evening meal. Sandra and I strolled toward the entrance gate and out into the courtyard. Here a merchant set up tables and fed an evening meal for those who could not make it back to their families to break their fast. We leaned against a stone wall and watched the activity. A shiver raced up my spine as Sandra's hand moved a couple inches over to gently grasp mine. We stood like that for a long while, holding hands, watching the feast preparations, feeling something grow between us. Finally, I dared to turn my head to look into her eyes, searching for some sign that she felt as drawn to me as I was to her. The smile appeared first in her eyes and then began to crease her mouth. Her words wafted up to my ears as she said, "Bren, it's time to go back to the hotel."

I groaned as I realized she'd once again left me to interpret an ambiguous statement. I longed for something straightforward, like, "Please, Bren, take me to the hotel and make me yours." Or, more to the point, "Please, Bren, take me to my room and fuck me." That would just about be clear enough, and certainly welcome enough for me. I held her hand tighter and led her through the crowded plaza, as we headed toward a main street in hopes of finding an available taxi. I hailed a passing cab and elbowed a path to its door, ushering Sandra into the backseat and shouting our destination to the driver. Sandra almost immediately reclaimed my hand, then leaned her head on my shoulder, lying there quietly during our trip through the wild Cairo traffic.

As we waited for an elevator in the lobby, I felt I needed to break the silence. "I don't want to part from you," I said. "Can we have a drink or dinner or something?"

I held her purchases as she rummaged through her purse for her key card. When she looked up at me with a smile my heart thudded again. "Why don't you give me an hour to rest and clean up and then come by my room? We'll decide what to do then." I broke into a wide grin and she said, "But don't assume anything. I don't want you to assume anything about me."

She left the elevator, her room number her only parting words. I hurried up to my room to shower, change, and fantasize. Despite her warning, I assumed a great deal. I assumed she would be great in bed. I assumed she wanted to sleep with me. I assumed by the way my heart kept thudding this was something more than a casual encounter. I assumed we'd find a way to be together. I assumed we were going to live happily ever after. I assumed these things because that's what I do when I stand on the cusp of a new relationship. So sue me. I'm a lesbian.

And I love being a lesbian. It's the number-one thing about my identity. It's in the forefront of my mind and it colors much of how I see the world. I'm interested in everything about being a lesbian. I should be a professional lesbian. Not like a prostitute, of course, but something like the head of a lesbian publishing company, or a lesbian comedienne, or the director of a lesbian health initiative. Instead I'm traveling the world, randomly running into lesbians who have a 0–5% probability of being available for anything more than a ships-pass-in-the-night encounter. How am I supposed to experience the unheralded but true joys of being a lesbian if I live like a nomad my whole working life? How will I set up household with the love of my life, shop at the garden centers, fuss over our dogs and cats, go to potluck dinners, cheer on the dyke bar's softball team, have a commitment ceremony, conquer lesbian bed death, go on an Olivia cruise, curl up on the sofa to watch our favorite TV show, and know that finally, truly, I am with the one woman who has enabled me to be the best person I can be, the most me I can be? I wanted that. I hadn't realized how much I'd wanted that.

I arrived at Sandra's door exactly one hour later. I had changed into fresh jeans, a tank top, and an unbuttoned oxford shirt, my hair still wet from the shower. When Sandra answered her door, mere seconds after my knock, I made some kind of involuntary noise, loud enough to cause one of her eyebrows to shoot up. She looked fantastic. Her hair was loose and flowed down her back; her tanned body was draped in a linen A-line dress that was simple and elegant, with a beautiful scarf knotted loosely around her neck. Her feet were bare. I'm sure I was gaping at her, because she laughed and pulled me in by the arm, closing the door behind me and pushing me up against it, her arms coming up to wrap around my shoulders. No words were spoken, and I made my move before either of us could question what was happening. My lips met hers and our mouths opened and melded together, exploring each other; our arms pulled us more tightly together. The hovering arousal that had been with me for hours now skyrocketed. We started to devour each other, sinking to our knees and falling to our sides in our grappling. We broke our kiss with a gasp, drawing in air, looking at each other with wild eyes. Just as I started to lower the zipper at the back of her dress a knock sounded at the door.

"God, who could that be?" Sandra whispered, our faces inches from the bottom of the door.

"It's room service," I whispered back. "Like an idiot I ordered champagne."

"No, it's sweet. I'll sign for it and send him away."

We scrambled up, and I stepped in front of Sandra and out the door to take care of the delivery, cursing myself for having caused this interruption. I knew the momentum would shift, that now I'd hear why we shouldn't sleep together, or why sleeping together wouldn't mean anything. I turned back into the room and saw Sandra sitting in the suite's living room, staring pensively out onto the Nile.

"Would you like some champagne?" I asked, joining her on the couch and unwrapping the bottle's cork.

"That would be lovely," she said, watching me uncork the bottle and pour. When she took her glass from my hand she placed her other hand on my leg. "We have to talk," she said.

"Isn't this sort of early for the 'We have to talk' line?" I said, hoping for a laugh. I didn't get one.

"Bren, it's obvious I'm very attracted to you. Actually, I'm wildly attracted to you."

I let my breath out. *Everything else can be worked out,* I thought. *The important thing is she wants me.*

"But things are quite complicated with me. And it's only fair to let you know that." She pulled back a little and took a sip of champagne. I tried to stay still and just let her talk. "Most of it has to do with my past and some very big changes that have occurred recently."

"Do you mean your divorce? Does this have to do with Andrew?" I saw her take another nervous sip from her glass.

"It has to do with the fact that I *am* Andrew. Or I was Andrew." She looked up from her glass and tried to track my expression, which I kept as blank as possible while my brain imploded. "I had sex reassignment surgery—or the last of the many surgeries—about a year ago and my transition is complete. I am, in all ways, a woman named Sandra Milthorne."

I hadn't had the slightest inkling that she might once have been a man. I hadn't picked up on any physical hint at all. I stared at her with complete surprise and had no idea how to react.

"I know you're in shock right now. I don't want to do or say anything that will upset you more. But I had to tell you. I've never wanted anyone as much as I wanted you ten minutes ago when we were over there kissing. I've wanted you since you introduced yourself outside the hotel. But I haven't been with anyone since my surgeries were completed, and I'm scared to death. I didn't know whether to run to you or from you."

"Oh, Jesus," I croaked. I got up from the couch and drank straight from the champagne bottle. I walked to the window and stared out blindly. My mind was completely blank and my heart was numb. It seemed like forever before I could find something to say. Sandra stayed still on the sofa.

"Tell me more about wanting me since you first saw me," I said. I continued to look out over the Nile, watching a tourist boat head south on a cruise of Ancient Egypt.

"I first noticed you when I checked in. You were sitting in the lobby with a newspaper in your hands, but you were checking me out. That's the first thing I noticed. Then I saw your legs. They were crossed at the knee and you had a beautiful line of muscle running up your thigh. Something moved inside me."

I turned to her now. "And how does that feel? Having that something move inside you now, when it used to move outside you, as it were?"

Sandra looked down at her hands, clasped tightly in her lap, and then raised her head to look me straight in the eye. "I believe it feels the same way for me as it does for you when you're aroused by another woman."

"Well, that's what I'm not sure of, goddamn it. I rely on the fact that lesbians have certain shared emotional and physical experiences, certain similarities. It's one of the things I love about being a lesbian. I don't know how this fits in." I sank onto the sofa, suddenly exhausted. What I wasn't understanding about this situation felt too big for me. I didn't know if I had the energy to have the open mind and open heart I had always preached others should.

Sandra moved over to sit closer to me. She pushed me gently back so that my head lay on the cushioned sofa back. She hitched herself up and over, straddling my lap, holding herself up with her hands on my shoulders. "The third thing I noticed about you was your charm. You had a straightforward way about you that made me realize that you are, above all else, an honest person. Another part inside me moved, as if to say here is a person who will tell me what her thoughts and feeling are, who I might have a chance of working through this with. She may not stay, but she won't be cruel, she won't play games. I'll at least know more than I know now about how trying to be with another woman is going to play out for me."

"Huh. That doesn't sound very sexy, does it?"

A smile lit Sandra's eyes. "Oh, it's very sexy to me. And you've got plenty of sexy. Do you want me to tell you about it?"

"Yes. In detail."

Sandra drew a little closer, her hands moving into my hair, working their way to the back of my head. "You are gorgeously handsome, strong but not overbearing. Your voice has that low raspy thing that's always driven me wild, you're smart, you're funny, you're very attracted to me. All of these things are very, very sexy."

My arms came up to wrap around her back, and I found myself pulling her closer. "I'm scared," I whispered. "I want you, but I have to tell you it feels weird. I'm afraid of what I'll find. I'm afraid of hurting you."

"I know," Sandra said, moving closer. "I'm terrified too. But I want you. Can we be scared together? Can we try this together?"

I pulled her in for a kiss and found that it didn't feel any different than it had just a short while before. Sandra was an exceptional kisser, and soon my head swam and my body responded in all the usual ways. I eased Sandra off my lap and lay her down on the sofa, draping myself gently over her. "Is there anything I should know before I make love to you?" I asked with a smile. I watched as Sandra's face transformed, whether by love or simple relief, into an expression of happiness. She smiled widely as she pulled me on top of her, whispering in my ear.

"With all of the money I've invested in this body, you shouldn't notice a thing. Just do what you always do."

And that's something I understood how to do very well.

Two weeks later I knocked on the door of the field trailer at the dig site in Tel el-Armana. I heard some rustling inside before the door was thrown open and Sandra blasted through it and into my arms. I managed to keep from falling onto my rear as I held her weight and sought some balance. Just as I started to say something her lips found mine and we kissed as if for the first and last time put together.

"I guess you're glad to see me," I wheezed.

Sandra stood with her arms around my neck, heedless of who might be looking at us, taking me in top to bottom. All I could see was Sandra. The lover who had already given me the most explosive orgasms of my entire life. The person who seemed to love me for exactly who I was. The woman I was falling in love with, for exactly who she was. My mind and my heart were wide open.

"God, you don't know how incredibly glad I am to see you. How many days do we have together?"

"How about all of them?" I asked.

WLSB

Sandra Barret

A listener sent us an email that asks, *Is there room for masturbation in a committed relationship?* Signed, *Shy in Cheyenne*. Well, she who is putting the *shy* in Cheyenne, Dr. Mona says most definitely yes. And if you can get that special girl in your life to watch you, well, it's all that much more fun, isn't it? With that, ladies, it's time to end our nightly chat. This is Moaning Mona, signing off for WLSB, Lesbo Radio. Think of me as you sleep tonight, and I'll be dreaming of you."

Mona Hiriko turned off her microphone and leaned back in her chair. Her on-air persona drifted away like dry leaves in a breeze. She wondered how many of her listeners realized that the sultry Dr. Mona, Moaning Mona, or whatever flavor of the week she decided to call herself, was really a tired, divorced mother of three adult children who hadn't been with a woman, any woman, for the past two years.

Her boss popped his head inside the studio doorway. "Nice show," he said.

"Thanks. Here's to dreaming up something equally as wacked by Monday night." That gave her two full days, if you ignored the wedding shower for her only daughter, Janice, that would eat up most of Saturday. Mona stood up and cracked her back and shoulders. Sitting for an hour was all it took these days to stiffen her up. She grabbed her backpack and headed for the door. "See you Monday," she said.

"Have a good one," he told her.

Mona pulled her bicycle helmet out of her backpack as she walked down the creaky staircase to the great outdoors. A blast of damp air hit her as soon as she opened the outside door. Great, she thought. The rain couldn't have waited another twenty minutes. She paused in the overhang of the three-story brick building that housed WLSB Radio and strapped on her helmet. Then she stepped out into the steady drizzle to unlock her bicycle. It would take her less than ten minutes to get home, but between the wet roads and the rain, she'd be a damp mess by the time she got there. She gritted her teeth and pedaled off, knowing no one would greet her at her townhouse except one old, bitter cat. So much for Moaning Mona.

"Mom, you cut your hair again," Janice said.

Not a hug. Not a "long time no see." Just a dig at her short, salt-and-pepper hair. Mona smiled at her daughter and patted her arm as she walked by. "Nice to see you, too, dear." Janice wore her long black hair in an elaborate bun that must have taken hours to perfect. She'd wrapped herself in a formfitting kimono and had two of those chopsticklike things holding up her hair. Mona had no real appreciation for Janice's traditional attire. She was fourth-generation Japanese-American, and the closest she got to Japanese culture was an occasional bottle of Sapporo. Mona pondered how she'd ever managed to have such a complete femme for a daughter. Some apples just hurl themselves as far away from the tree as they can get, she supposed.

Mona's son David pulled her over to a side table where his twin brother Pete sat. Pete and Repeat, they called themselves. But she loved them. Every feature, every hairstyle, every laugh seemed identical to most folks. But not to her. Her twins were her sanity. They'd been her lifeline when she divorced their father and came out of the closet seven years ago.

"Speaking of your dad, do you think he'll come to the wedding?" she asked.

Pete gave her a puzzled frown. "Who was speaking of Dad?"

"Never mind. Will he show up?" she repeated.

"He'll make it," David muttered.

And that told Mona all she needed to know about her ex-husband. Not that he held a grudge or anything after the divorce. But if she were at a family event, he was sure to be absent. Mona pushed back her annoyance and scanned the hall her daughter had rented for the wedding shower. Janice had outdone herself, as usual. Some mothers would have been upset that their only daughter had refused their offer of help for the wedding plans. Mona watched the beehive of look-alike friends buzzing around the hall, catering to Janice's every whim. No, Mona wasn't like other mothers. The girly bonding thing just didn't come naturally to her. And that was one of the few things Janice recognized, if not fully accepted, about her dyke mother.

"Has the bar opened yet?" Mona asked.

Pete pointed to the far corner of the hall. "Just push your way through the rest of the boozers."

"Very funny."

Mona walked over to the bar. She stood there for a time, jostled by guests and relatives alike as she debated what to get. Someone brushed up beside her, and Mona got a whiff of the most delicious perfume. She stole a glance to the side.

A full-figured Latina woman turned to her and smiled. "You've been standing in front of the bar for a while. Making a monumental decision?"

The woman's dark brown eyes mesmerized Mona. She watched one eyebrow rise and realized she hadn't replied. "Sorry. I'm debating whether to go for the secretive rum and coke or just get a beer and accept that I'm drinking before noon on a Saturday."

The woman leaned in closer. Her long brown-black hair brushed Mona's cheek. Mona's breath caught. "Go for the beer, and I'll join you," the woman said. Her voice sounded honey sweet so close to Mona's ear. A light shiver ran through Mona. The day was looking up, she decided, as she ordered two beers from the bar and handed one to the other woman.

"I'm Carmen, by the way."

"Mona. Nice to meet you." Mona shook Carmen's hand, feeling the heat from that contact sweep into her core.

Carmen held her hand a moment or two longer than necessary as she studied Mona. "Have we met before?" she asked.

Mona pitched her voice low. "And here I was about to use that line on you."

Carmen's eyebrows lifted. "Dr. Mona! I knew I recognized that voice."

Mona glanced around to see if anyone had heard Carmen. No one seemed to be paying them any attention, but she guided Carmen to a side table away from the bar, just to be sure. "Yes, that's me. Well, not me really, but my radio show." She looked around one more time. Janice was at the opposite end of the hall, not looking her way. "I'd appreciate it if we kept that little gem between us. My daughter's barely on speaking terms with me right now. If she finds out about my radio show today she'll be insufferable for weeks."

Carmen stifled a laugh. "You always hear about the parents who can't handle when their kid is gay and not enough about the kids who can't handle their gay parents."

"Thanks." Mona glanced away from the dark brown eyes that still threatened to overwhelm her.

"I need to get back to my table," Carmen said. She leaned in to whisper in Mona's ear. Her breath caressed Mona's neck, and Mona barely registered what she said. Something about meeting up after the party. Mona nodded and watched as Carmen worked her way through the maze of tables. When the other woman had disappeared from view, Mona decided she ought to return to her sons before they started looking for her. She left her beer on a table as she went. Something told her she'd want to be sober when she met up with Carmen later.

A half hour after the party ended, Carmen pulled to a haphazard stop outside an apartment building that Mona recognized. "This is where you live?" Mona asked.

"How do you think I know Janice? She lives across the hall from me." Something in Mona's shocked expression must have registered for Carmen. She patted Mona's leg. "Don't worry. She won't be home for another hour at least. And we're just stopping here so I can change out of these heels. They're killing me."

Mona rather liked the three-inch black heels Carmen was wearing, but she didn't dare mention it. She followed Carmen up the side staircase to the second floor and down the hallway. The third door on the left was Janice's apartment, and on the right was Carmen's. Mona resisted the urge to fidget while she waited for Carmen to find her apartment keys. She stepped inside right after Carmen and shut the door.

"You really don't want to be seen, do you?" Carmen asked.

"Am I that obvious?"

"Why is it such a big deal? I mean, Janice knows you're a lesbian."

Mona stuffed her hands in her pockets. "It's just easier if she doesn't see me *being* a lesbian. There's knowing in theory and then there's having her face rubbed in it." The frown on Carmen's face made Mona regret her words. "Sorry."

"Do you still want to go out this afternoon?" Carmen asked.

"Yes, definitely." Mona let out a long breath. "Definitely. Just ignore me."

Carmen walked to her and lifted Mona's face with her hand. "Ignoring you wasn't what I had in mind." Carmen's full lips curved in a smile that sent Mona's libido into overdrive. She stared unabashedly as Carmen kicked off her heels and padded barefoot into a room in the back of the apartment that Mona assumed was the bedroom.

Now if Mona really were like her radio personality, she'd be kicking off her own shoes and following. But Mona and Dr. Mona were decidedly different. *It's easy to be gutsy on the radio,* she thought as she pulled out a chair in the tiny kitchenette to wait.

When Mona had waited far longer than she thought necessary for changing a pair of shoes, she began to wonder if Carmen really was expecting her to follow. It wasn't the first time Mona had been picked up based on her radio persona. But relationships like that inevitably failed when she turned out not to be the sex goddess her radio fans had assumed. If that's what Carmen had in mind, she was in for a grave disappointment. Mona didn't play that game anymore.

She was relieved when she heard movement and glanced up as Carmen emerged from the bedroom. Her eyes took in the white blouse that stretched over Carmen's large breasts, and the

black jeans that hugged her hips. *Now* that *was worth the wait,*
Mona thought.

"Ready?" Carmen asked.

Mona nodded. Her voice wasn't up to answering just yet. She
wasn't sure where Carmen was taking her, but looking like that,
it wouldn't matter. Mona had all the eye candy she needed to
keep herself entertained for the afternoon.

Mona managed to keep the fact that she was dating Carmen a
secret from Janice for the first two weeks. Since Mona didn't
own a car, Carmen came to pick her up for their dates. And
that meant that the nights they spent together were at her townhouse, where Janice never came to visit. But the night before the
wedding, Mona's luck ran out. Carmen invited her over for the
night. It wasn't the first time she'd asked, but Mona had run
out of excuses for not returning to Carmen's apartment. She put
on a brave smile and said yes. For the short drive to Carmen's
apartment, Mona sent up a silent prayer that Janice would not
be around. She felt like a rabbit waiting for the fox to pounce
and knew Carmen sensed her nervousness.

Carmen parked in her usual spot but didn't make a move to
get out of the car. "This is killing you, isn't it?"

"Of course not."

Carmen let out a sigh and placed her hand on Mona's. Carmen's
touch never failed to send a shiver through Mona. "Look," Carmen said. "I don't want to preach to you, but at some point you
have to make a choice. Do you live your own life, or do you let
your daughter dictate how you live?" Carmen opened her door,
giving Mona's hand one final squeeze before she let go. "I'll be
upstairs, if you decide you want to stay the night." She stepped
out of the car and walked toward the staircase that led to her
apartment.

Mona watched until Carmen disappeared up the stairs. Then she dropped her head into her hands. What if Janice saw her entering or leaving, what then? And right before the wedding. Janice would never forgive her. Mona looked around, realizing she was still in Carmen's car. She stepped out and pushed the door shut a bit harder than necessary. She took a step toward the stairs. Did Janice's opinion really matter? Mona had all but slipped back into the closet when it came to handling her daughter, but it hadn't helped in the end. "Don't ask, don't tell" might work for the government, but it wasn't working in Mona's family. She took another step toward the stairs.

Taking a deep breath, she decided it was time to cut that twisted apron string Janice had been using to strangle Mona's love life for the past seven years. Mona broke out in a trot, hoping to get to Carmen before she disappeared into her apartment. When Mona emerged from the staircase on the second floor, her luck failed completely. Carmen was nowhere to be seen, but Janice was in clear view, along with two of her bridesmaids. Mona ignored that little voice in the back of her mind that told her to duck back down the staircase. She thought of Carmen, of the way her touch electrified her. Carmen deserved better than to be treated like something Mona had to hide.

Mona pulled the staircase door shut behind her. The thud of the heavy metal door caught Janice's attention. She turned and locked her gaze on Mona, her face masked in confusion.

Mona walked up to the small group and smiled.

"Is there a problem?" Janice asked.

"No. None at all." Mona tapped on Carmen's door. She looked over her shoulder, catching her daughter's cold glare. "See you at the wedding tomorrow," Mona said as Carmen opened the door.

Mona stared in the mirror as she fumbled with her deep yellow tie that matched Janice's wedding colors. She saw Carmen come up behind her.

Carmen brushed her hands aside. "Why is it that the people who wear the ties are never the people who know how to tie them?" She knotted the tie, then eyed it for a moment, making a minor adjustment. "There."

Mona stared into her lover's eyes, then wrapped her arms around her, not caring that it would crease her gray suit or Carmen's silky dress. "Thank you," she said, leaning in and capturing Carmen's lower lip in her own. Carmen melted into her, opening to the pressure of Mona's tongue. No matter how much time they spent together, it never seemed enough to Mona.

Carmen's hands gently separated them. "At this rate, we'll never make it out the door."

"Would that be such a bad thing?" Mona's mischievous smile earned her a teasing pinch.

"You know it would be. Now let's get going before Janice sends a search party for you."

"At least she'd know where to find me," Mona said as she opened Carmen's apartment door and led her down to the limo she'd rented. If she was going to her daughter's wedding, out and proud, she was determined to do it with the style befitting the mother of the bride.

When they got to the chapel, Mona left Carmen to the care of her sons, then proceeded to the back dressing room to face Janice. To her surprise, Janice graced her with an even smile and an expression that said if Mona didn't bring up the topic of Carmen, she wouldn't. It wasn't perfection, but as Mona gave her daughter a peck on the cheek and took her place in the wedding party, she realized it was a compromise she could live with, at least on Janice's wedding day. As she walked down the aisle and saw Carmen give her a wink, Mona wondered why she'd ever considered hiding such a beautiful woman from anyone in her family.

The on-the-air light illuminated in front of Mona. "Good evening, my lovelies," she said. She shut her eyes, as she always did at the beginning of her broadcasts. "Before we open up to callers, Dr. Mona wants to have a little talk with all of you about how to be true to yourselves. It's a lesson she learned this weekend, compliments of a gorgeous, dark-eyed beauty who wishes to remain nameless." Mona peeked at Carmen, who sat outside the studio, smiling at her and shaking her head. Mona closed her eyes again. "Let's call this chat, 'Love means never having to hide from your offspring.' "

PRETTY

Leslie Anne Leasure

Maggie MacAllistar lived in a three-story, cedar-shingled saltbox facing the harbor. I imagine her in her mother's garden, the silver king and artemisia white in moonlight, lilac and wisteria cascading over the latticed tops of the privacy fence. Her mother spoke with a slight Scottish burr and was never home. The iron spiral staircase that led up to the third floor was like a New England fire escape. I dreamt of slipping into her room at night and carrying her down the spiral into the garden. In these moments I thought of making love to her there, amid the broadblade lavender and Queen Anne's lace. We would taste the night and the northeast wind that would carry the marsh smell downtown, leaving the air heavy with the scent of desire.

The morning everything changed, fog rolled off the ocean and whirled up State Street like dry ice blown through a movie set. It was summer before senior year. My windowpanes framed gray, and the stoplights leaked wet red and green, light waves turning liquid. I could only see the sign at Fowles, neon script like the after-burn of a sparkler. Yellow light spilling out onto the sidewalk, beckoning like the only warm place in the winter world. But that morning, it was going to be hot. It was right around the Fourth of July, because the shops were lined with red, white and blue bunting.

Maggie sat in my section at work, ordered coffee, said no to eggs. She was bent over a *New York Times,* leaning forward slightly like a runner at a block.

I set a mug on the table and held up the pot. She had long curly red hair, and was wearing a tight white tank top and jeans. Her face had a slight asymmetry, or maybe it was her crooked smile. A wry expression, I thought.

She flipped the edge of the paper toward her and stared up at me. "Coffee. Please god. And an ashtray."

"Food?"

"In the morning?"

"Yeah, it's called breakfast," I said. "You know, eggs, toast?"

She lit a cigarette and held up her mug. "Breakfast of champions."

She was transferring back to my high school, after getting kicked out of Philips. For incorrigibility, she told me at the time. I was acutely conscious of her presence. I noticed she read every story all the way through, flipping the paper forward and back again. When the paper bent wrong, she snapped it like smoothing a stubborn map. She ended up hanging out through most of my shift, reading the paper and cracking jokes when it was slow.

Jason worked the grill, oblivious in his cook's whites and cigarette smoke. At the end of our shifts, he pulled me upstairs "for a quickie." We leaned against the prep-room door, with his knee between my legs and his hand on my tit. Just as he was about to push us inside, we heard someone coming up the stairs and separated guiltily. It was Maggie, headed for the bathroom just across from the prep room. She coughed, shot me a quizzical look and said, "Excuse me."

We let her pass, and Jason laughed and reached for me again. I ducked and mumbled something about taking care of my customers downstairs. Maggie came back down after a bit and started packing up her paper. I filled her coffee mug.

"Sorry about that." I gestured toward upstairs.

She shrugged. "Don't worry about it. Is your shift about over?"

"Yeah," I said.

"You doing anything now?"

"Nothing, except taking a shower, why?"

"Uhm. You want to go to Salisbury Beach and hang out?"

I said yes and we left the restaurant together as if we always did. Maggie squinted in the sun and put on her sunglasses. I tried to wipe the kitchen grease off my hands. Somehow I felt like my life had suddenly begun. Light cut across the street between the shops and burnished the brick. The mica in the asphalt winked like stars, and I imagined we were walking across the sky.

I took the key from the chain around my neck and led her inside, up the stairs to our apartment.

"Yeah, my mother works in Boston and doesn't usually get home until late," Maggie said with a grimace. "She has a new boyfriend there."

I wondered what it would be like if my father had a girlfriend. He did have one, once, a few years after my mother died, when I was very small. It only lasted a short time and since then, he hadn't had another. When I thought of that, it seemed strange. It seemed like a long time to be single. Maybe he had never gotten over my mother. I showed Maggie my room, grabbed some clothes, and headed to the shower. When I was in the bathroom I looked at myself in the mirror, wondering if I would look different, but I didn't.

"Your closet's like a morgue." Maggie pushed through my clothes. "You know there are other colors in the rainbow besides navy, khaki, and black, right?"

"Yeah, brown," I said and tossed the wet towel on the hook behind my door. My hair was still damp, and I combed through it with my fingers.

"Jesus, Zayne, your whole room is the same way. What, do you subscribe to *Jail Cell Living*? Where the hell is your lampshade?"

I shrugged. I didn't say how I held the bulb until it burned my palms.

She sat on my bed. "So is the cook your boyfriend?"

I could see the outline of her bra through her tank top. I turned to the stereo before she caught me looking. "I guess."

"Well, you kissed him," she said.

"You want the Cure or Jane's Addiction?"

"Christ! Hide the razor blades, will ya? The Cure." She flopped backward and groaned. Her legs were freckled like her arms, and I noted the outline of her calf muscles. "So what do you mean, 'you guess'?"

"Well, we mess around and stuff." I popped the cassette in and punched PLAY. I didn't know where to sit.

Maggie sat up and gave me an arch look. "Really?"

"What?"

"I thought—" Maggie looked down and then sort of shook herself. "Nothing. So how far have you been with him?"

I tossed the cassette case onto my desk. A hundred miles. I could pass the test. "We had sex."

"Zayne." Maggie faked horror and struck the girl-talk pose,

patting the bed beside her. "Sit. So did you like it? Tell me about it."

I sat next to her, careful not to touch her. "I guess."

"That's it? When did you?"

"After freshman year," I said. "In the prep kitchen."

Maggie paused for a minute. "But he's like thirty or something, right?"

"Twenty-seven now," I said. "Have you?"

"Me?" Maggie shook her head. "I have the Catholic girl's terror of getting pregnant."

"Oh wait, I know that one—kiss a boy in a swimsuit and Daddy gets his shotgun, right?"

"God, that too? Good thing I didn't do that!" She laughed and put her hand on my knee. "And here I was worried about wearing short skirts."

I froze when she touched me. "Yeah, you gotta watch out for short skirts."

"So was he the only one?"

"Yeah." I shifted with the lie and she took her hand away.

We played games at Salisbury Beach—it was a small-scale Coney Island; I placed a quarter on a square and waited for the roulette wheel to land on our numbers. I won a carton of Camels, and we smoked ourselves sick while trying to blow smoke rings. She kept saying the lighthouse was phallic, and poked her finger through the smoke rings laughing, "Don't let it die a virgin."

I told her about the gypsy wars in Seabrook and Salisbury. The families who set up competing tarot and palm-reading stands. There were five major beaches near Newburyport, each with its own culture and each with its own tribe. We had our palms read by Madam Debussy in Salisbury. Debussy stared at me awhile after reading my palm, made the sign of the cross and said I might live a very short life and that the hand of God was upon me. Maggie didn't tell me what the gypsy said to her.

I started blowing off Jason, just so I could hang out with Maggie. We'd meet after work and drive to the beach, or go to the park. Sometimes when it was really hot, we'd just hang out at her mother's air-conditioned house and watch television. When I think of her, I remember sandy asphalt, beachfront pizza. The sound of a Pac-Man game turned up too loud. Me and Maggie were tough, like Southie kids, and dropped our r's consciously when we took the train into Boston.

No one had been buried at the Olde Town Hill Cemetery since 1946, at least that we could tell. World War II sent the last bodies home to be buried near the iron canon and green bronze sculpture of Washington at Valley Forge. These graves were uniform like soldiers—square and printed in the same sans serif lettering. Name, rank, date of birth, date of death. No serial numbers. No epitaphs.

These were not the graves Maggie was interested in. She wanted the older ones, the ones so old that to the naked eye they were just stones standing unnamed, erased like amnesia. She collected death angels; had pages she kept in a huge book, charcoal rubbings matted on black paper.

We passed the ones inscribed with images of ships. I pointed to one that had a woman in a long dress holding a giant anchor. *"Dolly Picket, wife of Captain William Picket,"* I said. "Why do you think she's holding an anchor?"

"Maybe Willie died at sea and she drowned herself with an anchor," Maggie said, deadpan. "Probably because it was a popular design. Every few decades there are new trends. Like in the seventies they had graves shaped like trees or piles of logs.

The natural look."

"Oh," I said.

"The best are the ones they did in the seventeen-hundreds," she told me. She knelt in front of one marble headstone and pressed a page of onionskin paper over the angel. "Can you hold this?"

I stood behind the grave and held the sheet in place. She selected a thick chuck of the rubbing pencil and started to color the paper black.

"You need to keep still," she adjusted my hands. "Like that. Stay."

"Woof," I said, laughing.

She winked and continued to blacken the paper. "You know, someone did try to rob these graves a few years ago."

"Really?"

"So these guys broke into the mausoleum up at the top of the hill; you know, Mike Richards?"

"Didn't he die last year?" I watched as the etching textured the page.

"Uh-huh. Of tuberculosis. So the grave they went into—that's what the people had died of...TB."

"Come on. No way."

"Well, that's what they say anyway. Okay, who are you?" she asked the stone. The imprint of the name started to show darker than the rest of the page, the sunken letters just enough to make a reverse impression: *Samuel Blake, 1742.*

Maggie pulled the page away. "Not the right date." She shrugged and looked around, then headed for a white stone that was cracked and leaning against a tree.

"Okay, can you hold this again?" She handed me the edges of the sheet.

"What are you looking for?"

She began to cover the page, and I could see the angel in black relief. These angels of hers were odd—they had huge skeleton heads with curly hair and bat wings for bodies.

"This is like the style they used for the Salem witches," Maggie told me. "Only I've been to Salem and a lot of those stones have been vandalized. That's the bitch about headstones—they're too thin and the marble erodes quickly."

The slight breeze blew strands of Maggie's hair over my fingers. I could feel her breathing. Maybe through the stone. From above, I could see the edges of her ginger eyebrows. The slight scar under her right eye that you could only see when she squinted. The shadow of throat meeting hollow.

"Here, stand behind me. What do you think?"

Maggie held the rubbing, and I came around the headstone and stood behind her.

"I think I like the stones with the ships better," I said.

"All the time you spend on water," she murmured, not moving.

She leaned back against my shins and looked up at the headstone. Her shoulders were slight and like bird wings and for a minute, I thought she would sprout death wings and carry me off to hell.

"Cigarette?" she asked. I lit one and handed it down to her. I lit another for myself and kept standing so she could rest against me. I smoked and waited for her to surface.

The grave said:

> *Here lyes buried ye body of Capt. Joseph Little who departed this life September ye 6th, 1740 & in ye 87 year of his age: Come mortal man & cast an eye come read thy doom and prepare to die*

"Uplifting, isn't it?" She shook herself and stood up. We

headed back down the hill toward town. Maggie had shown me
her death angel book soon after we started hanging out. I hadn't
mentioned my family's album. Even to someone who collected
grave rubbings, I thought it might be weird. She walked slightly
to the left, and kept nudging into me. We joked about Weebles,
the wobbly toys that look like eggs.

We sat on the roof of my apartment building. It was starting to
get dark earlier at night again. It would be fall soon, and time to
go back to school. The roof was pebbled and erupted with metal
heating units smeared with tar. I had brought out a tarp and a
blanket, and we had been talking since dinner. Maggie's mother
had decided to marry the boyfriend. I met him once—we had all
gone out to dinner together. His name was Dino, like the Flint-
stones' dog. He wore one of those puka shell chokers you got at
the beach and had a mullet haircut. He was tan and muscled and
younger than her mother.

"And his name? Jesus." Maggie shook her head. "You'd
think that alone would wise her up enough not to marry him."

Maggie said it seemed like her mother was trying to match
her father in some midlife crisis. Her father had married the
former secretary with the bright fingernails in the spring. The
secretary had decided on a peach and organdy wedding. "It was
like a goddamn citrus stand," Maggie told me. She was relieved
her mother and Dino would go to a justice of the peace and not
have another big church wedding.

"It's not even like she's known him that long," Maggie said.

"Maybe she's lonely or something," I said.

"God, Zayne, this guy is just so disgusting. He gives me the
creeps, you know?"

"What do you mean?"

"I don't know," she sighed, and then suddenly got up and

paced the roof. She seemed so tiny; her body was sharp and angular. "You can see all the way to the ocean from here." Maggie leaned on the rail and stood on her toes.

"Cheese?" I asked. There was wine too.

"No, wine," she said without turning around.

"Wino," I laughed and poured a glass, setting it next to me as a lure.

"You should talk." She sat next to me and took the glass.

For a little while we drank in silence, watching the changing streetlights and listening to the vague sounds of traffic and waves. The echoes of cars going over the metal bridge, amplified by water. I wanted to touch her then, but didn't. I felt too filled with energy and stood up quickly, pacing to the edge. "Not really as romantic as a widow's walk," I said and turned to face her.

She stretched her legs and leaned on her hands, arching her back slightly. I envisioned holding her like that. It made my hands shake a little.

"What's the difference?" she asked.

"Colonial house versus apartment building. And usually the rail is a sort of white picket fence along the east side of the building."

"So why do they call it a widow's walk? Did men fall off while fixing the roof?" She smiled. I think she knew the answer.

"You know, the women would pace the walk waiting to see the ships coming in. I guess the widows would just keep doing it." Maybe they thought someday the masts would appear if they just kept vigil, kept the faith long enough. The fatal day she did not climb the stairs to the roof would be the day she let go, I thought.

Maggie got up and stood next to me. "How romantic," she murmured. "Hey, you can see my house from here. Look. We should work out a code of flashlight signals."

Her house, which was just off Water Street, stood like a step down to the river.

"It would take forever to spell things out. Do you even know Morse code?"

"No, but it's not hard," she said.

"I could just call you."

She shook her head, put her hand on my forearm. "Not the same. It could be our secret code."

I imagined the bat signal. Or two Dixie cups and a long, long string. *When I call you, will you come?* I thought. *Cuneiform, Braille, signs, Morse. In none of these languages can I really tell you I love you.* She set her glass on the ledge and took mine and set it down as well.

"Have you ever done mirror mime before?" she asked me as though she knew what I was thinking. She faced me and held her hands up. "Now mirror what I do, okay?"

Our hands did not touch—they were a centimeter apart—but we moved like a reflection of each other. One hand up. One down. Two hands together reaching up. She made a face and I copied her, but I couldn't meet her eyes. It was like glass between us, but I felt warmth in my palms. For a while we stood on the roof, playing follow the leader, until I didn't know who was leading anymore. Finally, we both were holding our breath so as not to break the silence and Maggie exhaled, laughing lightly.

Maggie slept over that night. She complained she was cold, so we shared my bed. She curled into me and I put my arm around her and could feel her fall asleep. I thought, *I would breathe for you.* I thought, *I would be your breath.* I dreamed of dancing silhouettes against the moonlight, our own code, but she could not see me from her windows.

Saturday nights, we'd cruise Hampton Beach and watch the guys from Revere play air hockey, arrogant in their thin leather ties and gel-spiked hair. Maggie wore neon bangles and miniskirts. Banana clips and bandanas. Me in leather and rivet bracelets. First communion gold-cross pendant-turned-earring dangling from right ear.

Maggie always wanted to look at clothes, even beach clothes with fringed edges and seashell embroidery. I followed her, holding the things she wanted to try on. She'd pull me into the dressing room with her, if it was big enough, and I would perch on the little seat inside and watch her change.

"What do you think?" She turned to me, one hand on hip, wearing a blue dress that fit her body like a sheath fitting a knife. I attempted a look of studied appraisal. Without waiting for a reply, Maggie turned to the mirror again, dropping her hands. "God, I look so fat!"

"On what planet?" I asked. Her body was like the knife, edged and sharp. Her skin glittered. She shook her head, ignoring me, and shimmied out of the shift. Standing in just her underwear, which was lace-edged silk, she pulled another dress off its hanger. I watched her through the mirror, trying hard to focus on her face, but sometimes straying to her shadowed cleavage. Her skin was so much lighter than mine, I thought cream. I thought snow. I thought, *Beauty is this.*

Nothing fit that day. She yanked her jeans back on and dove into her T-shirt. We wandered back out into the boutique, where the bored salesgirl refolded pants and listened to the top forty. Maggie wandered back to the sale rack.

"Check out this dress, Zayne."

It was a short red dress. I took it and held it up to her. "Not really your color," I said.

"*Hello*, as if I'm gonna wear red," she winced. "No, I meant for you."

"Funny," I said and handed it back to her.

"You'd look great in this. Come on, just try it on," Maggie said. "It won't kill you to not be wearing denim."

"It might," I said. She held the dress up to me, looking at it critically. I pushed it away.

Maggie put a hand on her hip. "You know, I don't think I've ever seen you wearing a dress."

I shrugged and looked down. I willed her to stop looking at my body. "They look dumb on me. Come on, I want a cigarette."

"No." Maggie shook her head. "You're trying this on. I want to see you in it."

"Fine." I took the hanger like taking a dare. In the dressing room, I pulled off my T-shirt and pulled the dress over my head, dropped my jeans and kicked them off. There were straight pins and hangers on the floor.

"How's it go—" Maggie slipped into the room. "My God, Zayne, you look great."

She stood behind me and we both looked up into the mirror. I felt too heavy, too short. My socks looked silly. My black hair fell to my shoulders and my chest seemed startling. We stared for a moment, me watching her reaction, she watching me. I stopped breathing.

"Damn." She was staring at my breasts, and then she blushed when I caught her looking. I wanted to crawl under the bench and hide.

Instead I shrugged and reached for my jeans. "Can we go now?"

"Yeah." She didn't say anything else, just backed out of the dressing room.

We walked the near-empty beaches that night, when the kelp and clams washed up with the breakers. I remember men fishing from the jetty. Bonfires on the beach. Fishing poles stuck in the sand like birch trees, their blue lines reflected by translucent rays of moonlight.

We sat under the boardwalk, picking shells up and chucking them into the surf.

"Why'd you freak out so much in the store?" Maggie asked.

"I didn't freak out."

"Yes, you did," Maggie laughed. "You always dress kind of like a guy, all baggy shirts and jeans and stuff."

"It's comfortable." I shrugged. I felt that panic I always did when my friend Joan nagged about my clothes. "Anyway, I grew up on my brother's hand-me-downs. Not exactly miniskirts and halter tops."

"They'd look good on you. I mean, you're really pretty." She turned to me and watched my face. I looked out at the running lights, which skated the surface of the horizon. I didn't know what to say. "That makes you uncomfortable doesn't it?"

I wanted to be able to explain it to her. The feeling of being unable to breathe when she looked at my body that way. It was different with Jason; I just didn't feel anything when he looked at me, when he touched me. But when a woman looked at my body that way, it was like sliding down into darkness. It was this out-of-control feeling. But I couldn't tell her. Couldn't tell her how sometimes I wanted my mother to come back and show me how to do all that, how to wear her clothes and makeup. How I wanted her to tell me I was beautiful. How I knew it wasn't going to happen, ever, and wanting to be that, to be pretty, would just kill me somehow. It's like when you so desperately want something you know you can't have, why admit it?

"I just...don't like wearing that stuff," I said. "I'm not really a girly-girl."

"Yeah, you're so tough," she laughed.

"Yeah." I lay back in the sand and stretched my arms. "You know, you can make sand angels, like snow angels."

"Uh-huh." Smiling, she watched as I pushed the sand into the shape of me with wings. I stopped and our legs were touching and it was like we knew it, but didn't.

"Your feet are so small," she said, trying to line up our arches.

"The foot-binding, you know."

"Ah."

She dug in her pocket and pulled out a pack of mints. "Hey, you know, when you bite into these, they make sparks. Try it."

We sat there, chewing wintergreen Life Savers in the darkness with open mouths so we could see the green spark. Maggie sat next to me, legs crossed Indian style and touching mine, poking my arm to make a point. Sitting in the dark with my longing, the sparks lighting like fireflies, random and startling.

When she kissed me, her lips tasted of mints and cigarettes.

"Oh," I said. It was all I could say.

"Oh?" Maggie laughed a bit and brushed her hair from her eyes.

"That was nice," I said. I leaned forward and our foreheads touched. We both looked down at the sand.

"I wanted to do that when I met you," she said.

"You knew?"

"I didn't know if you would," she said. "You had that whole boyfriend thing going on."

"I've never…" I pulled away and lay back in the sand, looking up at the rough wood of the boardwalk. "I've wanted to."

She rolled next to me, and slid her hand lightly across my breasts. I shivered.

"What if someone sees us?" I said.

"They won't."

We kissed again, and all I wanted to do was touch her. It didn't matter that it was starting to get cold, or that I could hear people walking above us.

"You're not so tough, are you?" she said lightly, when my

body trembled under her hands. "Don't worry, I won't tell any-one." She smoothed my hair back from my face and slipped her fingers inside me. I held on to her and she gently covered my mouth with her free hand when I couldn't stop from making noise.

"So pretty," she whispered in the darkness.

ABOUT THE AUTHORS

SAGGIO AMANTE is a fun-loving and passionate raconteur who lives, loves, and writes in the deep South. She is a writer of fiction and poetry and an avid reader of lesbian romance, adventure, and erotica. Her fiction appears in *Stolen Moments: Erotic Interludes 2*. When not reading or writing (or loving), Sage is found pursuing sometimes disastrous but always interesting culinary adventures.

SANDRA BARRET lives in New England with her partner, children, and more pets than are probably legal to own. She is an avid reader of fantasy and lesbian fiction. Her passion for different genres has led her to pen her own stories in fantasy, science fiction, romance, and horror. Her first novel, *Lavender Secrets*, is due to be published in February 2007. Visit her website at www.sandrabarret.com

CHEYENNE BLUE combines her two passions in life by writing travel guides and erotica. Her fiction has appeared in numerous anthologies, including *Best Women's Erotica*, *The Mammoth Book of Best New Erotica*, *Best Lesbian Erotica*, *Best Lesbian Love Stories*, *Aqua Erotica 2*, and on many websites. Her travel guides have been jammed underneath chocolate wrappers in thousands of glove boxes. She divides her time between the state of Colorado and Ireland, and is currently working on a book about the quiet and quirky areas of Ireland. You can see more of her writing at www.cheyenneblue.com.

SARAH COATS lives in Seattle where she enjoys the soggy weather and constantly uses it as an excuse to watch movies and write stories.

AUNT FANNY has published stories in the Lambda Literary Award–winning *Stolen Moments*, and the upcoming anthology *Extreme Passions*. Her stories also appear in *Ultimate Lesbian Erotica 2006* and *Wild Nights: True Lesbian Sex Stories*. Aunt Fanny claims she was born during a flying-carpet ride, a bumpy start at best. She currently lives quite happily in America's heartland with her rainbow family and friends, fighting the good fight against discrimination. Professional inquiries for Aunt Fanny can be addressed to: auntfannystories@yahoo.com.

LISA FIGUEROA is a Chicana writer from the Los Angeles area who received an MA in English/Creative Writing in 2001. Her stories have appeared in *Lesbian News*, *Harrington Lesbian Fiction Quarterly*, *Sinister Wisdom*, and *Lessons in Love: Erotic Interludes 3*. In addition to writing, she loves spending quality time with her beautiful, amazing partner of six years and their three adorable cats.

JEWELLE GOMEZ is the author of seven books, including the lesbian vampire novel *The Gilda Stories* and a collection of short stories, *Don't Explain*. Her poetry and fiction have appeared in anthologies such as *Dark Matter: An Anthology of African American Fantasy Fiction, The Oxford Treasury of Love Stories*, and *Best American Poetry 2001*. You can visit her website at www.jewellegomez.com or read her blog at www. hillgirlz.com.

LYNNE JAMNECK is the author of the Samantha Skellar Mystery series as well as several short stories that are featured in a host of anthologies. Her speculative fiction has appeared in *H. P. Lovecraft's Magazine of Horror* and *Best Lesbian Erotica 2003* and *2006*, and she has works slated for *So Fey: Queer Faery Fictions* and *Sex in the System: Stories of Erotic Futures, Technological Stimulation, and the Sensual Life of Machines*.

MAGGIE KINSELLA is an ex-nurse living in the west of Ireland. Her work has also appeared in *Best Lesbian Love Stories 2005*. She sells Wexford strawberries by the side of the Sligo Road, which gives her plenty of writing time.

LORI L. LAKE has published six novels (*Gun Shy, Under the Gun, Have Gun We'll Travel, Different Dress, Ricochet in Time*, and *Snow Moon Rising*) and *Stepping Out: Short Stories*. She edited the 2005 Lammy finalist *The Milk of Human Kindness: Lesbian Authors Write About Mothers and Daughters*, as well as *Romance for LIFE*, an anthology benefiting breast cancer research. Lori and her partner of twenty-five years live in Minnesota, where Lori teaches queer fiction writing at the Loft Literary Center and is currently at work on her eighth novel. You can visit her website at www.lorilake.com.

TERESA LAMAI lives in the Pacific Northwest. Her stories can be found in many anthologies, including *Best Lesbian Erotica*, *Best Women's Erotica*, and *The Mammoth Book of Best New Erotica*. She recently completed a collection of dance-inspired erotica called *Swayed to Music*.

ANNE LAUGHLIN helps people buy and sell homes in Chicago. When she's not in her car driving from property to property, she's working on her first novel. Her erotica pieces, written under a pen name, will be published in fall 2006 by Bold Strokes Books. Anne lives on the Chicago River with her partner of nine years.

LESLIE ANNE LEASURE's fiction has appeared in *Blithe House Quarterly*, *Best Lesbian Love Stories 2005*, and *Blood Sisters: Lesbian Vampire Tales*. Leslie recently finished her MFA in fiction at Indiana University and was a fellow at the Ledig House International Writers' Residency in 2003. She received an honorable mention in the Emerging Lesbian Writers Award in Fiction competition from the Astraea National Lesbian Action Foundation and served as the assistant director for the Indiana University Writers' Conference.

ELSPETH POTTER lives in Philadelphia. Her fiction has appeared in *Best Lesbian Erotica 2001–2004*, *Best Women's Erotica 2002* and *2005*, *Tough Girls*, *The Mammoth Book of Best New Erotica* volume 5, and *Sex in the System: Stories of Erotic Futures, Technological Stimulation, and the Sensual Life of Machines*. She is a member of Science Fiction and Fantasy Writers of America.

RACHEL ROSENBERG is enrolled in Montreal's Concordia University Creative Writing Program. When she was eight years old, she began jotting down handwritten *Darkwing Duck* fan fiction. From that, she realized how much she loved writing. She tends to be influenced by the various details she notices while people-watching, as well as by fairy tales. At age fourteen, she had a piece published in *Chicken Soup for the Teenage Soul 2* and is glad to be published again, so as to avoid becoming a literary child-star has-been.

KATHERINE SPARROW likes words and the many ways to manipulate them. She is a recent Clarion West Writer's Workshop graduate and spends her time working with mentally ill people, going on urban hikes, and imagining all kinds of strange things that aren't but could be.

K. I. THOMPSON began her writing career when her first short story, "The Blue Line," was included in the Lambda Literary Award–winning anthology *Erotic Interludes 2: Stolen Moments*. She also has selections in *Erotic Interludes 3: Lessons in Love* and *Erotic Interludes 4: Extreme Passions*. Her novel, *House of Clouds,* a romance set during the Civil War, is forthcoming from Bold Strokes Books.

FIONA ZEDDE moved to the United States from Jamaica as a sweet yet misunderstood preteen. After spending a few years in Tampa fooling around with incendiary women of all types, she moved to Atlanta, Georgia, where she currently lives. Fiona is the author of two novels, *Bliss* and *A Taste of Sin.* Find out more about her at www.fionazedde.com.

ABOUT THE EDITOR

ANGELA BROWN is the editor of *Mentsh: On Being Jewish and Queer* as well as more than thirty anthologies under her own name and pen names. She and her grouchy one-eyed dog Harry live in Atwater Village, a lesser-known pocket of Los Angeles near Griffith Park, where they dodge coyotes and skunks on a nightly basis. Her short stories, essays, and reviews have appeared on NPR, Pacifica Radio, LA.com, and in *OUT* magazine, and she's recently completed *I Fall to Pieces: A Kit Gunning Mystery*, the first book in a country music–themed crime series.